MOON MOURNING

/ / / /

J.R. RAIN
&
MATTHEW S. COX

SAMANTHA MOON ORIGINS

New Moon Rising

Moon Mourning

Published by
Crop Circle Books
212 Third Crater, Moon

Printed in the United States of America.

ISBN-13: 978-1983715525
ISBN-10: 1983715522

Dedication:

The authors wish to dedicate this book to Eve, Mariah and Clarissa.

Chapter One
Denial

Disintegrating flecks of wood lay scattered on the tiles in front of the bathroom sink. The cabinet door looks expensive, but under the veneer, it's particleboard.

More of the bathroom's flaws leap out at me: a misshapen corner, a lump in the wall, an error in the sponge paint I did almost a year ago. I look again at the crumbling cabinet door. Is it a metaphor for my life? Fine and normal on the outside, but no substance inside? Had I been lying to myself, to the world? On the outside, my family appears perfect, but on the inside…

Stop it. Being tight on money doesn't mean there's anything wrong with my family.

At least, nothing wrong with Danny, Tammy, or Anthony. I'm the problem. Now, the very big problem. I take some breaths, steadying myself. The kids' voices seep through the bathroom door from the living room, both singing along with Barney. A flash of night sky fills my memory, cold air wafting across my throat. Those few seconds had been so precious when I thought I would never see my children again.

My inability to explain or even rationalize what's going on with the mirror brings me right back to how I felt that night. I grip the side of the bathtub, trying to shake off the lingering terror that keeps my head down. Whatever happened out there didn't take me away from them. No explanation comes to mind—at least, none that make sense—but I do know one thing: my kids still have me, and *nothing* will ever make me feel like *that* again. If I can somehow brush aside even death for my kids, anything else this world throws at me will be trivial.

Another squidgy heartbeat registers to my ears.

Right. Here I am taunting the Grim Reaper and I'm still too much of a chicken shit to lift my head and confront the mirror again. Minutes pass. I take slow, careful breaths—that is, when I think to. If I don't make the effort, my breathing, well… ceases.

What's happening to me?

Still too freaked out to feel much of anything but numb, I lift my gaze once more to the mirror and stare at the hollow opening at the top of my nightgown. Off-white hovers in front of the black tiles surrounding the bathtub behind me. No head. No trace of my flesh appears in the reflection anywhere. The mirror is tormenting me, mocking me. If not for the memory of how much work I put into hanging the bastard thing myself, I'd smash it.

"This is just too…"

I shake my head. No, I can't really be seeing this. I mean, *c'mon.*

I'm not sure how I can win a staring contest with emptiness. My butt isn't even numb from the cold porcelain edge of the tub I've been sitting on for who knows how long. Like a fatal car accident I don't want to watch but can't help but stare at, I remain transfixed on the mirror while rising to my feet. When I lift my arm, an empty sleeve floats into view in the reflection. I keep reaching, fingers outstretched toward the lying thing in front of me. A second before contact, a soft knock at the door makes me jump back and cringe like I've been caught with a boy in my bedroom at fifteen.

"Hon? Are you okay?" asks Danny through the door.

My bare feet appear ghostly against the fuzzy black bathmat, so pale they're almost luminescent. Each of the four giant bulbs over the mirror cost us $24.99. LED you know… saving the environment one socket at a time. "I'm checking the bandages."

The knob rattles. Danny hesitates. He knows I never lock the bathroom door, so something *must* be wrong. A change of pitch in his breathing gives away his concern.

How the hell? My hand flies to cover my mouth before I can gasp.

I'm hearing him breathe!

The rush of air, in and out, as loud as if I'd laid my head upon his chest, mesmerizes me. His scent permeates my senses, too, strong and musky, pungent. His taste lingers on the roof of my mouth, though my tongue hasn't been near him in days. Longing and dread, both simultaneous and overpowering, collide. I want to burrow into his embrace and have him tell me I'm crazy, that this is some strange, hallucinogenic dream; but, I also dread how he'll react. My gaze shifts to the mirror. Telling him and having him see this… would just make it real. Surely, it's all in my head.

It's gotta be all in my head.

"Do you need a hand with them?" asks Danny. "Can I help you with anything?"

A strange crunching rustle follows, then repeats. It takes me a few seconds to realize the meaning of the noise—he's scratching, probably at his chest from the texture of fabric. How am I able to hear his nails raking over his shirt from here, like my ear is an inch away from him?

"I'm okay… I won't be in here much longer." I lift my hand and subconsciously mimic his gesture, scratching at my shoulder.

Rip.

A small cut appears in the reflection of the nightgown, making me gasp and stare at my… pointed fingernail. *No… that didn't just happen. My nails are not sharp enough to cut fabric.*

He lets a heavy sigh out his nose. The *thud* of his forehead on the door makes me jump. "All right. I'll be in the living room if you need me."

"Thanks. I…" I stare at my feet. "I won't be in

here much longer."

The squish of his shoes on carpet recedes to silence.

Danny, wait! I yell in my head and dart to the door, but I barely manage to get the lock undone before fear stalls me. What am I going to tell him? *Hey, hon, I think our mirror's broken. You see, I don't have a reflection anymore.*

After backing up to face the lying slab of glass again, I lift my nightgown to my chin and gawk at the nothingness in the mirror. Defeated, I let the satin fall from my grip and stumble backward until my heel strikes the tub.

I sink back to sit on the edge, shaking my head. None of this can be real. That night jog? Never happened. I'm still in bed having a wickedly awful dream. Maybe I even died at Nick's Super Burger when that kid unloaded his .38 revolver. What are the odds he'd miss all six shots from like fifteen feet away? The first one killed me and everything I think happened after that has all been in my head, the last-hurrah theatrical production of a dying brain gasping for oxygen.

My hair flies back and forth as I shake my head harder and harder. Nope. I don't believe this is real. No one has their throat torn open like I dreamed happened to me and walks out of the hospital a few days later. No one goes days without peeing. And no one can survive with a heartbeat in the range of three to six beats per minute.

It's impossible.

I'm impossible.

This mirror is impossible.

Wake up, Sam.

Grief pulls me forward and I wrap my arms around my legs, my head against my knees. Every ounce of my being wants to cry, but either shock or some unknown physical impairment gets in the way. So, I hug my legs to my chest, gazing down at my far-too-white feet.

"This isn't real. This can't be happening. I've *got* to be dreaming."

Chapter Two
Off-Limits

Disbelief, fear, and wonder swirl around in my head. I can't tell if I'm lying in bed caught in a nightmare or sprawled on the semi-paved front lot of Nick's Super Burger next to the half-eaten mess of my lunch I'll never finish. Surely, I can't *actually* be sitting here in my bathroom, while *not* appearing in a mirror, and *not* having used a toilet in days, or eaten… or…

A pathetic squishing *thud*, my heartbeat, echoes in my head.

I can't remember the last food I had before the egg burrito in the hospital that wound up flying straight back out of me. Aware of a palpable hunger, I scratch idly at my stomach, mindful not to shred my nightgown. The sensation is odd, though; deeper, the craving for nourishment is entwined with the very fiber of my being. A fleeting thought of the hamburger that may or may not be lying beside me as the last vestiges of warmth leave my bullet-riddled body does nothing to pique my appetite.

This can't be real.

The Barney sing-along stops. Ad jingles carry on for a minute or three. My kids' voices trail off to silence once the high-pitched chattering of cartoon children fill the vacuum the purple dinosaur left behind.

My head snaps up and I lock eyes with my non-reflection. Dreams don't go on for this long, do they? Could the final five seconds of consciousness in my dying brain feel like a week passing? And if I hadn't died at Nick's Super Burger, surely I had died in the park that night. If this *is* happening, if I'm really awake, aware, and in my bathroom now, then what's happened to me? How could I possibly not have so much as a mark on my neck that had been torn clear open? And what explanation could there be for how I look like I'm in my twenties again—or as pale as a corpse? I could totally rock a Morticia Addams outfit for Halloween.

The thought catches me off guard and I wind up laughing at the stupidity of cracking a joke when my brain's lost in a spiral dive. I could be dead or dying and I'm thinking of stupid crap like costumes.

I am hungry, yes, but none of my usual go-to ideas for food tempt me in the least. Maybe I'm having a craving for something weird, but I couldn't be pregnant… could I? They'd have said something at the hospital… assuming any of that hospital stuff really happened.

"Oh, what the hell do I want to eat?"

Metal scrapes on my right.

I lift my head and peer toward the sound. Tammy peeks around the door, one hand grasping the edge, one tiny bare foot creeping into view. She's still in her nightdress, a grape jelly stain on her chest.

"Mommy? Are you okay?" she asks.

The sight of my daughter pushes away the doldrums shadowing my heart. I start to smile at her, but my gaze fixates in on where her delicate neck meets her shoulder. Long, fine strands of black hair stand out in perfect detail, almost down to her elbows. A thin line swells and fades, her carotid artery thrumming with each beat of her heart. The child's scent floods my senses. Warm. Alive. Her young flesh mixed with the fruity essence of the jelly stain, green apple shampoo, and a hint of oatmeal cookie.

My stomach twists, growling, hungry. Tightness spreads across my face, below my eyes. Not quite pain, the unpleasant sensation makes me flinch. Seconds later, it cramps my lower jaw. What is wrong with me? Why am I staring at my child like she's filet mignon?

No… veal.

"Mommy?" Tammy steps all the way into the bathroom, pushing the door aside. "What's wrong?"

No! "Gah!" I force myself to look away. *W-*

what have I become? My body shakes with horror. *I will not.*

Tammy's feet patter over the tile. I about scream like someone's throwing boiling water on me when she leaps into a hug, snuggling tight to me. Her breath washes over the side of my neck, little fingers clutching my nightgown. My daughter's heartbeat echoes in my mind. She smells… appetizing. The tender skin of her neck waits inches from my lips. This hunger demands to be sated. All I'd need to do is lower my head and lean to the right.

No!

"Get better, Mommy," says Tammy into my shoulder. "I love you."

I close my eyes and pat her on the back, rocking softly side to side. "I love you too, sweetie. More than anything."

No way in hell. I will not *harm my children.* Something dark and evil slithers around the back of my consciousness, a vague, shadowy presence that doesn't belong there. More and more, the sense that I'm being watched, or that my thoughts are not purely mine, comes on. *It* wants food.

"*Barney*'s over, Mommy. Anthony and me were singing with him. Like this…" Tammy starts belting out the theme song, almost even on key, a first.

The strange cramping tightness starts in my face again.

No. I will not. A tear runs down my cheek. *Not my kids. Not my family.*

I don't understand what's happened to me, but the instant I believe I might be a threat to them, I will end it all, no hesitation.

I stand, cradling Tammy in my arms, and shy away from the mirror. She wraps her arms and legs around me, mostly sitting on my right arm. Listening to her voice hits me like a knife; this is one of those precious moments I almost lost. My four-year-old singing her heart out to make me feel better. How many more little random things from either one of my children would I have missed if I died that night?

I'm not dreaming, or dying. I'm home—with my family.

The temptation to devour her fades for a moment, but returns when I kiss the top of her head and catch a strong whiff of her scent. Jaw clenched, I ease my face away from her so she doesn't notice me recoiling.

No goddamned way. My family is off-limits. One more tiny inkling of temptation, and I will find a way to destroy myself. There is nothing I will not do to protect them. Nothing.

"That's the song, Mommy." Tammy leans back enough to grin up at me.

Whatever inner strength let me overcome the darkness lurking in the hallway that night and rush into Tammy's bedroom pulls me out of the mental pit I've sunken into. The slithering *ick* in my consciousness recedes, and I no longer feel the least bit of anything toward my child but protectiveness and love.

She tilts her head in confusion. “Why are you crying?”

Tears in my eyes, I heft her up and brush at her hair. “You sang so beautifully.” I wink. “Thank you for cheering me up.”

Tammy grins.

“Come on.” I set her down on her feet and take her hand. “Let’s go see what kind of trouble your brother and Daddy are getting into.”

She giggles, and pulls me along toward the living room.

Chapter Three
Still Me

Tammy leads me down the hall, walking past memories as much as physical space.

Every bit of molding makes me think of the hours we spent painting. The doorway to Tammy's room triggers an image of Danny laughing with a blotch of white on his forehead; the paint roller had fallen off the ladder and beaned him. A small uneven spot along the hallway near Anthony's room catches my eye. The master bedroom had a section of wall that the previous owner had damaged so severely we had to basically rebuild it. Danny had been carrying an armload of wood down the corridor when he tripped over the baby's toy. The lumber went flying, and one 2x4 gouged the drywall here. I can still see him lying in a heap, wood everywhere, laughing at himself. Good times.

At the end of the hall where it opens to the

living room, my mind next conjures an apparition of Danny kneeling, cursing up a storm at the tool he'd rented to staple or nail down the carpeting. It took him hours to figure out how to get it to work, but at least we saved a few hundred bucks. Once he got the hang of it, he did a fair job… and only stapled his finger once.

Anthony's sprawled on the floor near the TV, playing with action figures. I think the Blue Power Ranger is wrestling a triceratops. He looks up at us as we enter, and sits back on his heels, giving me a suspicious eye. Only his head moves, tracking my progress across the room to the couch, where Tammy crawls up to sit beside me.

"Hey, hon. You okay?" asks Danny from the kitchen.

"Yeah, I think so." I settle into the cushions, gazing around at my home. AC/DC's *Thunderstruck* blasts in my memory. All the furniture vanishes, replaced with drop cloths and ladders. I daydream about Danny in an old white T-shirt and jeans, the two of us dancing and messing around to the too-loud music on a Saturday afternoon. In my memory, Mary Lou had the kids; we had a buttload of housework. And I had lead singer Angus Young getting me through it all.

Anthony keeps staring at me like he's not sure who I even am.

"Hey, kiddo," I say, smiling at him, trying to project the love I have for my son into a physical radiance he can feel. "What's the Blue Ranger doing?'

"Stopping monsters," says Anthony, still giving me a measuring stare.

Danny drifts back and forth in the kitchen, muttering low about legal stuff. Probably has his cell phone in the apron's pocket, using headphones. For now, he's home to take care of me, yet still working as much as he can. I can't fault him that. We really do need all the money he can get. I'm grateful that he's here for me and has the freedom, for now, to work from home. Without him, I think I'd be lost.

"Are you still sick?" asks Tammy, her voice more whisper than speech.

I thread an arm around her and snug her close to my side. "I… think I'm just tired now."

"But you've been in bed all day." Tammy blinks.

"Well." I *boop* her on the nose. "Sometimes if people sleep too much, they feel tired. Funny, huh?"

"Yeah, funny. But not ha-ha funny."

I grin. "No, sweetie, not ha-ha funny."

Chopping noises start up in the kitchen. The fragrance of fresh mushrooms, garlic, and scallions hit me hard, but it doesn't activate my hunger. My nose even picks up the aroma of uncooked rice. Guess Danny's making a pilaf.

The feeling that I'm an impostor—another person entirely, who snuck into this family's house—gnaws at the edges of my consciousness. That sense I don't belong here worsens at my son's uneasy stare, as though I'm a stranger dressed up to look like Mommy.

My daughter appears to get the hint something isn't quite right and cuddles at my side the way she did after I'd been shot on that drug raid. Truth is, I'm groggy and out of it, and I'm sure it's showing on my face. No, I can't see myself in the mirror to check, but the idea that someone could've written a nasty word on my forehead and I'd never be able to tell strands me on an island between wanting to laugh or freak out.

"Do I haveta go to peeschool?" asks Tammy.

I snicker to myself and comb my fingers through her hair. "Not until next week, sweetie. But you do need to go to *pre*school."

"Why?" asks Tammy, while rubbing her nose. "I already know how to potty."

Giggling, I explain the difference between pee and pre. "So you can learn things and grow up to be smart and do amazing things." I worm a finger under her arm, tickling her side until she squeals into giggles.

"Your finger's cold, Mommy! Like ice!"

I stop tickling, her words cutting straight to my heart. She's right, of course. My fingers are cold. And so are my hands… and everything. Cold, like a corpse. I fight a new wave of depression. What the hell is wrong with me?

No, I think, shaking my head. *Time to move forward. Time to reclaim my life, my happiness...*

Anthony nods to himself, like some great matter

of cosmic justice wound its way to resolution inside his mind. His coolness evaporates and I get a silly grin before he scampers over to continue playing with his toys at my feet. “Dino Man tried to eated the city, but Bwoo Ranger pra’tect the people.” My little boy prattles on about Dino Man’s attack, telling me how none of the other heroes could stop him (likely the other figures scattered about the floor). In between the sometimes-hard-to-decipher sentences of a two-year-old, Tammy peppers me with questions about preschool, her dread increasing moment by moment until she hits me with a bomb that makes me want to laugh and cry at the same time.

“How long’m I gonna haveta stay there?” Her eyes widen to epic cuteness. “Why can’t I stay living here?”

“Oh, sweetie!” I give her a squeeze. “You’re not going to *live* there. It’s just a few hours a day. Like when Daddy and I go to work. We come home every night, right?”

Her fear fades somewhat as her pleading stare notches back to an expression of contemplation.

“Not every night,” mutters Anthony, looking down.

I scoop him up too, and hold the pair of them in a hug, kissing them both atop the head. “I’m sorry for scaring you two. I’ll never be away from you like that again.”

“Mommy wanted to come home, but she got hurted,” says Tammy in a matter-of-fact tone. “She hadda go doctor."

Anthony nods. "'Kay. Mommy, don' get doctor 'gain."

"I won't, kiddo." I poke him in the tummy.

I'm pretty sure I can keep this promise; that is, if what's happening to me is really happening to me. And if it is happening to me, well, I doubt even doctors can help me.

That, of course, begs the question—what is happening to you, Sam? I shake my head and push the thought aside.

Loud sizzling in the kitchen precedes the smell of heated butter, garlic, and mushrooms wafting in. With each quite-audible scrape of a wooden spatula over Teflon, I become increasingly aware that all is not as it should be in Sam World. At least I don't have any distracting awareness of Anthony or Tammy's heartbeats; holding them in my lap feels about as normal as it ought to. The pair cuddle with me on the sofa, watching some crazy cartoon. I swear I'm getting old. This show makes utterly zero sense to me, but the kids are enthralled.

Okay, I had a really bizarre series of events happen to me. I'm not sure exactly *what* any of it means… especially that bit with the mirror. But, I'm here. This is my house and my family. I think that sense of not belonging here, the dread and anxiety, came from my being afraid of the unknown. Tell me a sane person could see their reflection in the mirror vanish—and stay gone—and not have at least a minor existential crisis.

Then again, would a sane person see their reflection vanish?

No, I think. No sane person would see their reflection vanish, because reflections don't vanish. Not in the real world.

I veritably itch to check my reflection again. Just one more time. But I can't bring myself to do it. I can't face the emptiness again, can't face the implications of what it means, either.

And what does it mean?

Well, it means that I've gone off the deep end.

Or…

Or what?

I don't want to face that either. Ever.

Tammy's gurgle tells me I'm squeezing them a little too hard. I ease back and mess with their hair a bit. Anthony keeps mashing the triceratops figure into Blue Ranger while staring at the TV. Tammy pulls a small blanket over and tries to wrap it around my shoulders. Smiling, I sit up a little so she can. Okay, crisis over. Or at least minimized.

I'm still me.

We watch the cartoon—a show about a kid named Arnold with a weird football-shaped head and blond hair—for a while in relative normality. The sizzling in the kitchen ceases, and Danny shuffles around amid the bumping of pots and the heavy, glassy clatter of a large baking dish. The fridge opens and closes. Hunger twists in my gut, but thankfully, it's not from smelling either of my children. I lift my head, drawn toward the doorway and the smell of… meat.

"Mommy needs a moment," I mutter, and scoot the kids off to the floor before standing.

Anthony dives back into his mess of toys while Tammy burritos herself in the blanket on the sofa, attention glued to the TV.

With one hand on my stomach, I drift like a ghost across the living room to the kitchen. The pervasive grogginess that's been hounding me since my eyes opened lifts somewhat as I hone in on the large glass baking dish on the counter full of beef brisket. Danny's hovering near it, mixing up something in a smaller bowl.

As if on autopilot, I glide to the dish, pluck the meat out of the way with one hand, and upend the baking dish to my mouth. Cow's blood hits my tongue with the awesomeness of a full steak dinner, sending jolts of electricity down into my core.

Danny lets out a startled yelp and jumps to the side.

Maybe I snarl a little, but not at him… I feel like a starving mongrel fed after days in a cage.

There's not enough blood here, but I keep licking the glass.

"Sam?" asks Danny, sounding rattled. "What are you doing?"

I glance at the empty dish in my left hand, the slab of meat dangling from my right hand. For a second, I feel like a tween caught watching an R-rated movie and my gaze darts about looking for an excuse, but all I can think about is my hunger. That trace of blood is a tease more than anything. I want more. I *need* more.

Again, I snarl.

Danny leans back. "Sssaaam?"

I shake off the feral urges orbiting the edges of my thoughts and blink at him. "Umm… Sorry." After rinsing out the dish, I plop the brisket back in it and… lick the blood from my fingers.

"Wow. It's good to see you've got your appetite back at least, though *that* was a bit weird." Danny approaches and slides an arm around my back. "At least let me cook it first."

The garlic-onion-mushroom aroma of the pilaf is near overwhelming; how hadn't I noticed that before? "Uhh, yeah, right. I'm still not quite feeling like myself."

"Sam." Danny grasps my shoulders and stares at me.

I give him my best innocent expression. "Hmm?"

He reaches up and caresses my neck, his fingertips sending tingles of lightning down my skin from the slightest contact. My eyes half-lid. Drinking in his scent gets me hungry again, but not for any kind of food.

"Your bandage is off," says Danny in a weak voice.

My sex drive freezes and bursts into a thousand fragments.

He brushes my neck, the warmth of his contact gliding down to my collarbone. "There's not a mark on you."

"That's good, right?" I ask, not quite able to look him in the eye.

"It's… something." His arm drops to hang at his side. "Yeah, probably good. Did that really happen? The attack?"

I lean against him, face pressed to his shoulder. "Now I'm not so sure. It's… surreal. Nothing makes any sense but I know I'm *home* with my family, and that's all that matters."

"I'm so glad you're all right." Danny wraps his arms around me. He starts in on a deep kiss, but pulls back faster than I expect, still smiling. "How do you feel?"

"Little tired. Hungry."

"No soreness? Pain?" His eyebrows rise with hope.

"Not really." I feel like yawning, but it's as though my body forgot how. I could *so* go to sleep right here standing up, leaning on my husband. "Just tired… and hungry."

"Well, dinner'll be ready soon." He tickles my sides. "You're as bad as Tammy hovering around when there're cookies in the oven."

I laugh. Parents who complain about their kids pulling the 'are we there yet?' thing in a car have never been in the house with Tammy while baking is going on. "Yeah, yeah… That smells amazing, by the way."

"Thanks, babe." He kisses me on the lips, and again pulls back. "Are you sure you feel all right?"

“Other than groggy, yes, why?”

“Not cold at all?”

I shrug. “Not really, no.”

“Hmm.” He half shrugs and turns back to continue mixing up the seasoning for the brisket. “Strange.”

“Danny… everything about these past few days is strange.” I meander back to the living room where the kids remain engrossed in the TV.

Tammy grins at me and holds up the blanket as an invitation. I pad over, sit, and snuggle with her.

“Have we spent all day in our jammies?” I ask.

She nods, shrugging.

Ah, what a normal, lazy thing to do on a day off. ‘Normal’ being the operative word here. I can’t help but think everything about my life is about to get quite far from normal.

Quite far, indeed.

Chapter Four
Chilling

Since I met Danny, the smell of his cooking had always made me ravenous.

I guess it's true what they say about some people having a knack for certain tasks. In his case, it's cooking. Sometimes, I think the man ought to have become a professional chef instead of a lawyer, but his parents would never have approved of that.

I tease my fork around the mushroom rice pilaf he made, eyeing a few strips of brisket I snagged from the middle where the meat appeared rarest. As if I hadn't been worried enough about what's happened to me, that I can sit here and stare at this wonderful food and think on an intellectual level 'yes, this is beautiful and smells appetizing,' but I'm not experiencing any physical reaction, bothers me. The red meat comes closest to triggering a hunger-like response, though I ought to be inhaling this meal.

Instead, I take my time dicing Tammy's portion of brisket into teensy cubes while Danny does the same for Anthony. We've still got the applesauce backup in case the boy decides he hates the real food.

Danny finishes cutting and gets Anthony started on his first mouthful. He emits a happy murmur and grabs a handful of pilaf before stuffing it in his mouth, rice dribbling down his cheeks onto his bib. Tammy takes her time, meticulously stabbing one cube of brisket on each tine of her fork before raising it to her mouth.

Not until Danny glances at me do I take my first bite. I don't feel sick or anything, but something about this food is giving off a warning. Not knowing *why* I think eating it is a bad idea, I force down a mouthful of the rice—which is pretty good, but unsatisfying. A hunk of brisket appeals somewhat more, but within ten seconds of swallowing, World War Three breaks out in my gut.

Anthony starts rolling a mushroom around his plate, which distracts Danny away from noticing me gag. I grab the napkin, cover my mouth and fake a sneeze so Tammy doesn't question why I made a funny face.

"Be right back." I stand.

"Everything all right?" asks Danny.

"Oh, fine." I force a smile over my rapidly building nausea. "Nature's calling, and she dialed collect."

He nods.

I hurry off down the hall to the bathroom with Mount Vesuvius rumbling inside me. Within seconds of the door closing, I start retching… but a couple forkfuls of rice and a hunk or two of meat does not contain much fluid. I have horribleness stuck inside me and it can't go anywhere. My face hovers over the toilet for a moment, surely as red as a tomato. Panic starts to set in due to the feeling of a brick wedged in my throat, but it's not because I can't breathe…

Fumbling at the sink, I grab the plastic cup, fill it to the top, and force myself to chug it. I barely get the cup away from my lip before the geyser starts, spattering the mirror, sink, floor, and toilet.

Rice and meat bits go everywhere.

I swoon to my knees, hugging the toilet. It's been a few years since I found myself in this position… not since college. Convulsions rock me for a little while more. After they stop, I cough and pluck rice out of my hair. The room spins, and I catch myself gasping for air. Wait, did vomiting fix something?

What if…

Holding my breath stabs a dagger of sorrow into my heart. There's no sense of urgency; I feel like I could sit here for hours and be fine. Guess that panic while throwing up didn't come from not being able to breathe.

Damn. Better get back out there before Danny

worries.

I spring to my feet, grab a fistful of TP, and wipe down the spray as best I can in a rush. The truly strange part of this is the vomit doesn't stink like anything repugnant. It smells no different from how it had on the plate. Granted, it hadn't stayed down very long, but there ought to at least be a trace of bile or something.

What is *wrong* with me?

Once the bathroom no longer looks like a drunk college roommate exploded all over it, I hurry out the door, but grab the cup on my way. Danny and the kids look up from their food as I swoop in and resume my seat. Both my husband and daughter give me worried stares until I take a giant forkful of rice and brisket and make enthusiastic 'mmm' sounds.

As soon as Danny looks away to check on Anthony, I spit the food into the bathroom cup, which I conceal under the table. There's no sense alarming the children, and I'm not quite ready to make Danny feel bad, thinking I don't like his food. Faking it isn't too difficult, since as long as I don't attempt to swallow anything, it does actually taste pretty good. Eventually, the kids are back in the living room and Danny's at the dining room table on his laptop doing work stuff. As is our usual routine, since he cooked, I deal with the dishes and cleanup. And by cleanup, I mean dumping my chewed-up mush into the trash. I'm tempted to throw the whole damn cup in there, too, but I suspect many more uneaten meals were going to end up in this thing.

I'm so distracted by worry, it doesn't occur to me that I've run the water ridiculously hot until the steam wafting up from the sink is thick enough to interfere with my vision. It's near-painful to touch, but not so much that I jerk my hands out of the water. It's also not turning my skin red.

My brain can't process any more weirdness tonight, so I ignore it and wash.

Danny glances over the laptop screen every so often. He seems haunted, or worried, but doesn't do anything more than cast furtive glances. Rapid key clicking continues for most of the time I wash dishes, pots, and such. I'm still hungry, but I've got no temptation whatsoever to pick at the leftovers.

With the dishes complete, I head to the living room and toss on *The Lion King* for the kids. Danny rushes typing another line or two, probably in an email, and darts over to join us on the couch. For about an hour and a half, the four of us snuggle on the sofa and I almost manage to forget my attack.

At least, until a sudden onset of anxiousness grips me.

I fight through it, gasping at times, running my fingers through my hair at others. My toes curl. I blink and rub my eyes and wonder what the hell is happening to me. I want to get up and pace, but that would only attract more stares and more worry. I fight through it—until I reach a point where I am certain I will need to stand and make an excuse to leave the room… and then, just like that, the feeling leaves.

And I know. Boy, oh boy, do I know why.

I can almost see it in my mind. How, I don't know, but there is a part of me that knows that the something planetary had just occurred. Something epic and beautiful and perfect. The sun had set.

And I couldn't be happier.

***

I am perplexed, horrified, intrigued.

After all, the veil of pervasive fatigue that had been weighing on me all day evaporates right around the time the windows go dark. A few hours ago, I couldn't help myself and slurped up blood. The daylight is painful to my skin… Now, I feel *alive* as soon as the sun goes down.

My mind leaps to the obvious conclusion, but I wind up laughing in my head since I'm not a character in a silly horror movie. *Oh, wow, Sam. Really? I am definitely going crazy.*

Danny's got his arm around me like he usually does for 'family movie time,' though he keeps giving me strange glances. Mostly, he appears worried. He'd sensed my anxiety a few minutes ago, of course. He had to have. Or he noticed me faking eating dinner. I push that knot of worry aside and allow myself to savor this time with my family. Time I almost had stolen from me.

"It's not a sad part," whispers Tammy, peering

up at me. "Don't cry yet."

"I know, Tam Tam." I ruffle her hair. "Sometimes people cry when they're really happy."

She grins and snuggles against my side.

The movie is over all too fast. Danny and I help the kids get ready for bed, tuck them in, and drift down the hall to our room. A white elephant follows me in. I just know Danny's going to hit me with something awkward, the only real question is if he's potentially hurt at my not eating, worried about my not eating, or something worse is coming.

"You… look better." Danny pulls his shirt off, his hair fluffing as it bursts from the neck opening. "All day you've had this… I dunno… *sick* air about you, but you look like yourself again now."

It's obviously a pure coincidence that I felt better as soon as the sun went down. What possible connection could there be for that? Since I don't want my husband to think I've slid completely 'round the bend, especially since I didn't know what to expect next, I say, "Thanks. Yeah, I do feel better."

He wings the shirt at the hamper and sets his hands on his hips, standing there in only jeans and socks. Despite the physical hunger still swirling around my gut, the sight of his bare chest lights a fire in my soul. I shouldn't be feeling like this and so revved up a week after I almost died. Then again, my neck shouldn't be healed either. At the very least, I *should* be sporting a rather serious scar, but…

I glide across the room and grasp Danny's sides, a wicked grin pulling my lips open.

"Sam?" Danny raises an eyebrow. "I know that look. Are you sure? It's barely been a week. You're… not in pain?"

My lips trace across his chest, kissing around his collarbone. "I'm feeling more alive now than I have in years. It's like being eighteen all over again. All that energy." I lean back and look into his dark blue eyes. "I almost lost you. I almost lost everything. Life is precious." Again, I cling to him, my cheek against his shoulder. "Every second of it."

He wraps me in his arms and we drift to the bed, groping each other and making out on the way. I sit on the edge and stretch out on my back, Danny sliding up beside me. His eyes radiate love, but also confusion. Feeling self-conscious, I slip away and pull my nightgown off.

"Wow, Sam, you're so damn beautiful." Danny flicks his belt open, shoving his jeans off onto the floor.

I grin and lay back. "You're no slouch yourself, Danny Moon." Looking at him, *smelling* his scent, is already driving me to the brink. The brink of what, admittedly, I'm not entirely sure.

He rolls closer, brushing a hand over my head and pulling me again into a kiss. His body, pressed against me, is deliciously warm, like a hot pie just removed from the oven. The coarseness of his fingers on my neck and shoulder sends a tingle down my spine. I swear I can feel every ridge and valley of his fingerprints. The sheets at my back, a legion of caressing hands, ignite my nerves. *Everything* is so much more intense than I can remember.

I moan into his mouth, grabbing at his boxer briefs, pushing them down while his scratchy chin glides across my shoulder toward my neck. When his lips make contact with my skin, a shudder of ecstasy runs through me, rattling the headboard. My eager hands search deeper, lower while I flatten on my back, pulling him up on top of me.

My fingers close around his length in a gentle, eager grasp; it's so hot, tingles dance up the backs of my arms. Something's come over me, and I *can't wait* to have him deep inside.

He groans and curls up, falling sideways off me. "Oof."

Not the reaction I was expecting.

"Danny?" I ask. "What's wrong?"

"Umm." His eyes are huge, a mixture of freaked out and turned on. "Your umm. Fingers." He rubs himself. "Little cold… and sharp."

I laugh and roll onto him. "So now it's my hands too? Not just my feet in the winter?"

Danny rests his hand on my shoulder for a moment before gliding it down to cradle my left breast. "It's not just your hands. You're a little, umm. Chilly. Everywhere."

"Sorry." I look down. His words hit me harder than they should, and I go from horny to crying in an instant.

"Hey." Danny sits up and brushes a thumb across my cheek. "I didn't mean it like that. You're still the most beautiful woman I know. The kindest, most loving, caring person I've ever met."

I sniffle, relaxing. He's got too much confidence in his voice to 'just be saying that.' A smile peers out from under my shame. "I'm so lucky to have you, Danny."

He leans in and kisses me. After a few minutes, it evolves to groping, and then more. He lines up and we start going all the way; a shaft of intense heat strikes through my core like a lightning bolt. My fingers dig into his shoulders; my back arches, and I let out a low moan of desire tinged with a sultry growl.

"Ngh!" Danny pulls back like someone punched him in the groin. His confusion flickers to disgust for an instant and then abject bewilderment.

The mood's done. Dead and buried.

Sheepish and dejected, I crawl after my nightgown and pull it back on over my head. For a few minutes, I sit at the foot end of the bed, staring at the rug. Danny remains curled up on his side, cradling himself.

Eventually, the silence is too burdensome to bear.

I whisper, "I'm sorry."

"It's… not your fault, Sam."

"What's wrong?" I ask, my gaze still locked on the rug.

The bed jostles as Danny moves around, likely

pulling his boxers back on. "I—maybe it's just too soon. I keep seeing you in my mind all torn up and…"

He's almost lying. Not quite. He doesn't have to say it though; I'm not *that* obtuse. My heart's beating a couple times a minute. Danny's skin is hot to my touch. I must be corpse-cold to him, especially *down there*. That flicker of revulsion in his eyes was brief, but telling. Maybe this will improve with time? I have to hope I'll get better.

Danny shuffles closer and sits beside me, an arm across my back. "Hey… I still love you. We just need to figure out what's going on. You will recover… whatever this is."

"I hope so." I lean against him, grateful he's not pulling away.

"So, I was doing a little research about that whole sun thing."

"Sun thing?"

"You got a sunburn in a few seconds when I took you home from the hospital. I'm not sure how exactly you wound up developing a condition like that out of the blue, but it sounds like xeroderma pigmentosum."

"Bless you." I look up with a wry smile.

He chuckles at my sneezing joke. "It's an autosomal disease. A genetic disorder of the skin. Usually, it manifests immediately after birth." He tickles my side with one finger. "You know they call victims 'moon children' because they can't tolerate any sunlight. Even minute exposure causes horrible burns."

Moon children. I'd laugh at the irony if I didn't want to curl up into a lonely dark place out of shame. Will my husband ever want to touch me again? Have I become disgusting to him?

I trace my fingers back and forth across my left forearm. "People don't spontaneously develop genetic conditions, Danny." *Of course, it makes more sense than what I'm thinking... but what I'm thinking makes no sense at all.*

"Well, something's going on." He rubs my back, squeezing my shoulder. "I'm not giving up on you, Samantha Moon. Not now. Not ever." He pulls me into a two-armed hug, forehead pressed to the crook of my neck.

A hitch in his breath tells me he's on the verge of crying, and a lump swells in my throat, too. All the guilt I imagined at Danny learning of my death hits me again. "I'm sorry… I should've never gone jogging out that late. That's the dumbest thing I've ever done."

"It's not your fault." He squeezes tighter for a second, then sits up and wipes his eyes. "Even with your training and a gun, you couldn't have done much against… well, whatever it was that came out of the woods and got you."

A man. I felt his fingers on my flesh, his breath against my skin... his teeth piercing my neck like icepicks. Gold flashes in my mind's eye, the dangling medallion, inches from my face. "Maybe you're right," I say, distracted.

He would've come for me anyway… and he might've killed my whole family had I not gone out.

No. I'm not even going to think about what might've happened if it attacked me at home. But it had come for me, I was sure of it. If so, then I needed to stop feeling stupid for going out alone at night. It wound up being a *good thing.* Perhaps by total chance, but I did save Danny, Tammy, and Anthony's lives by doing that. I believe that with all my heart and soul.

I remember the voice again… the voice I had heard inside my head.

Hello, Sssamantha.

Yes, it had come for me, whatever or whoever it was.

I sit there while Danny goes to clean up and brush his teeth for the night. Maybe in a few days, if I'm still cold to the touch, I'll suggest we get frisky in the shower. Hot water might help. Soon, he's back in the bedroom and we lay in bed beside each other, cuddling under the blankets. At first, he's stiff and a little standoffish, like a boy who still thinks I'll give him cooties. Though, after a few minutes, the normality of the arrangement settles in and we cuddle.

Once the lights go out, Danny fades off to sleep. I remain awake and alert. Other than a distracting sense of hunger, I feel ready to take on the world—like it's 11:00 a.m., and I've downed five Red Bulls or something. There's no reason I should be this wired at almost midnight. Then again, I did sleep late. Maybe my circadian rhythm is totally jacked up since my throat had been torn open. Yeah, that's gotta be it.

Allergic to the sun.

Groggy during the day.

Awake at night.

The mirror hates me.

I healed a severe injury within hours.

My body's rejecting everything I try to eat except for blood.

I'm cold.

I don't need to breathe.

My heart's beating too slow to possibly keep me alive.

...and I'm completely insane for even thinking what I'm thinking.

Get a grip, Sam. Vampires don't exist.

Chapter Five
The Inferno

Hours drag by in a solemn march of boredom.

When it becomes clear I'm not sleeping, I slip out of bed and pace the house while Tammy, Anthony, and Danny remain lost to their dreams. Watching my kids sleep makes me smile, at least until I think about how close I came to being gone from their lives.

Hunger pulls me to the kitchen, but nothing in the fridge appeals. I open and close the door a dozen times, as if something that hadn't been there before might suddenly appear and pique my interest.

The crunch of someone walking outside invades my silent kitchen, like I had a movie turned up way too loud. I follow the noise to the living room window and catch a few seconds' glimpse of a man in a T-shirt and track pants. He twists toward our side of the street, a flashlight raised.

Oh, it's Chet Perry. He lives two houses away at the opening of our cul-de-sac, and I bet he's looking for his dog again, no doubt cursing his wife for talking him into agreeing to a Cairn terrier, which is totally a real thing. I chuckle to myself. The man always complains about it, but he'd probably jump in front of a car to save that dog. Never understood why some men express affection by complaining.

With a sigh, I retreat to the dining room and sit by Danny's laptop to throw a couple hours at *Yahoo!*, hoping I can find something about insomnia. I read for a while about that, as well as that xeroderma pigmentosum business Danny mentioned. Information is somewhat sparse, but it does look like a genetic disorder that people are born with. It's unlikely I've had it my whole life and only now has it become symptomatic, but a strange medical anomaly sure makes more sense than me becoming some fictional monster.

One article described a small boy who has to load up on super-strong sunscreen and heavy clothing if his parents take him out of the house during the day… even when it's cloudy. Oh, that poor child. It's difficult for me to feel sorry for my situation when I'm looking at a photograph of a five-year-old covered in burns he got from three minutes' exposure to direct sunlight. According to what I'm reading, the condition also results in dry skin, hardened lumps forming, and lingering scar tissue.

Well, I burned the hell out of myself the day I came home from the hospital, but within an hour, I looked fine again… like nothing happened. I don't like the sound of 'keratinized lumps' and I'm not sure what they are, but I don't think I have them. Maybe I've got a new and undiscovered disease. Or Danny could be on to something. If my condition ever becomes an issue, I could always claim to have XP.

Ugh. I'm going to have to go out in the day for work. I wonder if the sunscreen method will help?

You'd think with a hundred channels on cable there'd be something worth watching… but not at three in the morning. Channel-flipping lands me on the opening sequence for a movie, and I sit there stunned by *Hell Comes to Frogtown.* It's so ridiculously bad I can't stop watching it. Days ago, I lay wounded, lamenting every second passing by as so precious… Now, it feels wrong to waste them on *this*.

I go back to the laptop and check the web for any information about my attack, but find little other than a mention that the suggested coyote hunt got called off after an 'unknown source' determined the animals weren't to blame. Hmm. I've never been an unknown source before. Makes me feel like I'm in a spy movie. At least no one hurt the poor animals. They really did have nothing to do with it.

With a sigh, I get up and roam down the hall to Tammy's room. There, I sit on the floor by her bed and watch her sleep for a while. I drift into

Anthony's room next, idly picking up a few toys. He stirs at my approach, but doesn't wake. A huge smile forms on his face, which is probably a reaction to something in his dream, but I can't help but believe he knows Mommy's here to protect him.

Eventually, I find myself back in the kitchen staring into the fridge.

Still the same stuff. Plenty of food… but as soon as I think of eating anything, I go from hungry to nauseated.

"Ugh," I mutter, and shut the door.

Since it's 5:40 a.m., I decide to give sleep one last shot, and crawl back in under the blankets next to Danny—who, as it turns out, snores. He doesn't rattle the windows, just makes these little soft snorts like a dog having an exciting dream of chasing chipmunks.

Nothing that's happening to me makes any logical sense. Ideas and theories circle my brain like buzzards waiting for something to die. Or maybe something already is dead. Me. Totally not a good thought when you're trying to sleep. Like, at all.

They say intelligent people have a more difficult time falling asleep at night because their minds won't shut down. I find myself thinking about this theory, which either proves it… or proves that I'm a glutton for punishment. When it comes to my family, I might be on the smarter end of the spectrum, which didn't necessarily say much. (Hey, at least I'm not a narcissist.) Anyway, I figure my brother Dusk's probably smarter than me, but he's been cursed with our father's lazy gene. I wonder how his European wandering is going. What else does one do with an art degree other than teach or roam the globe? I guess he could like work at a gallery or something. Mary Lou and I are probably about equal, but I bet she considers herself a little smarter than me. That's fine. I'll let her have it, and hey, maybe she's right after all. My sister didn't go jogging at midnight, alone. I can't help but note how quickly Danny always seems to fall asleep. Does that say something about my husband's intelligence? I doubt it; I mean, he's a lawyer, right? Probably more a statement about how exhausting his days are.

Finally, I start to feel tired, like sleep might be a possibility, so I clear my mind and try to think of nothing at all.

The next thing I know, I'm sitting on the beach with the sun bearing down on me. Tammy's nearby, burrowing a hole in the sand while Anthony is shoveling it bit by bit back into the hole. Danny's maybe thirty feet away, closer to the water, and talking to a light-haired woman in oversized sunglasses, an orange bikini top, and a sunflower-patterned wrap.

I have the strangest feeling that Tammy's about to punch Anthony on the nose, but I can't pull my attention away from my husband. He's having an innocent-looking conversation with that woman, but I find myself hating her. Jealousy rises out of nowhere, a toxic darkness saturating my emotions.

Who is this bitch and why is she smiling at Danny? Why is he over there with her and not with me and the kids?

Livid, I grab the armrests of my beach chair and start to get up, but freeze in terror at the sight of smoke wisps peeling up from my hands. What? It's a perfect day with a clear blue sky, and I adore the beach, sunbathing every chance I can get. My arms are… burning.

The instant the word 'burning' crosses my brain, my legs and stomach go bright red and blistery. Small black spots on the backs of my hands expand to smoldering patches of char. I'm no longer sitting in the sun; I'm sitting under an unforgiving ball of flaming death.

Agony like nothing I could've imagined paralyzes me.

I let off a weak, whispery squeak, my body in too much pain to even scream.

"That's not good fire," says Anthony.

Tammy lifts her gaze from her excavation and peers at me. Utterly calm, she tilts her head like a bewildered puppy. "Promise you won't give up on me? Or Anf-nee."

Most of my fingers crumble away to ashes, the black seep crawling up my wrists onto my forearms. My feet disintegrate. Skin on my thighs and stomach bubbles and melts off. Neither of my children reacts whatsoever to my apparent spontaneous combustion.

Again, I try to scream, but only manage a

wheeze.

Danny notices the smoke billowing away from me and frowns. He gestures at the woman in the orange bikini as if to say 'hang on a moment,' and comes walking toward me, looking annoyed.

"You're going to hurt them," says Danny, while snatching Tammy and Anthony off the beach and backing away from me.

No! I try to scream, but my body won't listen. What's left of my arms dissolves into a cloud of black ash particles as I sit up and try to reach for my children. Danny pulls them away, back to the woman I can't stand.

Finally, the agony trapped in my throat flies into the world on an anguished scream. The force of the sound wave that blasts out of me swats Danny to the beach. He lets off a strangled gurgle and curls up in a ball. Seconds later, he collapses into a mass of inky vapors, the tendrils of which whirl around Anthony until he breathes them in.

Horrified, I stare down at myself, watching flesh immolate away. The sky I so adored has gone from blue and cloudless to a rolling inferno straight out of *Dante*. I'm in so much pain I can't even feel it anymore. In seconds, my body's nothing but a set of blackened bones in the smoldering remains of my bathing suit.

I jolt upright in bed, shaking, but somehow not screaming.

Danny's no longer beside me.

The clock on the nightstand reads 11:14 a.m.

Gasping for air, I raise my hands, terrified of what I may find, but to my relief, they're only shaking. No ashes, no burns.

I'm not even sweating.

"Not real," I mutter to no one in particular.

Minutes pass in silence of me doing nothing but staring at my hands, basking in the relief of seeing myself whole and not crispy-crittered. I think my heart's even racing. It's beating about twenty times a minute.

Figures, it had been a nightmare.

Chapter Six
Dusk

My eyes open again at the ring of the house phone. I don't remember lying back down after that horrible dream, but I've clearly been sleeping since the clock has leapt to 1:52 p.m. The space between staring at my still-intact hands and losing a few hours passed in an instant. Well, I guess no dreams beats bad dreams.

"Sam?" asks Danny from the doorway. "Are you feeling all right? I figured I'd let you sleep since you seemed so out of it yesterday."

I raise a leaden arm to my face and wipe at my eyes. The bed's like a magnet, trying to pull me back down. My eyes don't want to stay open, but I can't sleep all day, dammit. Grunting, I swing my legs over the side and stand.

"Sam?"

"Yeah… I'm okay. I just feel… overtired or

something."

And I don't have to pee. Again.

That truth alone gets my hands shaking from fear. It's almost five days now and I haven't gone to the damn bathroom once. *This isn't normal.* Hah. As if peeing represented the entirety of how *not-normal* I am right now.

"Umm, there's a guy on the phone for you. Says he's your brother." Danny points with his thumb toward the kitchen.

"Wow. Really?" I force myself to walk down the hall.

In my groggy half-aware state, I don't notice a patch of sunlight on the rug from the bathroom window until I put my foot in it. Like I'd stepped on a hot frying pan, I let out a yowl and leap forward, hopping on one leg. My right foot's lobster red and wisping smoke.

Danny catches me before I fall over. "Whoa! Sam…"

"Mommy?" calls Tammy from the living room.

"I'm fine," I half-yell, before gritting my teeth against the pain. "Just stepped on something painful."

"What on earth?" Danny stoops to examine my injury.

The redness, and the feeling my skin's coated in a layer of boiling oil, fade in a few seconds, leaving us both stunned.

I blink at my again-unhurt foot. "Guess I've got that xeroderma thing you were talking about yesterday, huh?"

"That's…" Danny stares into my eyes with the look of a frightened boy. "I don't even know what I just saw."

"I don't either." I cling to him. "We're in uncharted waters."

"Hey." He lifts my chin with one finger and smiles as soon as we make eye contact. His fear's gone, replaced with the same outward confidence he throws off in court. "We're going to get through this. Whatever it takes, I'm not going to rest until we've got this handled. Okay?"

I wasn't buying it. After all, he'd sounded this self-assured before when facing his first judge, and I knew for a fact he'd been terrified. It was his first case, and I'd gone along to lend moral support from the audience seats. The whole car ride there, he shook, sweat bullets, and muttered about how everything could go wrong… but as soon as he got going, he'd turned into the super cool, poised litigator who's smiling at me now. Like that day, he's probably terrified. Then again, I am too. Can't fault him.

"Yeah," I say.

"Something's burning?" asks Tammy from the archway to the living room. "Stinky."

"It's nothing." Danny nudges me toward the phone and scoops Tammy up. "I was cleaning the stove."

Tammy glances at me as if she doesn't quite believe him. And she shouldn't; after all, her daddy just lied to her face. All because of me and my condition. I go a different route and try to convey the idea that 'you're too young to worry about it' with my facial expression. She shrugs, looks at Danny, points into the living room, and starts telling him about something Barney's doing.

In the kitchen, the phone's balanced sideways on the cradle. I grab the handset, lean against the wall, and say, "Hello?"

"Sammy," says Dusk, my middle brother and one year my junior. "How ya doing, kiddo?"

His voice is tinny and the line crackles with static. "Kiddo? I'm only one year behind you. And I've been home from the hospital for about three days. Nice of you to finally check in on me."

"Aww, don't be like that, Sammy… I'm in friggin' Belarus. Not the easiest place to get news. What happened?" A pair of older-sounding female voices argue in the background, not using any language I can recognize.

I twist my finger around the phone cord while jabbing my big toe at the kitchen floor. It's a touch bitchy of me to snap at him for waiting so long to make contact considering he's on the other side of the globe… and no one else I'm related to aside from Mary Lou has even bothered. Again, my family's not exactly what one could call 'close.' As far as I know, there's no active animosity anywhere… we just drifted apart and never looked back.

Except for my sister. *Damn! What am I going to*

tell her?

Danny mentioned he'd gotten through to River, my eldest brother, but he's in Louisiana working on some construction project. Out-of-state contractors do some bizarre thing where they work twelve hours a day for weeks without a day off, then take a couple months off. I remember hearing once that he goes all over the country for these jobs. He's away so much his wife must feel like a widow getting a pension from a mysterious benefactor.

"Sorry," I say, and mean it. "I've been having a crazy couple days of it."

A horn blares by in the background over the phone. "I'm sorry, sis. What happened?"

I don't have a ready answer for his question. Hell, I don't have ready answers for my own questions. "I'm still not entirely sure. Something or someone attacked me when I was jogging—"

And that's all I get out before my younger brother veritably leaps through the line. I spend the next few minutes reassuring him that I'm all right. He goes off on a tirade of swearing, and I remember all over again just what a hothead Dusk can be.

Dusk would be a helluva name for a vampire.

Where the heck did that thought come from? Talk about a non-sequitur.

Anyway, when I've calmed him down—and appreciating his feisty, brotherly concern more than I care to admit—I finish up with: "I guess it looked a whole lot worse than it was. I'm home already and I feel okay. Lot of blood but the wound was shallow. It's almost gone now. No one looking at me would even suspect I'd been mugged. So… Belarus, huh? How's the art thing going?"

The arguing old ladies get louder. Even not understanding a word being said, I get the feeling someone's about to get clubbed over the head with a purse.

"Eh, it's all right. Kinda living off the kindness of strangers at the moment. Doing odd jobs here and there. Seeing the world before I'm too old to walk. Been emailing this guy in New York about the evil."

I raise an eyebrow. "Did you say 'the evil'? And what are those women fighting about?"

"Huh? What women?"

"The ones arguing behind you somewhere."

Rustling comes over the line for a few seconds. "Oh, holy crap, this phone's sensitive. There're a couple old women down at the corner. Looks like they're trying to choke each other."

Eep. A normal person wouldn't have heard them. I let it go. "So, uhh, what's 'the evil?'"

"Ahh." Dusk laughs. "A day job."

I blink. "*You* are contemplating a day job?"

"Well…" He sighs. "I'm almost thirty-five. Figured since I haven't become a famous European painter by now, I could try a different approach."

"Doing what?"

His voice exudes a smile. "Art teacher. What else?"

"And be stoned all day in class like Mr.

Haltemeyer?" Who was, of course, our high school art teacher. Stoner or not, he had set Dusk on the path of art and travel. Or getting high and wandering aimlessly.

He cackles. "Well, yeah, but I'm not going to spend my days quite as blazed as he was."

Hah! Back then, all the kids floated the rumor he had a giant bong in his desk. I still don't know for sure if the man had been toking between periods or if he just smoked so much at home he stayed high all day.

"Oh wow. You know, I heard he's *still* there. Guess Principal Monroe never searched his desk."

Dusk laughs. "I'm sure things won't be quite as laid back in New York as they were in Cali." A sharp *click* comes over the line. "Oh, crap. About out of money here. So, you're really okay?"

"As far as I know. Nothing hurts and I seem to be alive." Mostly. "New York? Seriously?"

"Yeah, it's the only nibble I've got so far. And, cool. Hey, I gave Danny an address you can use if you need to get in touch with me at least for the next few months. If you need—"

The line drops.

I sigh, whispering, "Thanks for thinking of me, Dusk."

After hanging the phone up, I trudge into the living room. Danny's sitting on the floor with his back against the front of the couch, Tammy beside him. Mercifully, they've dethroned the purple dinosaur. Danny's put on an old movie: *The Black*

Cauldron, which might be a little much for a four-year-old, even though it's a cartoon.

Anthony wobbles across the room and goes face-first into the pot of our giant fake plant to the left of the TV. I start to go after him, but he grabs the curtain to pull himself up and yanks it open a few inches, blasting me with the glaring late-afternoon California sun.

Like I'd had a pot of boiling water thrown on my face, I scream and jump back, scrambling for the safety of the hallway. Everything is a panicky blur until I'm on my hands and knees a few feet inside the master bedroom, coughing on smoke. It feels like air is moving in and out of my mouth through holes in my cheeks, but that *terrible* sensation stops after a second or two.

"Mommy?" Tammy runs in behind me. "Why did you scream?"

Anthony's frightened wailing reaches my awareness.

I sit back on my heels, keeping my arms in my lap so Tammy hopefully can't see the burns. Lying to my kids bothers me, but she's not equipped to deal with this. Hell, I'm not sure *I* am. "I saw a big spider."

Tammy gasps and runs back down the hall to the living room, shouting for Daddy to get rid of the spider.

Without thinking, I dart to my feet and run to check myself in the bathroom mirror—and stare at a hollow nightgown.

Crap.

I recoil from that horror and hurry out to the bedroom, waving my arms to clear the smoke. Once the crazy itching in my face stops, I test my cheeks with probing fingers and all seems to be smooth and where it should be. My arms aren't red anymore, either. Whew. Only seconds in the sun and I felt like I'd body surfed a hibachi grill. Incredulous, I gaze at my unblemished arms for a moment more, and let them fall slack at my sides.

"Yup. This is definitely *not* normal."

Chapter Seven
Scary Sam

By the time I get back to the living room, Danny's mostly got Anthony calm. The poor little guy thought I'd yelled at him for pulling on the curtain; luckily, neither one of the kids realized I'd turned into the Amazing Combustible Mommy.

It would be funny if it wasn't so sad.

With the kids calm again, Danny talks a little about work. He's going to need to go to court in a few days to represent his client. That part, he can't do from home. I'm fine with him going back. The last thing I want is for him to feel trapped here because of whatever's happened to me. And honestly, I'm not helpless or even sick. Just… tired. Well, during the days. Last night… well, last night I could have done anything. I really believe that.

He's seen me burn twice now, and it's probably out of the question to ignore that it happened. While the kids are engrossed in the movie, I lean close to him and mutter that I read a little about XP and saw that some sufferers use sunscreen.

"Worth a try," says Danny with an appraising frown. "We should probably get you back to the doctor's for a look."

"Maybe."

He gives me a parental smirk. "More than maybe."

"Look, it might clear up." Staying positive. That's me.

"I"—the doorbell rings, saving my ass—"got it," says Danny.

Not taking any chances with errant rays of sunlight, I get up, too, and move around behind the sofa, edging backward into the hallway.

Danny opens the door. "Oh, hey. Come in."

Mary Lou walks in with her brood. Or maybe spills in might be a better way of putting it. Ellie Mae, her six-year-old, beelines for Tammy while Billy Joe zooms down the hall for the bathroom, both hands clamped over his butt. Mary Lou starts to smile at me but a curious glance at all the drawn curtains distracts her. It's the first time she'd been here since I got back from the hospital… which had only been two days ago.

Her youngest, Ruby Grace, stops short a few steps inside the door and stares at me. "Mom?"

Mary Lou twists around to look down at her. "Hmm?"

"Why is Aunt Sam scary?"

"What do you mean scary?" Mary Lou glances at me for a second then back to her.

Ruby Grace fidgets. "She's got scary eyes now. I don't think she's mad at me, but if she was mad at me, I'd be really scared."

"I'm not mad at you, sweetie." I put on my most reassuring smile.

As soon as Danny shuts the door, muting the sunlight, a tangible wave of relief sweeps over me.

"Aunt Sam was hurt a little while ago and she's still feeling sick. You know how grumpy Daddy gets when he's sick."

"Yeah." Ruby Grace nods. "He's a grump."

The two-year-old (months shy of three) joins the other kids on the rug. She's already talking like a four- or five-year-old. Smart kid. She'll either be a scientist when she grows up or a holographic radio host… or whatever it is that the future holds for us.

Mary Lou gives Danny a 'need a minute' glance before taking me by the hand and pulling me down the hall to the master bedroom. Once we're inside, she eases the door almost closed, faces me, and half-whispers, "Okay, spill."

"Spill what?" I ask, wrapping my arms around myself.

"Sam." Mary Lou hugs me. "You're white as a ghost. You've got the curtains drawn on every window in the house, and you're on edge. I can see it all over your face." She leans back and stares into my eyes. "Yeah, you look different even from just yesterday. Sweetie, what's wrong?"

I look down, knowing she's right. Hell, I could almost feel myself changing hourly. "I'm not really sure what's going on, Mary Lou. Danny thinks I might have some weird skin condition that's making me sensitive to sunlight."

"Porphyria?"

"No… Xeroderma pigmentosum. I'm getting sunburned in seconds now."

She gasps. "But you're a beach bum!"

I let out a wry laugh. "Not anymore… at least, not unless whatever's going on with me is temporary."

"Well, we can get you to a doctor and have them check everything out." Mary Lou fusses over me. "Let me get a closer look. And why are you out of your bandages already?"

I reach across my chest with my left arm and idly scratch where I'd been torn open. The doctors had told Danny the extent of my injuries, even if he hadn't seen them. And, Mary Lou had been there as well. Both had heard the doctor say I'd probably never speak again. I could always downplay the extent of the injuries, hoping Mary Lou accepts the idea the doctor may have been wrong. Then again, maybe I should come clean to Mary Lou. Coming clean is the least-desirable option, because not only does it make me sound insane, I still haven't figured out what is happening to me. And if she sets her mind to it, Mary Lou could pry every last tidbit of information out of me. She's had years of practice at it from her job as a claims examiner. Worse, she's not working at the moment so she can wrangle three kids full time since Rick's doing well enough that they don't *need* two incomes. I bet she'd jump at the chance to get into that old mode. Once Ruby Grace is older, I'm sure she'll go back to it. She adores doing the stay-at-home-mom thing for her kids, but she's itching to keep her mind busy.

Anyway, I'm too… exhausted to deal with all of this now. Maybe tonight, when I have more energy. A thought that gives me pause… I'm accepting truth in knowing I'll have more energy tonight *after* the sun goes down. Whoa, Sam, dial it back a bit. Reality check.

So, I say, "I think the doctor was a bit overly conservative. I went to change them yesterday and, well… look. There's not even a mark left. It was a knife, I think, but it must've been really sharp. The cut was small. Lot of blood."

"Sam…" Mary Lou grabs my hand and cradles it in both of hers. "Even a small cut wouldn't be *gone* in a week. And the last I saw you—granted you were sleeping at the time—but still, the last I saw you, you had this huge bandage around your neck. Like huge. I remember, because I nearly lost it. They said the injury was bad. Like really bad. But… there's nothing, Sam. Seriously, what the heck?"

I sigh, knowing there's no one in this world I trust more than Mary Lou. I guess my late-night confessional was getting moved up, energy or no energy. "I… don't understand either. Maybe you can help me make sense of it."

"Sense of what?"

"You're staring at me the same way you stared at me before I told you what I did at Jensen's farm."

She puts her fists on her hips. "Damn right, I am. Sam, what's going on? You're freaking me out."

Jensen's farm. Right, my hippie family living in the woods needed food and I'd snuck onto his farm at night to steal vegetables. Figured the worst that would happen being ten years old at the time would've been an ass whipping. More than likely, Mr. Jensen would've felt bad for me, a wild-haired scrawny ragamuffin trying to steal food because her parents failed at life. Luckily, I never got caught that summer, even though I went back there dozens of times. Mary Lou hadn't told on me… in fact, once or twice she'd helped carry stuff. Not that the Jensens missed it. They had a *lot* of land and sold most of their produce to some giant company.

Anyway… I have to trust her.

At the realization I haven't taken a breath in a few minutes, I suck in a deep one and let it out slow. "I'm confused and a little freaked out myself." I motion for her to follow me. "C'mon."

My turn to lead her by the hand. The kids and Danny are all still in the living room. We creep down the hall and duck into the bathroom. Mary Lou folds her arms, like she's expecting me to lift up my nightgown and show some wound, blemish, or other some such body issue.

"Promise me you won't scream, okay?" I say.

She smiles. "You didn't sprout a penis, did you?"

I cackle and wind up laughing uncontrollably for a moment. "God, I needed that."

"So no extra body parts, then?" she asks.

"Nope. I think it's more like something's *missing*." I wipe the laughter tears, grab her by the shoulders, and try to steady myself. "This is going to be weird. Weirder than anything you've ever seen."

"So you *did* sprout a—"

"No." I shake my head. "My plumbing's just fine." Head bowed, I close my eyes. "Look in the mirror."

Mary Lou gasps. "Sam… what?"

Cat's out of the bag now; no sense hesitating. I open my eyes and lift my head, standing beside my sister with an arm around her. Mary Lou's in the mirror next to my floating nightgown.

I pull up the front, 'flashing' the mirror, but only expose the inside of the garment for a second.

"Oh my God…" She puts a hand over her mouth. "Is this a trick mirror?"

"No. This is really happening." I pick at her hair, which in the mirror appears to be jumping on its own.

"You mean this joke is happening. Not funny, Sam. In fact, I'm a little pissed off. No, a lot pissed off. Here I am worrying about you, and what, you guys have been busy installing this bullshit mirror—"

"It's not a joke, Mary Lou." I rummage through one of the cabinet drawers and find a small handheld mirror. I hold it up, curious myself to see if my refection would be in it… but nope. I angle it so Mary Lou can see, too. In it, I see the tears on her face. In it, I see my sister oh-so-very-close to losing it. That made two of us.

"Sam, where are you?"

"I don't know. But I'm here. I think." And despite myself, my voice constricts, and something close to a sob comes out.

Mary Lou, without thinking, pulls me in close. As she does so, I feel her turn her head to the mirror. She says "Jesus" under her breath, and holds me tighter. Soon, we are both sobbing. Mostly—and bless her for this—she lets me know that I am here, that I am alive. And that this is really happening.

***

"So, what do you think?" I ask, when we get a handle on the tears.

"Funky," mutters Mary Lou, leaning closer to the mirror. "Damn funky. Has Danny seen *this*?"

"No. I'm a chicken." I manage a weak smile. "I haven't told anyone else about my mirror shyness."

She snickers. "Interesting term for it. Is anything else going on? Do you feel different?"

"A little tired… all day yesterday too. I could *so* crawl into bed right now and zonk. And… I'm kinda having sunburn issues."

Mary Lou narrows her eyes, tapping her finger on her chin.

That's her thinking face… and it usually doesn't end well.

Chapter Eight
Anger

Mary Lou listened while I talked about most of what had been going through my head since the attack.

As I spoke, my sister didn't flip out or say much at all, which was a good thing. Because I needed to get it all out in a bad way. When I finished, when I heard how nuts I sounded out loud, my sister gave me a warm, supportive hug… and a look that suggested she'd gone down the rabbit hole and was in crazy land. It was, I thought, a fitting look. We agreed to discuss it later—basically, when I had more information—and, after I got dressed, migrated out to the living room. As if I didn't already feel like the helpless sick girl, spending two full days in a nightgown only made that worse.

Her husband, Rick, arrived a little after six. My sister and I made dinner. I don't think she caught me drinking the blood out of the ground beef package, but I'm pretty sure she did catch me faking eating later—not that she said anything.

So, yeah, that was my day.

Now, it's nearly one in the morning. I'm wide awake again. Danny's out cold. The kids are safe in their beds. My perfect family sleeps. Only, I feel like I'm not supposed to be here anymore. Everything isn't as it should be. No, I should be dead. In fact, Danny should be a grieving widower trying to wrangle two kids and a career.

I can't help but sense that a serious fray has developed in the fabric of my life, and it's going to unravel in a big way.

To avoid disturbing Danny, I slip gingerly out of bed. We didn't bother attempting to get intimate tonight, just went to bed like some old couple. And, yes, I know not *all* old people are so boring. But if I start thinking about oldsters getting frisky, that'll make me think of my parents and just… no.

Minutes drag into an hour of pacing around the bedroom, watching Danny sleep. Memories of our life together flood my thoughts in a torrent of snapshot smiles. The confused/worried expression he had on when he ran up to me on the beach only weeks ago lingers. He hadn't noticed I had lost track of Tammy, hadn't seen what a failure of a parent I'd been. Mere seconds. I'd looked away for mere seconds, transfixed by—something evil.

I've read countless crime statistics. I *know* what can happen in 'mere seconds,' and yet, I still fell for the trap. I lost her. By sheer luck, she'd found a kind old man and not a dangerous one.

And I'd failed her again when I decided to go jogging in the middle of the night. Why was I so freakin' stupid!? Why did I do that to my family? To Danny? What did I do to deserve this? Why me? I get pissed off at the universe all over again.

Rage boils up inside me. My fists clench. I storm out of the bedroom so my stomping doesn't wake Danny or the kids. Around and around the sofa I go in the living room, muttering curses. I want to get my hands on the piece of shit who attacked me. I want to bang my head on the wall to punish myself for being so *stupid* to go out alone. Never mind that I've already determined that by going out alone, I had possibly saved my family from an imminent attack. Screw that. It had to have been random. It had to have, dammit. And I put myself in harm's way, and now my life was… over. I felt it, sensed it, knew it. Everything I had ever wanted or hoped for was being taken from me, one blood-filled package of raw beef at a time.

Shimmering crimson seeps between my fingers. The pain is minute, but it sneaks past my fury.

Eight small red crescents line my palms from where my fingernails bit in. The wounds close before my eyes, even as the sight of blood stirs hunger within my gut. Before I know what I'm doing, I lick my hands clean.

Hungry, and still furious, I stand there in the kitchen feeling like a home-invader.

With each passing minute, anger builds. I have to do *something.* I have to… kill the monster that did this to me. A part of my brain laughs at the idiocy of the idea, but I'm far too pissed off for rational thought. How dare he do this to me! How dare he ruin my life! Sure, it wasn't perfect, but it had been mine. Thirty-one years it had taken me to stop feeling like I *needed* to hang on to someone else for support to get by. I'd *finally* become a functioning adult.

And this son of a bitch tried to take it away from me.

I swoop down the hall to the bedroom and change into a tank top, sweatpants, socks, and sneakers. Curses stream past my lips in constant whispering. In mere seconds, I'm already jogging, nearly running, away from the house, the same path I took that night. No explanation for what I'm doing comes to me. My body's just going.

I may have even left my front door open.

Rage drives me. My sneakers pound the pavement. Snarling, I push myself up to a full run, somehow convinced that if I get back to Hillcrest Park fast enough, I'll get revenge. I swing a right onto Virginia Road and head west for North Lemon Street. Straight ahead of me, a small ramp leads up into Hillcrest Park, and a six-foot concrete retaining wall at the base of the rounded hill I'd tried to run across to escape just a few nights ago.

Not even close to winded, I hurl myself at the wall, scaling it with ease and claw my way up the curved, grassy slope to the top. It takes me only a few seconds to dart across to the west, leaping down the hilly face on the other side dotted with tiny trees. There, I stop on the bend in the road where that *thing* caught up to me.

I just ran as hard as I could for about a mile and I'm not breathing hard.

Hell, I'm not even breathing.

This little road bends around a bell-shaped curve with an offshoot leading northeast at the top… That creature picked me up and threw me into the woods, straight north. I take a few steps off the road onto the dirt, turning, scanning the area for any sign of motion.

Nothing.

I feel like a lioness. I hold my arms out, fingers curled like claws, my teeth bared. If that man is here, he is going to die. It doesn't bother me that I ran down here and didn't get tired. I barely process the notion that I'm unarmed. It doesn't seem like a problem. I feel utterly invincible.

"Come on, you coward!" I scream into the trees. "What are you hiding from?"

I turn, glaring death at the sad little moonlit excuse for a forest. It's all so clear to my eyes. There's nowhere anyone could hide and I wouldn't see them. Did someone turn the moon's dimmer switch all the way up?

"Where are you?!" I roar.

After a moment of no answer, I turn my rage up at the heavens, at God. "Is that what happened? Are you real and you're laughing your ass off at me now for *not* believing? Come on! If you're real, show yourself!"

My voice echoes into nothingness.

"Why me?" I shout. "What the hell did I do?"

A strong twinge of hunger gets me even angrier. Since neither my attacker nor God is bothering to show up for me to vent upon, I stomp around the woods until a potato-sized rock catches my eye.

Overcome by mindless rage, I grab it and hurl it off in a random direction with everything I have, stumbling two steps forward after letting go.

Even that doesn't make me feel like I've burned off any of this excess energy.

I point at the trees, thinking of my attacker. "Where are you, coward? Why me? What did I do to you? And *you!*" My glare turns skyward. "You're not real. Or if you are, you're a sadistic bastard! Benevolent, my ass!"

Too angry to think straight, and having no targets to absorb my wrath, I collapse to my knees, seething at the ground. Frustration at not being able to do anything gets me angry-crying. This isn't fair! This is completely messed up and *so* unfair.

A growl, inhumanly deep, slips from my throat. I spring to my feet and plow my fist into a nearby tree, cracking the wood and breaking two knuckles. The pain doesn't bother me.

It just makes me angrier.

Chapter Nine
SPF Nine Million

Danny comes through for me, having caught the hint I dropped.

When I manage to force myself out of bed around noon the next day—I think it's Thursday—there's a plastic bag on the bureau with a few bottles of extreme sunscreen.

I'm a little hungrier than I was yesterday, which unnerves me. I haven't kept food down since the attack. Even that egg burrito Danny got me in the hospital jumped ship in minutes. I shouldn't be *a little hungry;* I should be starving.

After trading my nightgown for a T-shirt, jeans, and sneakers, I snag the sunscreen products and stagger down the hall toward the kitchen. Danny's at the dining room table working on the laptop. Tammy's sitting nearby, her attention on a coloring book while Anthony sits on the floor under the table with his toys.

"Morning, hon." Danny stands into a kiss, smiling. "Are you feeling any better?"

"Same as I have the past few days. I feel fine… just tired."

He rubs his chin. "Hmm. I've never known you to sleep past nine in the morning before. Maybe you've got some kind of flu?"

"No congestion or anything… and you didn't know me during high school. Mary Lou practically had to drag me out of bed in the morning. I wasn't a happy camper."

"Huh." He chuckles. "I always thought you were a morning person."

"I am, but it took me a while to outgrow the staying-up-too-late thing." I hold up the bag. "Thanks. Gonna see if this helps."

"You need me to help with anything?"

"Yeah." I wrap my arms around him and nuzzle at his neck for a moment before kissing it and whispering in his ear, "Keep an eye on the kids in case this sunscreen idea goes south…"

"Right."

I spend a few minutes with Tammy and Anthony before slipping away with a, "Be right back."

Once I'm in the kitchen, I set the bag on the table and pick among the options. Might as well start at the top. I grab the highest-rated one, a Coppertone lotion, and apply a moderate amount to my left hand. Since I'm not looking forward to turning that beach nightmare into reality, I decide to test small first. Using my 'protected' hand, I tug the curtains blocking the window over the kitchen sink aside an inch, creating a patch of sunlight in the steel basin.

"Well, here goes nothing," I mutter.

It takes me a moment of staring at my shaking hand to find the courage necessary to slide it forward into the light. The glare on my overly-white skin is blinding and the heat is intense. Clenching my jaw, I force myself to keep holding my fingers in the light. Miraculously, I don't break out in red, smoking blisters. Though, I can't call it pleasant. It's as if I've stuck my hand right at the opening of a toaster oven. Uncomfortable-teetering-on-painful.

Maybe the knuckles on my right hand turn white from clenching the sink's edge, but I'm so pale I can't tell. At the start of a faint cracking noise from the Formica, I stop squeezing. Oh, hell no. We just redid this whole kitchen. I am not breaking my countertop.

Wait.

Breaking my countertop?

I shouldn't be strong enough to crack it without a hammer, much less one-handed. Gah! I must be hearing things. Okay. Sunblock SPF maximum might just work. If I can avoid spontaneous combustion, I might be able to cope with this condition.

Finally, some hope.

***

Friday and the weekend pass in a surreal mixture of boredom, unease, and gratitude (for still being with my family). Danny runs to Albertson's for me again, and I'm the proud new owner of a wide-brimmed hat, sunglasses, and some loose-fitting but long dresses. Pity I can't wear them at work. Whatever's happened to me has resulted in my not being too concerned about overheating or being too cold. Mostly, I need to keep the damn sun off my skin.

Experimentation on Saturday revealed that clothing helps but doesn't outright stop burning in sunlight. Exposed skin covered in the super sunblock hurts less than fabric. A combination is best. I also discover that I can make myself sorta appear in mirrors using a coating of foundation makeup. If I'm going to try and keep my job, that's going to need to happen. I'm sure the building security people would freak out if they saw empty clothing walking around on the CCTV feeds. Another bonus is the foundation has more skin tone than I've been showing lately, so it'll keep people from asking why I look like a marble lawn statue.

At some point over the weekend, a thought occurs to me: If I'm now some sort of magical creature who doesn't appear in mirrors, then why don't I have a strong enough enchantment that it hides whatever I'm wearing too? I mean, shouldn't such craziness extend to my clothing? Argh! I don't understand any of this. Did I seriously just think 'enchantment' and be serious?

When I catch myself starting to dab foundation on my bare butt so I can see it in a mirror, I know it's time get away from the evil reflective thing.

By Monday—Tammy's start date for preschool—the constant sense of hunger that's been dogging me has grown from simply irritating to, 'I will eat your family pet.' Alas, a few attempts at food on Sunday night when everyone slept resulted in a sprint to the kitchen trashcan.

Danny jostles me awake at 7 a.m., which is about when I used to set my alarm for work, but at present, I can barely function. Only thoughts of my daughter's first day of preschool keep me motivated, and I eventually get myself dressed after covering my face, neck, shoulders, arms, and legs from the knees down in sunscreen. Makeup, sunglasses, and scarf later, I collect Tammy from her bed, get her dressed, and carry her to the kitchen while telling her how much fun she's going to have today.

"Why are you dressed like that?" asks Tammy.

"Well…" I fix her a bowl of cereal and sit in the next chair. "You know I was hurt. Something I don't understand has happened to me, and I've become allergic to the sun."

"Like Uncle Rick and cats?" asks Tammy.

I laugh. "Something like that, only I don't wind up sneezing like he does when he's around cats. The sun hurts."

"It's okay. I like the beach, but we don't have to go if it hurts you, Mommy." Tammy shovels Kix into her mouth.

Aww.

Carrying Anthony, Danny walks in, grinning at me.

"What?" I ask.

"You, uhh, look like an eccentric wealthy recluse from France or something." He winks. "The only thing missing is a little step-on dog in your handbag."

"Step-on dog?" I raise an eyebrow.

Danny sets our son in his high chair, then holds his hands about eight inches apart. "You know, one of those little suckers, always under your feet. Smaller than a cat? Shih Tzu or something?"

"Ooo!" Tammy gasps. "Daddy said a bad word!"

I snicker, and spend a few minutes explaining it's a type of dog while my husband feeds Anthony.

Giant, angry butterflies swim around in my stomach, but I do my best to ignore them. I have to. In only twenty minutes, I'll be leaving my daughter at the preschool. One stage of her life is ending, another step toward adulthood. She doesn't mind me hovering and fussing at her hair and dress. Danny makes faces at me for being overly clingy. He's right, though. It's not like I'm sending my child overseas never to see her again, so why does it feel that way?

Since I still don't quite trust myself out in the

day, Danny agrees to drive. Hell, even looking at our curtained windows hurts my eyes. Sure enough, when we make our way out to the Momvan, the world is painfully bright like I've just come out of the eye doctor's office. Despite sunglasses, I can't keep my eyes open all the way without it hurting. My hat/scarf/sunscreen getup keeps the sun down to a light microwaving. It's highly unpleasant but doesn't burn so much that I can't keep a straight face. Still, I sprint to the van and hop in, giving serious consideration to getting the windows tinted.

Safe inside the inconveniently unattached garage, I crawl into the mid-row and buckle the kids in once Danny sets them in their car seats. He hops in and starts the engine. Once I'm back in my seat, we're on the way. The whole ride to the preschool, I keep telling Tammy how much fun she's going to have and not to be scared. It's only a few hours and she'll be home soon.

Danny knows I'm talking to myself more than Tammy. For her part, my daughter's as blasé as it gets.

"I know, Mommy. You don't have to cry."

For some reason, that gets me crying harder.

We arrive at the preschool after a short ride. I step out into the inferno and force myself to walk at a normal pace across the parking lot, holding Tammy's right hand while Danny holds her left. Anthony toddles along on Danny's left, clinging to his other hand. The sun rains down on me like a hail of hot needles. Every fiber of my being is screaming at me to run, almost to the point of a panic attack and losing conscious control of my body. The searing pain is so bad, I weep in silence. That horrible dream of watching my arms and legs disintegrate to ashes comes to mind.

A subtle glance over myself confirms no visible flames or smoke, just dump trucks full of pain. My legs wobble, knees threatening to give out at any moment. I'm not about to run for the awning over the front doors and watch Danny and the kids like some outsider. No. This is *my* family. I *have* to be here for Tammy. This is her first day, and I won't ruin it no matter how much pain I'm in.

Tears are full on streaming down my face by the time we reach the shelter of the concrete awning over the area in front of the doors. Danny looks over, but he likely thinks I'm crying about sending Tammy off to school. And, yes, a few of these tears are mourning my daughter hurtling onward toward no longer being my little Tam Tam, but alas, the majority are an involuntary reaction to the most pain I've ever experienced.

He puts an arm around me and I lean on him for support as my legs are about to mutiny; as in, I may not be able to control myself, no matter how hard I try. Mercifully, we soon we make our way to the front office and wonderful cool air conditioning. The place is fairly big despite being only a preschool. While it has the appearance of containing multiple-grade classrooms, it's really separate groups of four- and five-year-olds. We confirm the registration, sign some last-minute paperwork, and accompany the administrator to Tammy's new classroom.

I can't help but think of my first day at school, though it wasn't pre. I was eight or nine when the homeschooling stopped by court order. My brothers were all terrified of other kids, and their fear took the form of aggression. Clayton, the youngest, *hated* that he had to wear clothes to go to school. I remember being thrilled at a chance for a 'real' education, though I hadn't been fond of other people much. Mary Lou took to socializing the best, though always struggled to get decent grades. I wound up the invisible kid, neither popular nor unpopular with decent-to-good marks.

Tammy hugs me, hugs Danny, and marches straight into a cluster of about eighteen other children. Wow. Fearless. Perhaps a third of the little ones fall silent and all stare at me. I can't help but feel like a big ol' alley cat who's just walked into a nest of baby mice. One tiny Indian girl bursts into tears after a few seconds of petrified staring and begins screaming for her mother.

"Wai go too." Anthony starts charging after her, but Danny picks him up. The boy reaches both arms out toward the classroom, squirming.

Tammy plops down on the rug amid a group of seven or eight other kids and just starts talking. I watch for a moment with tears in my eyes, then cling to Danny and stifle sobs. At the rustle of fabric approaching me from behind, I turn. A thirtysomething woman with shoulder-length black hair approaches.

"First time?" asks the teacher. "I'm Miss Larson."

I nod, sniffling.

"I can tell." She grins. "By second grade, you'll be throwing her out the car window at school, barely stopping outside, glad to be rid of her for a couple hours."

I've heard that joke before, but that's not going to be me. I'm never going to be glad to 'be rid of' my kids. Still, no sense making a scene. "Yeah, so I'm told."

We get a brief explanation from the teacher about the lesson plans, nap time, play activities, and so on. She asks about any allergies, favorite foods/activities, and if Tammy is on any medications. For the first two weeks, classes will be finished by noon to ease the kids into the concept of going to school. After that, we're to pick her up at 2 p.m.

"Great. Thank you." Danny shakes the teacher's hand.

"Do you mind if I ask about the… umm, hat and such?" asks Miss Larson.

For an instant, I feel like my mother just walked in on me touching myself, but I manage a smile. "Oh, not at all. I've got a skin condition that doesn't agree well with sunlight."

"Oh." She touches a finger to her chin, eyeing Tammy. "Is it something hereditary? Should we keep an eye on her?"

"No. We're still trying to work out exactly what it is, but it's a reaction to another medical issue that's definitely not genetic."

Danny puts an arm around me. "We're thinking it might be something like xeroderma pigmentosum, but we haven't gotten an official diagnosis yet. It only started a short time ago."

Anthony pulls my giant hat off. Since we're inside, I don't make a big deal of it, but I do pry it out of his little hands and put it back on. *Please don't let him do that to me when I'm under direct sunlight.*

"Oh. I'm sorry." Miss Larson purses her lips. "I hope you get some good news."

"Me too." I glance over at Tammy, who's fully integrated herself with a pack of chatty kids.

"C'mon." Danny tugs at my arm. "We're supposed to go now."

I fake a whine, but smile enough that the teacher knows I'm kidding. This time, at least, I can run across the parking lot without tearing my heart in little bits. As soon as Danny gets me back out to the Momvan, I burst into tears. I start rambling and worrying about her. Any of a million possible things could happen when I'm not there to protect her and… well, I won't be there to protect her, dammit.

Danny grins and bears my neurosis as he drives, muttering reassurances that she'll be fine. When he says that every parent feels like I feel the first time they drop off a kid at school, I glare at him… and notice he's got tears brimming in his eyes too.

It's a little tricky with the wide-brimmed hat, but I lean against him and cling to his arm.

Danny flips on the radio, perhaps to mask his own sniffling.

"…police continue to investigate reports of a rock thrown through a fifteenth-floor window of the Fullerton Towers building last night. According to Sergeant Rafael Guzman, they have no leads. Anyone with information is urged to contact the police."

I eye the radio.

"Wow," mutters Danny. "Who the hell chucks a rock through a window? Probably stupid teenagers."

Of course, the real question was… who can throw a rock up fifteen floors? The problem here being that the Fullerton Towers sit adjacent to Hillcrest Park. And, yeah, I had thrown a rock just last night… in the direction of the towers, too.

Crap. Well, at least I can hope I didn't leave fingerprints on it. Mine are definitely in the system from being a federal agent, but if this ridiculousness going on with me is true, I can't leave prints anymore. I know from my forensics studies that a dead body has no oils on the skin, hence, if I *am* an undead creature, I'd leave no fingerprints unless I got stuff like oil, paint, or ink on my hands. Besides, it's pretty damn difficult to get fingerprints off a dirty rock.

Wait… Fullerton Towers? That's got to be over a thousand feet away from Hillcrest Park. Sure, it's somewhat downhill… but did I really throw a stone that far? I couldn't have. It's not humanly possible.

Humanly being the operative word here.

***

My body objects to being awake, and the next thing I know, I'm lying on the sofa and Danny is shaking me by the shoulder.

I do the sunscreen and stupid outfit thing again, and we pick Tammy up. I'm a veritable zombie the whole time, barely managing conversation with anyone. My hunger's only getting worse, and I find myself not wanting to look at Danny or the kids, though I am beyond thrilled/relieved to have Tammy home in one piece. Who knew day one at preschool could be such hell on a mom?

I lose chunks of the day, finally breaking out of my stupor a little past six when the sun weakens in the sky. Tammy's curled up beside me on the sofa, cartoons blaring from the TV.

"Hey, it's… oh, what the hell?" blurts Danny, a hair shy of yelling.

"Huh?" Groggy, I force myself to sit up.

Anthony's sprawled on the floor in his birthday suit. A handful of paper towels lay nearby smeared with unmentionable brown horribleness. His loaded diaper is near my feet, wide open.

"Umm…" I feel like I've come out of a thirty-year coma and can't even recall my own name. My blank stare seems to worry my husband who starts shaking his head while gesturing at our little Nature Boy. "I don't know what happened…" I mumble to no one in particular.

"We're not hippies, Sam," says Danny. "Our kids wear clothes *before* the age of ten."

"I didn't do that…"

Tammy pushes herself up to sit. "Anf-nee diaper dirty. Mommy sleeping, so I changed him."

I lean forward, coming more to my senses. I mean, *really* coming to my senses. In fact, yes. The sun had just set. I knew it. Could feel it. Hell, I could practically taste it. Don't ask me how.

"That's very sweet of you!" I hug her. "Come on, I'll show you how to put a new one on."

Hopefully, that won't last too long… we really ought to get Anthony potty trained, but with everything going on, it's gotten lost in the mess. I take the kids into Anthony's room, clean him up with a wet wipe and demonstrate putting on a diaper. I'm not going too slow, since I don't really plan on having Tammy change him. With any luck, he'll be weaned off diapers soon, anyway. Unless he's like my brother, River. It took forever to potty train him. Mostly, because our parents told him to use the toilet—so he did precisely the opposite. He's always been like that with authority. Being their firstborn, they had no experience either, so yeah, I bet that was fun.

Anyway, after I get the kids back to the living

room, Danny gives me the eye from the kitchen. I drift over there.

"So, umm. What's going on with you and food?" he asks in a near-whisper.

It occurs to me again that I haven't been breathing all day, until hesitation makes me take a deep one. I trust Danny as much as one can trust another person who didn't pop out of the same womb. "I… umm. Every time I eat something, it comes right back up." I explain everything that's happened with me and food. Including how the beef blood seemed to be the only thing to stay down.

He grasps my shoulders, looking worried. "You haven't eaten at all since we got you back from the hospital?"

I shake my head.

"How are you not starving?"

Probably for the same reason I'm not dead, despite having a single-digit heartrate, but I can't tell him that. I stare down and mutter, "I don't understand it either. I'm hungry, but everything I try to eat, my body rejects."

"Hmm." He stares at me, wary and worried. "Keep an eye on them for a bit? I'll be right back."

"All right."

We kiss, and he runs off out the door. I join the kids in the living room for a while, watching Nickelodeon. Tammy still appears to think I'm 'not doing well,' and tucks herself against my side. That makes me think back to when I'd been so much pain after being shot in my armored vest—another close call where my family almost lost me. It's also a time before all this unexplainable crap started.

Danny returns in about fifteen minutes with a paper bag, and heads straight to the kitchen while giving me a 'come here' look.

After easing Tammy aside, I kiss her on the head and follow him.

He peers around me, making sure the kids aren't following. Then, he surprises the hell out of me by extracting a half-gallon plastic bottle from the bag, with dark liquid in it. "I'm going out on a limb here with a crazy theory, but… sniff this and tell me what you think it is."

I take the bottle, pop the cap, and sniff. There's a faint hint of old milk, but the overpowering smell of blood rushes up into my sensorium. A distinctly uncomfortable tightness spreads across the middle of my face under my nose and in my lower jaw. The hunger that had been clawing at my gut surges, and before I can make any sort of conscious decision about anything, I've upended the bottle and I'm chugging.

Danny leans back, but I barely register the expression of surprise on his face. All that matters right now in the world is what's in my hands. I down a little more than half of it before I feel full, and stop. The strangest feeling comes over me as I lower the bottle. Warmth swirls in my core and spreads down my limbs in a flurry of tingles.

"Sam," whispers Danny. "You've got some color back in your face."

"I do?" I look down at my hands. Still pale, but not corpse-white anymore. The hunger's receded to a tiny, irritating presence at the back of my mind, as if I'd eaten too much oatmeal when I'd wanted filet mignon.

He grasps my hand. "You just drank beef blood."

That it didn't disgust me—in fact, it tasted quite good—disturbs me on a primordial level. "I suppose I did. What do you think that means?"

"It means we're both about to be fitted for straitjackets." He fidgets. "Let's, umm, keep this quiet?"

"Yeah, that's a good idea."

He gestures at the bottle. "Done?"

"For now. Where'd you get this?" I re-cap it.

Danny takes the blood and tucks it deep in the fridge, behind the milk, orange juice, and Diet Coke. At the moment, the kids are too little to go rooting around in there, but that won't last forever. Hopefully, I can recover from whatever disease I've gotten, but in a couple years, we won't be able to leave a half-gallon of blood in the fridge for the children to find.

"Represented this guy, Jaroslaw, last year in a lawsuit… he owns a butcher shop." Danny shuts the fridge door and faces me, his expression a swirl of confusion and curiosity. "Told him I was experimenting with British food and wanted to make a blood pudding."

"I realize what I just drank, but that phrase is

nauseating."

He chuckles. "That's about what he thought too."

"So what now?"

"Well." He hugs me closer, rubbing a hand up and down my back. "We'll figure something out. Eventually, we'll find a reasonable explanation. For now, we can tell the kids you've got to drink special milkshakes or something the doctor wants you on, and can't have solid food."

I chuckle. "Okay, that'll work for a little while."

Chapter Ten
Medical Leave

By the end of the week, I'm sure I've slipped into the early stages of going stir crazy. I *still* can't sleep at night, and staying up during the day is an uphill battle. To Danny's alarm, and the surprise of Nico Fortunato, my boss, I decide to show up for work the following Monday.

I had a brief phone conversation with Mary Lou about that, since I wanted her opinion. She asked me a bunch of questions about how I'd been sleeping, if anything weird had happened, and my 'relationship' with sunlight. She only usually gets that inquisitive when she's working on a claim. She's never pried into my life (or lack thereof) so much before, but her tone remained concerned, so I told her as much as I could think of. For now, neither of us mentioned the v-word. We treated this as a real disease, which it was. I was sure of it. I mean, it had to be, right?

Monday morning, I almost pound a fist onto my alarm clock to shut it up. I do *not* want to get out of bed at 7 a.m., but I do anyway. The walk to the bathroom makes me feel like a drunk college student the day after a party epic enough to trigger a police raid. My left leg won't bend at the knee and my right behaves like a tube of Jell-O. Unsurprisingly, I don't need to use the toilet, but I take a long, hot, glorious shower.

Once I dry off, I apply sunscreen, then a coat of foundation to my face until I look only a little eerie in the mirror. A pantsuit covers most of my body, which will help. Hopefully, the guys won't tease me too much about the stupid hat and shades.

Danny hovers over me during the time I'd normally have been scarfing down oatmeal or something for breakfast, continually asking me if I'm sure I want to do this.

"Sure? No… but I have to. Medical leave won't last forever, and we need the income." I kiss him on the cheek. His idea of butcher's blood helped my skin temperature issue, and we've gotten a bit more intimate, but he's stopped short of going all the way.

"All right." He shakes his head, staring down. "It doesn't feel like a good idea. You often have to go outside for your job, you know. What if something happens?"

I lean my rear end against the counter, arms folded. "Maybe I could tell them I have that xeroderma thing, and request some kind of office position that won't send me out into the field." I sigh. "That would probably change my classification and I'd no longer be a sworn agent. And it would be boring as hell."

He grins. "I thought your job right now is pretty boring."

"It is." I rub my ribs. "Except for when it's not. The problem is… I'd need an actual doctor to issue an official diagnosis before I can take any medical claims to them. This sunscreen seems to be working for now, so I think I'll play it by ear and see how it goes."

He sighs, but nods. "I don't have the best feeling about this, but I'll support you if it's what you want to do. Be careful, Sam."

"I will." I kiss him again.

His response is noticeably better since I seem to have some heat in my skin again.

"Sam?" Danny shakes me.

"Huh? What?" I lean back and blink at him.

"You just… like fainted on me."

Whoa. Total blackout. "I did?"

"That's not… Look, Sam. You should stay home. We still don't know what's going on with you."

"Maybe, but if I collapse at work, it'll help my case for extending medical leave." I wink.

"You've been groggy ever since the attack. I'm terrified this isn't going to get better any time soon." He squeezes me close.

I'm not groggy at night, though. In fact, I *can't* sleep when the sun goes down. Maybe I should get a job on the graveyard shift. Wonder if any career-type jobs exist with those hours, and if so, do they pay anything close to what I get now? Maybe air traffic control? Ugh. Way too much stress.

"You called your sister?"

"Yeah, she'll be here any minute. You going back to the office today then?"

He nods. "Yeah. First one out picks the kids up from Mary Lou's?"

"Right. Back to normal." I wink.

As if.

***

I hotfoot it to the Momvan and hop in fast. After a moment, I stop feeling like I've gone for a swim in a deep fryer. Ouch. At least I've got no visible signs of burning or smoke, but holy hell, that hurts! The sunglasses mostly let me see, though whenever sunlight glints off anything reflective, it's a needle jabbing me in the eye.

It's been some time since I had any contact with 'the guys,' though I have been on the phone with Chad a couple times since my discharge from the hospital. Nothing grand, mostly status updates about my health, office gossip, and a whole lot of playful bitching about him having to cover my workload. I offered to take some on from home, but without a special secure modem, I don't have access to the

HUD servers.

The ride past familiar landmarks gives me hope that my life might eventually get back to some semblance of normality. I get caught at the same red light that always snags me, and smile when the Starbucks comes into view. When it occurs to me that I may not be able to drink coffee again, I cringe like I've been told a family member perished unexpectedly.

Okay, maybe there *is* a good enough motivation for me to check with a doctor about my digestive issues. Life without coffee? Ack!

When I get to the office, Chad, Bryce, Michelle, and Ernie swarm me like I'm a wounded foal limping back to pasture. They all pepper me with questions about the attack, so I give them the 'sane' version, leaving out my thoughts that whoever attacked me had been too fast to see moving, or seemed to come out of nowhere, or had the strength to hurl me thirty feet.

Nico jogs over a few minutes into the conversation and pats me on the shoulder. "Sam! I didn't think you were serious about coming in. It's only been two weeks… How are you even standing?"

"The injury looked a lot worse than it was. The doctors were amazing." I rub where my neck meets my right shoulder. "I'm pretty much back to a hundred percent."

"Pretty much?" asks Chad.

"I'm still working out the particulars, but I seem

to have developed a sun allergy."

"Is that why you're wearing that, umm, hat?" asks Michelle.

I nod, sighing. "Yeah. I'm still not sure of the best way to manage it. For now, this seems to be passable. Ridiculous hat and all."

"You're not going to be able to wear that in the field," says Chad. "It's way out of regs."

"Any idea what it is?" asks Ernie. "I mean, the allergy? You look pretty amazing, Sammy. If I didn't know better, I'd accuse you of getting some work done." He winks. "You dropped a few years."

"Hah." I smirk at my former training partner. Ernie's the most senior of us, and I spent my first few months working with him. "If I didn't know better, I'd think you were hitting on me."

Ernie laughs, then shrugs.

"He's kinda right," says Chad. "You do look younger."

"Maybe almost dying made me so happy to be alive that I'm, like, supercharged with life or something."

Everyone chuckles. At least no one points out the silliness of my explanation. The truth is, it's the only explanation I have. Rather, the only somewhat sane explanation.

I resume explaining the attack, but the only detail I can give them about who did it—I make sure they all know it was a man and not innocent coyotes—is that gold medallion that dangled in front of my face. Alas, the way it all happened didn't give me a good look at his face. The only other description I can give them is he came out of nowhere, wore all black, and he was really damn strong.

Maybe twenty minutes go by before the 'welcome back' meeting breaks up and people return to their desks. Nico gives me the nod, and waves for Chad to follow us. We meander down a row of cubicles and into his office. Chad nudges the door closed.

"Sam, talk to me," says Nico. "What are we looking at in terms of your health? Are you *back* back, or is there anything I need to know about?"

"As far as I'm aware, just the sensitivity to sunlight. I haven't figured out exactly what's going on so far, but Danny thinks it's xeroderma pigmentosum." I ramble through an overview of it. "Yeah, I know it's a genetic thing, but the symptoms are the closest thing we've been able to find to what's going on."

"Have you been examined by a doctor for that?" asks Nico.

"Not yet. I was kinda hoping it would go away on its own, but a doctor is on my to-do list."

Nico fidgets. "Is it going to get in the way of your job?"

Based on my sunscreen forays, I'm in for a lot of pain, but I should be able to work past it. "I'm using some high-test sunblock, which seems to be working. I don't think it's going to be an issue, but if it is, you'll be the second to know. I'm not going to do anything that'll risk Chad or anyone's lives."

"All right." Nico smiles, evidently liking that answer. "I'll trust your judgment. Chad's too."

He nods.

I look back at my partner. "I'm sure he'll let me know if there's anything out of sorts."

"Absolutely." Chad pats me on the shoulder.

"I mean it…" I let out a long sigh. "If you think I'm a liability, I want you to tell me."

Nico tilts his head. "Do you think you'll be a liability?"

"I don't expect to be, but until I get some good answers, I can't say for sure." I look Nico in the eye. "Whatever happens, I do *not* want to put anyone's life in danger."

Chad holds up his hand, showing off a small red mark by his index knuckle. "I'm more than willing to jump in front of a paper cut for you."

I laugh. My partner can be such a jackass sometimes, but I love him.

"Might as well head over to Conference A," says Nico. "We'll be a couple minutes early for the department meeting."

"Right," I say.

Chad nudges me. "Coffee?"

I cringe. "I wish. Can't do it for a while. It's been pure hell."

"Ooh." He flinches. "Really? That's horrible. You sure you can't cheat it?"

"Yeah. I'm sure. Unless you fancy me pulling an *Exorcist* and projectile vomiting java everywhere."

"Ouch," says Nico.

I roll my eyes. "It's so annoying. Some kind of reaction to one of the meds they gave me. I'm stuck with these special nutrient milkshakes for a while."

Both men cringe.

Nico heads straight to Conference Room A, and I follow while Chad swings by the coffee machine. I can smell it from here and I desperately want some, but I know what will happen if I dare try. Another round of "good to have you back" goes around the room as I enter and flop in one of the open seats.

In the couple of minutes it takes for Nico to get his notes in order, I realize how comfortable the chair is.

"Hey, you all right?" Chad whispers, nudging my arm. "Nico's not *that* boring."

I force my head up, evidently having passed out. "Yeah." I scoot more upright in my seat and make eye contact with Chad, smiling. "Damn meds."

Wow, she looks beat, says Chad's voice in my head.

Huh, what? I blink at him. Obviously, I imagined hearing him speak. He has a look on his face that implies he thought me exhausted, and I just, you know, pictured him saying it. I lean my elbow on the table and rest my head upon my hand, staring aimlessly across the table at Michelle.

Such bullshit they haven't found the guy who attacked her, says Michelle's voice in my thoughts.

My arm falls away from my head, striking the

table with a *thump*. My eyes must be bugging out as everyone's looking at me.

"Something wrong, Sam?" asks Nico.

The instant I look at him, I hear, *She's hiding something. Damn, I hope she doesn't have terminal cancer. She even looks thinner.*

"Uhh. No, I'm okay. Two weeks off without an alarm clock. Just adjusting to waking up early again."

Nico gives me this sad little frown, but nods.

...damn pain in the ass with the forms... Ernie's voice dances across my brain.

"All right, where is everyone with their current cases? Resolve rate?" asks Nico.

I sink into the chair and catch Bryce staring at me.

Who in their right mind goes jogging at night anyway? What was she thinking? Damn lucky she's not dead.

With a soft grunt, I bow my head and focus my attention on the crappy fake wood grain in the table. What is this new hell? I'm hearing people's thoughts now? I clamp a hand over my mouth before I laugh aloud at my insanity. Of course, I'm not hearing them think. I'm delirious from lack of sleep and sliding into a new world of crazy. Hearing voices is a sign of psychosis, and I'm pretty sure insomnia can lead to mental issues.

Crap.

I sink into my chair, listening to everyone talk about their investigations. My body already doesn't want to be functioning now, but I can't pass out in the middle of a meeting. The whole point of me being here is trying *not* to lose this job. I busted my ass too much, put in too many hours to get where I am to let something like falling asleep in the office end my career.

They better find that son of a bitch. Or I'm going to start looking.

Chad's voice breaks the silence in my head. Dammit! I'm cracking. This isn't happening to me. I'm not allowing myself to go legit nuts, not after recovering from an attack that nearly killed me. I keep my head down for the rest of the meeting, avoiding eye contact with anyone on the way back to my desk.

"Chad?" I ask, with one foot in my cube.

"Hmm?" he mumbles from behind me.

I turn to face him. "Have you heard anything regarding the investigation into my attack?"

He scowls. "Not a damn thing. Pisses me off. Someone attacks a federal agent and it's like the FBI isn't even trying. I've never seen them take this long to turn up even one scrap of evidence. I swear I'm"—Chad pinches at the air—"*this* close to digging into it myself."

Holy crap! No effing way. I imagined him thinking that, and it's really on his mind!

"Sam?" Chad's anger evaporates to concern. "What? Are you okay? Does something hurt?"

"No. Why?"

"You, uhh, got this sudden look on your face

like you might be having a heart attack."

I back into my cube. "Oh, no. I was just, umm, thinking that the guy's still out there." Okay, Sam. Relax. You did not really hear his thoughts. Lack of sleep is messing with you. First day back at work—let's try not to leave in an ambulance and a straitjacket.

"Yeah." Chad sets his hands on his hips and shakes his head. "We'll get that son of a bitch. Don't worry."

"I'll try not to." Yeah right. Worry seems to be all I can do lately. I keep walking backward until my leg bumps the seat of my chair and I fall into it.

Great… exactly what I *didn't* need. Another unexplainable weirdness.

Well, I suppose hearing *other* people's voices in my head is better than going schizophrenic.

Maybe.

Chapter Eleven
Overdoing It

This part of the job had always been boring, but on top of my body wanting to shut down, it's intolerable.

Hours sink away as I slog through reports and cases that've backlogged during my 'vacation.' Every so often, the clock jumps ahead by twenty or thirty minutes, suggesting I'd blacked out and woke back up. Fortunately, the cube walls are high and no one can see me unless they peered into my workspace.

At 12:08, Chad does exactly that. Fortunately, I'm awake at the time.

"Hey, Sam?"

"Yeah." I swivel in my chair and smile up at him.

"Wow. You look like you could use some sun."

No, not really, I think. "Umm."

"Got a routine inspection scheduled for today. Wanna go?" He points over his shoulder with his thumb. "I can fly solo if you're not up for it."

"Nah. If I wasn't up for it, I wouldn't be here." I lock the computer, stand, and do a quick sunscreen check. "One sec."

As soon as I reach for the massive hat, Chad chuckles. "Are you really going to wear that?"

Umm. Drat. It's way out of regs and it *does* look ridiculous. At least I have long hair. "Not unless I need to."

I carry it to the car—painfully aware that some of the sunscreen might have been rubbed off the top of my ears—and leave the monstrosity in the back seat, letting Chad drive. On the way out, I tell him more about my sun allergy, because, well, he's looking at me kinda weird.

"Oh, that sucks. Hope that clears up. I don't think the brass is going to let you wear that on duty, though. Makes you look like some bat-shit crazy, hermit, old-lady author who lives with thirty-four cats alone in a castle somewhere you can only get to by riding a donkey up a steep cliff."

His comment makes me laugh until tears slip down my cheeks. "Wow… where did you come up with that?"

"I dunno. Out of the blue."

I chuckle again at the donkey part; truly inspired. "Danny said I needed a toy Shih Tzu to go with the hat."

He snickers. "The man's got a point."

"Well, you can both go to hell." I chuckle and close my eyes.

The next thing I know, the *whump* of Chad's door wakes me up. Yikes! I stumble out the door—and wake right up. Nothing like standing in a three-hundred-degree oven to keep a gal on her toes.

Chad's already on the porch of a smallish one-story home with a beat-up white fence along both sides. He probably spent the ride talking about it, but I'd zonked out. *Please don't let me have narcolepsy.* No, I've just been up all night, every night, for two weeks. I need to find a way to get my sleep schedule back to normal.

A faint, and wholly sinister, chuckle glides across the back of my awareness. I spin, but there's no one whispering in my ear.

Ugh. *Ignore it, Sam. You're not losing your mind.*

Chad rings the bell.

I jog over—okay, sprint—and stand beside him in the shade. "Remind me again what's going on here? Sorry, I kinda zoned."

He smiles. "Nothing beyond a routine check."

"Oh, goodie."

"Goodie?"

"That's how I talk now. Got a problem with it?"

He grins. "Not if you don't."

A young guy, early twenties, with long straw-blond hair and buff pectorals answers the door wearing only a pair of cargo shorts. His chest muscles are puffy and perfect, almost like someone blew him up with an air pump. A deep tan and slightly-high expression make me think *surfer*. Within seconds of looking at him, my attention gravitates to his neck, and a visibly pulsating line where the carotid artery runs.

"Uhh, hi," says the resident.

"Joseph Bell?" asks Chad.

"No one calls me that but my mom when she's pissed. I'm Joey." The guy smiles. "You guys selling vacuum cleaners or Jesus?"

An ache spreads across my face below my eyes, like a mild sinus infection, and also in my lower jaw. I pull my ID and forcibly shift my gaze from his neck to his eyes. "I'm Agent Moon, this is Agent Helling. We're with the Department of Housing and Urban Development. Just here to do a routine inspection of the property."

"Oh, right on." Joey nods. "Come in, I guess. You guys want any tea or something? I sun brew."

Strange thoughts play out in my mind. Seeing this handsome, nearly perfect young man is filling me with an inexplicable hunger. For a brief moment, I want to consume him—carnally and literally. The literal part shocks me back to my senses, and I shake my head to clear it. Eager to keep him out of my direct vision, I dart into the hallway toward the back end of the house and kitchen.

"Sorry to bother you, Mr. Bell, err, Joey. This is just a routine inspection. We do them at least once for a new resident, but occasionally, more often," says Chad. "That's a rather nice TV you've got."

"Yeah." Joey nods with a vapid smile.

Well, I guess he can't be perfect. All looks, not much between his ears. I stop halfway down the hall and return to the living room, keeping him in my peripheral vision to avoid any bizarre thoughts starting up again. Sure enough, he's got a huge projection TV. Looks like about fifty inches. Probably cost him about four grand or so.

"How'd you manage to swing a unit like that given your reported financial state?" I ask.

"Oh, I didn't." Joey gestures at it. "My parents got it for me as a housewarming gift."

Yeah, right. Parents who'd throw four grand at a television for their son wouldn't sleep well at night knowing their little angel had to rely on government assistance to swing a mortgage. My special tingly senses tell me he's probably selling drugs, or at least has some undeclared income.

I leave Chad talking with him about the parents and continue deeper into the house.

A golden retriever bursts out of a doorway and growls at me.

"Easy, boy." I raise my hands. "Good dog. I'm only looking around."

Whimpers mix with growls. The dog's tail goes between its legs, and it backs away.

"Aww, it's okay, boy," I say. "I'm not going to hurt you."

The dog bolts back into what appears to be a

spare bedroom with an unmade bed (which it crawls under) and single, small dresser. Hmm. Friend or acquaintance spent the night recently. Other than dog, the room has the scent of a man in it.

Hmm. It's not strange at all that I can smell that.

Nope. Not one bit.

I sigh, and head to the kitchen.

The instant I'm through the archway, a yowling, screeching, furball scares the ever-loving crap out of me. By the time I realize it's merely a housecat objecting to my presence, I've already drawn my gun. Oops. Unlike the dog, this calico isn't retreating. She spits and hisses at me, raking her claws at the air from her perch atop the kitchen table. Since it's only a cat, I put my weapon away before anyone notices.

"Queenie!" yells Joey. "Be nice."

The cat hisses at me again.

An odd temptation to hiss back at her strikes me, but I ignore it and settle for a quick glance around a messy, but non-suspicious kitchen. Queenie continues hissing, spitting, and growling even as I retreat back to the front of the house.

We thank Chad for his time and head outside. I half-sprint to the car and dive in out of the inferno as fast as I can, gasping with relief as the roof shields me from the burning daystar. Ugh, this is cruel. I used to love the sun, now, it's trying to kill me.

"When did you start smoking?" asks Chad, as he climbs in.

"I don't."

He squints at me. "Oh, must've been dust or something. Thought I saw smoke. Heh. Maybe it's the guy across the street cooking. Kinda smells like grilled meat."

I fidget. "Guess you're hungry. Must be in your head."

"Mmm. Yeah, that aroma. Good idea." He starts the car. "Lunch?"

"Knock yourself out. I wish I could, but… special diet."

He nods. "Hope they let you off it soon."

"Yeah. Me too."

Chad winds up driving to Nick's Super Burger. Lovely. The last time we stopped here for lunch, it came with a side of .38 special bullets. My knuckles whiten as I grip the seat. Could this be the end of the dream? Maybe I *did* die there, and this circular path is bringing me back to the beginning. My brain runs away with the idea that everything since the shooting has existed only in the seconds between my taking a fatal bullet and being clinically dead. By the time the car stops, I'm terrified.

As soon as we walk past the table, I'm going to realize I'm dead.

"Want me to get it to go?" asks Chad.

"Up to you. I'll go in if you want to eat here, but can we sit inside, out of the sun?"

He leans forward to look at my face. "You okay? You sound a little odd."

Great. He hears me being afraid. "I'd forgotten

how early 7 a.m. arrives. I'm only tired."

"Welcome back, Sam." Chad pats my leg in a purely buddy-cop platonic sort of way. "It's good to see you're okay." His voice cracks a little. "Wasn't looking good there for a while at first."

"So I hear. Guess I'm tougher than I look."

"The toughest." He grins. "I'm going to eat, and possibly tempt you with the forbidden fruit of greasy perfection. If you should find your willpower slipping, I promise not to tell your doctor."

I laugh. "Glad to hear you've got me covered. Probably not going to happen, though. I've had enough intense vomiting for a lifetime, thanks."

"Ugh. Tragic."

My thoughts go to Starbucks. It's been two weeks since I've had coffee. Maybe that's why I'm going crazy. "Yeah, tragic."

I hop out and run across the lot, refusing to look at the table that's still got a silvery gouge in the green paint where a bullet hit it. How many people have sat at that table, noticed the dent in the steel, and not had a clue what caused it?

By the time I'm inside, I feel like I've been broiled. There's a lot of shiny metal in here. The wall behind the counter area is covered with polished metal that functions like a crappy mirror, blurring everything. My makeup is more than adequate to keep my reflection from being too suspicious. The skin-toned blur of foundation above my shoulders appears no different from any of the other barely-recognizable blobs in the 'mirror.'

I grab a seat while Chad goes up to the counter and orders. It takes him only a moment before he thanks the clerk and hurries over to join me.

"It's the table outside, isn't it?" asks Chad.

"Huh?"

"Wanting to go inside? You asked me to be honest with you, so… if you've got PTSD or something, it's worth talking about."

"Oh. No… it's not the shooting. The guy missed, remember?" Evidently, he did, since my theoretical postmortem wild dream didn't come to an abrupt halt once we got here. "I really have a nasty sunburn issue. I got some kind of infection in the hospital that's made my skin overly sensitive to sunlight. It's extremely uncomfortable."

"Oh, porphyria?"

"No… Danny thinks it's this thing called XP, but I'm not sure since that one's genetic. I've never had any symptoms until recently, and I used to adore sunbathing." I laugh. "Maybe I overdid it."

When his number is called, Chad retrieves his lunch, a bacon double-cheeseburger that looks bigger than Tammy's head. His eyes sparkle with anticipation.

"Speaking of overdoing things," I say, "that's a heart attack on a roll."

"Yeah." Chad scoops the burger up in two hands. "But it's a tasty heart attack. You sure you're not tempted?"

"I'm sure," I say.

I remember cheating on my old diet for this

place every so often since the burgers *are* good. It would be a pity to waste one of these magnificent monstrosities by spewing it into a toilet. And, honestly, since the attack, food hasn't tasted the same. Everything's kinda bland. Then again, knowing that anything I eat is going to come flying out of me within fifteen minutes is quite the *de*motivator.

Chapter Twelve
Bargaining

My first day back at work didn't go too bad, all things considered. I'd expected boredom, and the job delivered and then some. However, the day went by much faster than I'd expected… probably since I kept blacking out.

I remember Chad's 'see you tomorrow' pat on the arm, a fleeting memory of Tammy and Anthony scrambling across Mary Lou's living room to leap on me, but nothing about driving or even getting home. One moment I'm at the office, the next, I'm lying in my bed staring at the ceiling.

Someone (Danny, I hope) traded my pantsuit for a nightgown. Hell, maybe I changed myself. Since I feel wide awake after a bout of restlessness, I'm sure the sun went down… but that still doesn't make any sense. I sit up in bed, listening to voices from the other end of the house: Danny and the kids talking over dinner.

More than ever, I feel like an outsider in my own home.

I curl up, arms crossed over my knees, and sob as quietly as I can. What's happening to me? Panic comes out of nowhere at not understanding anything. Am I alive or dead? Is this an awful dream or could any of it be real? Am I even now in a padded cell somewhere, mumbling incoherently to myself? Bits and pieces of the attack replay in my memory. I squeeze my legs tight to my chest, feeling like a little girl who sprang awake from a nightmare and desperately needs her parents, but they're nowhere nearby.

Then again, Mom and Dad weren't exactly the nurturing type. It would've been Mary Lou comforting me. And she wouldn't have needed to go far as we'd shared a bed.

A sense that I'm trapped in an impossible nightmare closes in on me. My emotions swing back and forth from terrified to crying my eyes out. The extreme *need* to be normal again, to go back to the way things were, hurts almost as much as the sun.

Storming emotions surge and ebb. Every *clink* of fork on plate from the kitchen rings like a cathedral bell in my mind, tolling to remind me that I am no longer part of this family or of this world.

No!

I scramble to my feet and start to rush out, but something makes me grab the doorjamb and catch myself. Shame and disgust roll over me. I recoil back into the bedroom, not wanting to let my family see this monster I'm turning into.

"Okay, so what if you *are* real, God?" I ask the ceiling while pacing around the room. "I'm sorry for doubting you. Please help me get back to normal?"

A moment or two of nothing happens.

"Please," I whine like a tween begging her father for a pony. "I promise I'll do whatever you want, just let me be normal again. *Please.*"

Scuffing shoes go by on the street outside, someone jogging. The *crunch* of their sneakers on paving hammers my brain, so loud it's as though they're running across the top of my skull. Again, I pace about my bedroom.

This can't possibly be real. People can't be alive with such a sluggish heartbeat. People don't disappear from mirrors or drink blood or stay up all night long feeling totally awake. I have *got* to be stuck in a nightmare.

"God, fate, the universe, whatever is out there, *please* let me wake up."

I flop kneeling beside the bed, my upper half sprawled over the mattress, sobbing into the blankets.

Pathetic... whispers a sinister voice at the back of my mind.

"Yeah, well, fuck you too, schizo hallucination."

Another image of the attack flashes to the tip of

my brain: a mostly human face of an older man in his late fifties, dark curly hair, pale. His lips part, revealing stark white teeth, and canines that grow out into fangs.

I snap upright, shaking my head to throw away that ridiculous image. Insomnia and starvation are making me psychotic. Maybe I *should* call my father. He might be able to suggest some herbal remedy on the down low. Nothing that'll show up in a report at work and get me dismissed for drug use.

My eyes snap open wide.

Wait a sec. In order to complete a drug test, I'd have to pee in a flask, and it's been two weeks since I've peed. In a panic, I run to the bathroom, barely able to get a grip on the cup, and choke down water, filling and chugging five or six glasses' worth before leaping onto the toilet.

"Come on. Pee. Damn you…"

I stare down at my non-working plumbing, trying by sheer force of will to make things happen. Churning in my gut sends a warning.

No!

I clench my jaw. No way, water. You're not coming up. Take the usual route. Be normal.

Moments later, a convulsion rocks me, water streaming out between my teeth. Instinct takes over and I lurch forward, thrusting my head past the edge of the tub in time for the torrent to blast out.

Once the eruption stops, I drape there, neck against cold porcelain, head dangling into the tub, staring at the trails of water running off toward the drain. What do I have to do to wake up from this?

"I swear I'll quit my job if that's what it takes." I push myself up and wipe my mouth on the back of my arm. "Anything… what do I have to do?" Sniffle. "Not my kids. Anything but hurt or leave my family."

Water gurgles in the drain for a few minutes, then intermittent drips; a hollow echo from the pipe fills the air.

"What do I have to do to get back to normal? It's not like I ever wanted much. I never asked to be rich or famous or powerful… I only wanted a normal life and family." Tingles along the bottoms of my eyes announce an imminent explosion of tears, but I'm too fried to let them out.

Minutes pass, and it becomes painfully obvious that the universe, God, or fate are ignoring me. I pick myself up off the floor and stop by the mirror to make sure I don't look too much like I've been crying my eyes out—and stare at a hollow nightgown.

Head hung in defeat, I trudge out to the kitchen to be with my family.

At least I still have them.

Chapter Thirteen
Qwerty Sandwich

With the kids in bed and Danny snoring lightly, I spend another night roaming my house like the lost soul that I am, wishing like hell that I had more of that cow blood, which I had long since consumed. As the hours pass, I oscillate from wanting to hunt for my own blood—it should be that hard to find, right?—and cursing God, which, oddly, feels good.

Since I've got nothing better to do, I decide to get into a battle of wills with an inanimate object. Or in this case, water. When a pro athlete gets into a serious car accident, they don't leap out of their hospital bed and get back on the field. No, they take baby steps. My baby step is going to be water. This food thing has got to be in my head. So I sidle up to the kitchen sink, fill a cup and take a few sips.

The war starts off as usual, but this time, I

refuse to listen to the cramping and churning.

It's only water, I chant in my head. A little burbles up into the back of my mouth, but I hold it down.

Another sip.

And another.

At one point, I'm nearly in tears from the cramping, but I am determined to get my life back to something at least an inch closer to normal than things have been going lately.

I take a gulp, the icy liquid sliding down my throat. It's not what my body wants, but it's what I'm giving it right now. Both hands clutching the edge of the counter, I concentrate on thoughts of water going *through* me.

By 1:44 a.m., I've downed two cups and I'm holding it. Power of will for the win.

I'm proud of myself for all of six minutes before I notice a small problem—I'm standing in a puddle. It's not pee though—it's plain water, having run through me like I'm a walking, talking Brita filter.

Damn. I can't figure out if I should be happy for my small victory (I didn't puke) or worried that it's still apparently ordinary water. The next time the job wants a sample to prove I'm not on drugs, there are going to be some intensely awkward questions.

Still. I beat the water. And, like an athlete re-learning how to walk, apparently, I need to re-learn how to hold things in.

Well, I made some progress.

In the early hours of the morning, I wind up

standing at the living window, suddenly curious that I seem to intrinsically know where the sun is at all times… hyper-aware of its approach with or without the use of a window or a clock.

The sun. What is the deal with the sun?

One minute, I'm watching the sky turn from deep purple to pale blue, the next, I've gotten a face full of living room carpet.

"Sam?" asks Danny, shaking my shoulder. "What's wrong?"

"Huh?" I blearily blink at the beige blur in front of my eyes. My limbs feel like lead. Not wanting to move, I close my eyes again.

"Sam?" Again, Danny jostles me.

"What?" I don't move or look.

"You're collapsed in the middle of the living room."

"What time is it?" I mutter.

"Five after seven."

Damn. "I'm going to be late for work," I say, or think I say. There is a very good chance I might have incoherently mumbled.

"Yeah. Are you feeling up for it? I mean, I can call Fortunato and tell him you've had a relapse or something."

Most of me wants him to do that. Like, ninety percent of me. The idea of not moving is oh so tempting. Somehow, the ten percent wins. "I got it."

I struggle to push myself up to my knees, and squint at the curtains. They're heavy, and closed, but the feeble amount of sunlight coming through them is still enough to hurt my eyes if I look directly at the window.

Tammy zips by in a cute black dress with a panda face on the chest, the furry white parts filled with glitter. I swing out an arm and catch her in a hug, standing with my squealing daughter clinging to me. The warmth of her body is like a balm for my soul, and after spinning the giggling child around a few times, I feel like me again.

She runs to the kitchen when I put her down. Danny takes care of breakfast while I go get ready for work. I'm going to have to buy stock in a sunblock company at this rate. Today, I manage to only cook myself a little bit getting the kids loaded into the Momvan. I drop Anthony off at Mary Lou's, then swing by the preschool. To avoid a repeat of last time, I cheat and drive into the bus lane right by the front door, parking under the awning. If anyone gives me lip about it, I'll claim xeroderma pigmentosum and call it a medical need to stay in the shade.

No one bothers me, and I walk Tammy inside to her classroom.

By the time I get to the office, I'm so woozy and out of it, I give serious consideration to curling up on the break room sofa and sleeping. It would be much more direct to tell Nico 'I quit,' not to mention look better on my record, than to be fired for sleeping on the job… so I trudge to my desk. Bryce goes by with a Boston cream sticking out of his mouth. He points across the office and mumbles something, probably about there being donuts in the conference room.

"Thanks." I smile. "Still on a restricted diet."

His next mumble sounds like, "Your loss."

I fall into my chair and boot up the computer.

Reports and audits go by in a mesmerizing blur, until a sharp impact to my face startles me awake. I'm slumped over the desk. Damn. Not again. With a grunt, I sit up and resume working—after deleting three lines of gibberish from cheek-typing.

"Wow, you must be hungry," says Chad. "How's that qwerty sandwich taste?"

Except my brain has long since shut off. Like a zombie, I turn my head toward him and blink. "What?"

He mutes a laugh. "Qwerty sandwich. You went face down on the keyboard."

"Oh. Had a rough night." I fidget my fingers at my shirt like a kid caught doing something wrong. "Look, Chad… I've been having trouble sleeping since the attack."

"Would coffee conflict with your medical diet?" he asks.

"Probably, but…" I'm so tired I can't even yawn. "Maybe I'll cheat this once."

"I got it." Chad winks, and runs off.

I try to focus on the screen and muddle through the report of Joey Bell's inspection. I think he's involved with something 'off the books' that's giving him money he's not reporting to the government. His parents' tax returns don't suggest they'd have the kind of money to be able to buy a television like the one he had on a whim. Unless they've got money hidden away in a Cayman Islands bank or something.

"Here you are," says Chad, setting a paper cup on my desk.

The scent of coffee is so strong my eyes water. Because of it, I realize I'm not picking up Chad's musky scent as much. His scent? Great, I get attacked by a man-dog-something-or-other and now, I'm a bloodhound too. I should not be smelling *people*.

"Thanks." I pick up the coffee and take a long swig.

"Holy crap, Sam… How'd you do that?"

"Do what?" I blink at him. "Drinking is not difficult. Raise cup to lips, tilt back, swallow. Even Anders can figure that out."

"Bite me," says Bryce from over the cube wall.

Not something one should say to a vampire. I laugh internally. *Yeah, right. Vampires.*

Chad points. "That's, like, fresh. Just came out of the pot. It should be, you know, way too hot for you to chug like that."

I shrug. "Doesn't feel hot. Maybe I'm just so tired I don't care."

"Uhh, wow. Right. Maybe nerve damage from the attack or something?" Chad leans over me, looking at the screen. I get a strong hit of his scent again. Not cologne. Of *him*. Jesus. "Got anything?"

I next catch myself staring at his exposed wrist

where his plum-colored shirt has pulled up. Again, that odd tightness spreads over my face and jaw. The sense of blood flowing beneath his skin mesmerizes me. For a moment, I feel like he's a helpless little morsel who couldn't do a thing to stop me if I—*Get a grip, Sam!* And since when could I sense flowing blood? Good Lord. Wow. Did I just invoke God? Now I know I'm losing my mind. But then again… if vampires exist, who's to say…

"Checking on the parents," I mutter, before taking another long sip of coffee. "It doesn't look like they have the financial means to buy a TV like the one we saw out of the blue. I'm sure something's going on with Joey."

"Me too." He pats me on the shoulder. "I'm running down all his known associates, seeing if I can find anything."

"Sounds good," I mutter into the cup, keeping my eyes off his wrists or neck, or skin in general. That I saw Chad as something weak and pathetic, beneath me, prey easy for the taking, shook me to my core.

Chad returns to his desk, and I drain the coffee in three huge gulps. He's right. It's steaming, but doesn't bother me to drink. Oh, please, if anything about this nightmare can change… please let me be able to have coffee.

Whether it's the core of warmth in my gut or the actual effect of caffeine, I'm not sure, but I do feel more alert for a short while. Real short. Strong nausea slams me perhaps five minutes later. Two streams of still-hot coffee spray out of my nose, some spattering on the keyboard as I wrench my head around so my mouth is over the wastebasket.

Fortunately, I'd only glugged down an eight-ounce cup, so the eruption isn't epic. But ouch. Hot coffee in my sinuses stings. I cough, sneeze, and gag, and I think I may have shed a few java tears. I enjoy the fresh new hell of having still-steaming coffee pour out of my nose for a few seconds.

Chad appears in the cube opening. "You okay?"

"I've been better." I lean back in my chair, tissue clamped over my face, feeling spent.

He eyes the splatter. "Wow, you weren't kidding…"

"Ugh. My eyes are burning." Except, of course, the stinging only lasts a few seconds, and then I feel fine again.

Chad runs off and returns with some paper towels. Fortunately, my keyboard doesn't short out. After mopping up the mess, I dive back into the electronic investigation.

The next thing I know, a hand on my shoulder shakes me until I sit up. My cheek peels away from the keyboard, and I stare up at Nico.

Oops. I'm in trouble.

"Sam?"

"I, umm. Sorry. Been having issues sleeping ever since the attack. Nightmares and stuff."

Nico nods. "That's understandable, but we'll need to get that under control. Can't have you passing out at the desk."

I nod. "Yeah."

"Do you want me to set up a session with Dr. Burdine?"

"Not sure. I think I can get a handle on it. Week or two? If I'm still having issues, I'll take you up on that, okay?" What I'm going through would probably make our department psychiatrist go see a psychiatrist himself… or get me committed.

Nico hits me with his 'appraising stare.' The top of his perfect silver-and-pewter coif catches the light and glows, making the darker pewter highlights stand out. Chad's behind him, wearing an 'oh, shit' face.

"I need to see you two in my office, about the Brauerman case," says Nico. "Few minutes to collect yourself?"

"Thanks. Yeah. Be right there."

As Nico walks off, I lean back and wipe my face. I'm not really having nightmares, unless the one I'm presently experiencing counts. In fact, since the fiery beach one, I haven't dreamed at all. Whenever I do manage to sleep, it feels less like sleep and more like I've *lost* hours. Eyes closed and open in an instant, and time has vanished. None of it makes sense. I'm barely able to function during the day, but as soon as the sun goes down, I'm charged with the energy of an eighteen-year-old on crack. Heightened senses, aversion to sunlight, craving for blood… Wow, I sure do sound like a vampire, but that's so patently ridiculous all I can do is laugh at myself.

"How do I look?" I ask Chad.

"Hungover—oh, damn, did Nico catch you zonked?"

I look down. "Yeah. I can't help it. Staring at numbers and reports…"

Chad chuckles. "Right. This place would knock Jim Carrey out cold after five minutes. Maybe even Robin Williams, back in the day."

I laugh. "Hey, do I have keyboard squares on my face?"

"Nope."

"Well, there's that." I stand. "Let's go see what Nico wants."

We head down the cube row to the end, and into the office at the corner.

Nico hands us both a pair of blue subpoena folders. "The Brauerman case is going before a federal grand jury in a few days. You're both expected to testify."

Chad nods. "No problem. Did they subpoena Sam Moon or Lorelei Duke?" Chad, of course, is referring to my simple, country bumpkin alter ego I'd adopted to bust a HUD scammer last month. You know, back when I was normal. Pre-attack Sam.

I snicker. "Please tell me I don't need to put on that ridiculous outfit again?" Ugh. The mere thought of that makes me want to shiver in pain and cry in mourning at the same time. Not to mention, baring that much skin in daylight now would be agony… but I hate that I can't. Then again, I'd happily strut around in short shorts and a half-shirt if it meant I could have my old life back.

"We can officially retire Lorelei," says Nico. "And your work's solid on this one. Just tell it like it is and everything will be fine."

Yeah, right. Not *everything* is going to be fine. At least, not with my life. Truth is, I find myself barely able to care about the case now or the subpoena. In fact, I can't concentrate on anything right now except...

Sleep. And maybe, yes, just maybe...

Blood.

Oh, wow, this is getting strange.

I manage a smile and tap the subpoena against my hand. "No problem."

Chapter Fourteen
Depression

I have trouble focusing on anything much past staying awake for the rest of the day.

After picking the kids up from Mary Lou's, I drive home. Cartoons on, I flop on the couch with Tammy beside me and Anthony playing on the floor. She rambles about her day at preschool, hand-painting, learning some letters, naptime and so on.

In an instant, the show's changed and Tammy's gone. A car door closes with a *whump* outside, and dangerous silence fills the house. A house with a four and two-year-old should never be silent.

A gleeful squeal comes from the kitchen.

Danny opens the door. I flinch from the daylight, weak as it is, raising my arm to shield my eyes.

"Eeeeee!" Anthony runs by wearing only a coating of white powder, leaving small footprints across the rug.

"I see I've missed the party," says Danny. "Is the keg empty?"

I twist to my left. Tammy's standing in the archway between the kitchen and dining room in her underpants, also covered head-to-toe in white. Her hair's fluffed up, wild, and as grey as an old woman from the dusting. She looks like a refugee from ground zero at a flour factory explosion. Behind her, most of the kitchen floor and cabinets are white.

"Oh, no," I mutter.

"What happened?" Danny sets his briefcase down by the door and walks past me, chasing Anthony.

I sit up, forcing my non-cooperating muscles to move. "I must have blacked out."

Tammy marches up to me. Turns out most of her body isn't covered in powder, but a white slime, almost like plaster before it sets. "Anf-nee used potty!"

"What did you do in the kitchen?" I ask, horrified.

She holds up her hands, covered in what I believe is flour or maybe cornstarch mixed with water. "Hand paints!"

Ugh, they made their own 'paint.' Crap. This can't end well.

I grasp her under the arms and carry her to the bathroom. Anthony's abandoned diaper sits clean near the little potty chair. Danny's got him in the tub already, in a few inches of water. Add second toddler and stir until the water reaches an even whiteness.

"Sorry," I mutter. "Like you need this after working all day."

"You worked all day too." He leans over and kisses me on the cheek. "I'm more worried you're having blackouts."

I kneel next to him and begin scrubbing Tammy. "It's like I just can't stay awake during the day."

"Have you thought about seeing the doctor again?" Danny uses a little blue pail to pour water over Anthony's head, making him giggle. As soon as he hands it to me, Tammy clamps her hands over her eyes.

"Yeah. Still not sure if that's going to be a good idea. I'd like to wait a little longer…"

He nods. "We can't just keep waiting forever, Sam. We need answers."

"I know. I know… just another few weeks until I can make sense of this."

I leave him to watch over the kids playing in the tub, and dash to their rooms to grab a change of clothing for them. We dry them off, get them dressed, and set them on the couch with *101 Dalmatians* on DVD. I attack the mess in the kitchen while Danny gets going on dinner. Dammit, he's making spaghetti sauce. I love his spaghetti sauce.

The smell of it triggers a waterfall of memories

from the first time he made it for me when we were dating, to an awkward dinner with his parents, to countless nights before we had kids to my joke about his mother teaching the kids how to make the sauce. I say awkward because his mother had no qualms calling me ‘that godless hippie girl’ straight to my face, and talking about me to Danny as if I weren’t in the room. Memories of our college days, dating, and wedding flit and dart around my head.

I’m a silent wreck by the time I’m done cleaning up the white paste and thousands of tiny handprints on the cabinet doors.

To keep up appearances, I decide to join them at the table and have some of Danny’s spaghetti. A small portion, mostly because I adore it so much. Even after the attack, when food’s been reduced to blah, the fragrance of his sauce is still enough to tempt me.

Tammy’s gotten the hang of twirling pasta on her fork; meanwhile, Anthony’s gotten a handful and is shoving it in his mouth. Almost as much sauce winds up on his cheeks as inside him. I take a smallish portion and eat, but it doesn’t taste as good as I remember it. I know it’s not Danny—it’s me. Whatever God-forsaken thing has happened to me has taken me away from my husband’s affection, away from the sun, away from coffee, and away from his amazing tomato sauce.

I put a hand to my gut to quell the beginnings of churn. This *thing* will not take me away from my family. It’s devouring everything else, but I have to draw the line somewhere. This is all in my head. What possible explanation can there be for this? I'm a vampire. Okay, what possible *sane* explanation can there be for this? Rejecting food is some psychosomatic nonsense going on in my brain.

This sauce is my favorite meal in the world. If anything will help me get past this mental block, it's this.

A storm rages inside me. I press in on my stomach and let a belch slip, so laced with garlic it burns my nose. Obviously, I'm not a vampire or I couldn't have even consumed garlic in the first place, right?

Tammy grins. "Love sketti!"

"Da make bes sauce!" yells Anthony, right before I feed him another forkful.

Danny eyes me with concern. I'm sure the war brewing in my gut is evident on my face. I will defeat this mental block. There's no such thing as vampires. I've got PTSD or something. By some mechanism I can't understand, I've associated eating with the attack. At the moment, I stop trying to eat any more and keep my jaw locked, my face stoic. The longest I've been able to keep food down so far has been a minute or two. That's the wall I must overcome. Pain and cramping intensifies, but I refuse to let a crack show in my outward calm. Another two minutes, and I win.

Exactly at the five-minute mark, a spike of pain punctures my belly like a dagger.

The fork I'm feeding Anthony with tumbles out

of my fingers. Its contents spatter all over the high chair tray as it bounces off the plate with a sharp *clank* and falls to the floor. I double over, grabbing my gut with both hands. The back of my mouth fills with food that wants *out.*

No. Stay down. I can do this.

Whoever's holding the dagger impaled in my stomach gives it a twist.

"Mommy?" asks Tammy.

I manage a brief look of apology to Danny before flying out of my chair and sprinting down the hall to the bathroom. I can't bear to let him watch me hurl, certainly not the sauce he put so much love into. He made it, hoping it might help me overcome this… problem but…

My body crashes into the doorjamb. I shove away, stumble up to the toilet, and let fly. Chills and convulsions paralyze me. Unholy cramps pummel my guts, keeping me bent over and gagging for several minutes before I can move again under my own control. The toilet water inches away from my eyes looks like someone's head exploded in a mess of blood and brain squiggles.

The sight of it feels like I've rejected Danny.

I wind up sobbing, hugging the bowl.

A *click* to my left makes me look over and up.

Danny's crept in and pushed the door shut. He swoops in to kneel beside me, worry and concern all over his face.

"I'm sorry," I blub.

He takes some toilet paper and dabs sauce from

my chin. "Why are you apologizing? None of this is your fault."

"Because this is your sauce. And I *so* love it. I don't know why…"

"I know, Sam." He flushes the toilet, then hugs me. "I'm not taking this as an indictment on my cooking."

Except there's no consoling me at this point, and I'm sobbing and sniffling nearly uncontrollably. "I'm sorry. I love your sauce. I really do. I don't know what's happening to me. I need answers, and I need help. So much help…"

He holds me, rubbing my shoulder and rocking me for a few minutes.

"Kids are alone," I finally mutter.

"Yeah."

"There's going to be spaghetti sauce all over the cabinets."

Danny chuckles. "We haven't been away *that* long. They'll only have painted a couple of doors."

I pull myself together and allow a smile. "Heh."

After wiping my tears dry and doing my best to put myself together—without the benefit of a mirror—we return to the kitchen. Anthony's got two fistfuls of spaghetti, which he's attempting to jam in his mouth at the same time while Tammy's trying to give him back the fork I dropped. We lucked out. The kitchen's not a disaster again. Hooray for small miracles. I take the fork from Tammy and toss it in the sink since it hit the floor, and grab a clean one to feed Anthony. Neither

Danny nor I draw attention to my not finishing my plate.

A cloud of gloom hounds me the rest of the night. Every cute thing the kids do gets me crying, as does every concerned/worried stare from Danny. Soon after we put the little ones to bed, he hops on the laptop and starts combing the Internet.

"What are you looking for?" I ask, sidling up next to him.

"I'm not sure, exactly. Something… anything that might explain what's going on."

I squat beside him and rest my head on his shoulder, watching (but not quite watching) page after page on *Yahoo!* go zipping by. Snippets of text here and there almost suggest he's looking at occult references. Hmm. I guess we're truly screwed if he's starting to check out bullshit like that.

Still taken with guilt over throwing up his sauce, I snuggle closer, eyes closed. His scent teases at my awareness, a mix of his presence and cologne that I've always been aware of when he held me, but it's different now. Really different. The essence of *Danny* is so strong I can taste it. Temptation grows, an irresistible urge welling up from within. My head moves as if on its own, and I kiss the side of his neck.

He squirms, but doesn't pull away.

I keep kissing him for a while as he searches. He squirms again when I drag my tongue up the side of his neck, tracing the line of his carotid artery. The pulse resonates within my mouth, and that strange ache spreads over my face again.

The spell breaks.

No. Dammit! I said leave them out! I pull away, refusing to think of my husband as a food source. What in the eff is wrong with me?

Danny twists toward me and kisses me on the lips, oblivious to the bestial urge that had been forming in my mind. Seeing him interested in me again in a sexual way brushes that worry aside and I climb half into his lap, facing him, kissing and pawing.

We migrate to the bedroom.

"Wait," I whisper, breathless. "Let me try something real quick."

He nods. "All right…"

I rush to the bathroom, strip, and run the shower full hot. It's a shock to stand in, but not even close to painful compared to walking Tammy to preschool across Dante's Parking Lot. Spinning under the water like a rotisserie chicken, I give myself a few minutes before shutting the faucet and drying off. Wearing just the towel, I hurry back to the bedroom and climb in with Danny.

Since the sun's down, I'm wide-awake and *extremely* turned on.

***

Danny's sound asleep in bed.

I sit curled up, naked on the floor in the narrow space between the bed and the wall. Maybe I shouldn't have done this? The shower did warm me up enough, but as soon as we went all the way, Danny's enthusiasm receded. Trooper that he is, he kept going, but if the look on his face when we finished is any indication, he doesn't have much interest in doing that ever again… at least until we figure out why I'm so cold *inside* too.

He's never looked at me like *that* before, either. A 'what the hell are you?' kind of stare that chilled me straight to the heart. I don't think he meant it consciously, which makes it worse, since it speaks truth.

I think back to earlier, when I had knelt beside him out in the dining room; the temptation to *feed* on him had been undeniable. Terrible, just terrible. Head down, my hair cascades over my shins, spilling over my feet to the carpet. Tears run down my legs from heavy, silent sobs wracking my body. I'm a danger to the people I love. How can I be sure I'll be able to control myself? The attack *did* kill me. After all, it killed my family, my dreams, everything I'd ever worked so hard for and loved so much.

Truly, I don't deserve to still exist.

Sorrow consumes me. Visions of suicide dance around my head like the demon actors of Hell's variety show. The life I had is gone. I'm not sure what I am now, but it's not safe for my family. *I'm* not safe for my family, and that kills me all over again. I could disappear in the night, go somewhere far, far away. They'd all be better off. I cry harder, realizing that my family would've been happier if I didn't survive that attack.

I picture Danny's face, getting *the call*.

"We're sorry, Mr. Moon. Your wife was found dead this morning," says an anonymous voice, part Nico Fortunato, part Chad Helling, part generic cop. "We're investigating, but don't have any leads. But from all appearances, it was an animal attack. Maybe a pit bull. Maybe coyotes. Maybe a chupacabra."

Okay, that last bit gets me laughing. Great. Now I sound hysterical.

Tammy and Anthony are so young, they probably won't remember me after a while… that is, had I died that night. *Or if I run away*. Either way, I'm sure their lives will turn out much better without me around. Fragments of an imagined future, the kids getting older, living alone with their father haunt my thoughts. Surly Tammy, a high-school outcast, never quite right since her mother died or disappeared. Anthony, fourteen years old, scrawny and shy. No friends, gets bullied, obsessed with finding who or what killed his mother.

Or just finding his mother.

"Oh, stop it," I whisper to myself, sitting up and rubbing my eyes. "That's not how they're going to turn out." I know I'm only trying to talk myself out of doing what I must.

And what is it you must do, Sam? I ask myself.

The answer, of course, is simple. I just can't be

a danger to my family. If something happened to them by my hand… how could I live with myself? I couldn't of course. I couldn't live, at all. Better to spare them—and me, and just get the hell of out of Dodge. Or Fullerton.

Leaving feels right, but it all feels terrible too. Too terrible to contemplate for long. Which is why I sit in silence for an hour or so more, trying to come up with any rational explanation for what's happening to me. My line of reasoning keeps circling back to one illogical conclusion: I've become the unthinkable.

The truly unbelievable.

Which makes no sense at all. Vampires don't exist.

But, I can't argue with what my eyes have been telling me for the past two weeks. My eyes and stomach and skin and sleep patterns. And if I *have* become a fiend, if by some bizarre twist of fate that such beings really exist, then I really, really can't sit idly by and let such a monster threaten the lives of my children. Or Danny.

I stand and walk down the hall, not bothering to get dressed. This will probably hurt less if there's nothing between my skin and the sunlight. Silent tears run down my face, dripping onto my chest. I'm mourning my own death. Or, more to the point, I'm mourning the effect it will have on my family. I don't care about dying anymore. Protecting my children is all that matters.

The patio door from the kitchen opens with a

soft scrape of metal. My nakedness glows blue in the moonlight of a clear sky. What perfect weather to die in. A cool breeze lofts my hair and caresses me in the embrace of Mother Nature. Am I still even part of this world? Is death the end or will I haunt this place? Surely, if I am a vampire, I've been cursed and won't be welcomed to Heaven.

Hah. Of course. I've never really believed in God my whole life. At this moment, why do I find myself hoping He's real?

Grass tickles my feet as I walk to the middle of our backyard and gaze up at the moon. Like some ancient pagan priestess, I stand naked under the sky and raise my arms to the sky. I don't belong here anymore. My fingers stretch apart as I mentally command the cosmos to take me. Nothing matters but protecting my family.

Nothing.

I've only a few hours to wait.

Chapter Fifteen
A Small Hope

Soft grunts and mumbles coming from the house make me twist around.

Tammy's little voice reaches my ears despite the distance and an exterior wall between us. She must be having a nightmare, tossing and turning in her sleep. A weak scrap of thought coalesces in the back of my head that she's aware of what I'm going to do. I bow my head.

She'll be better off without me.

A soft wind lifts my hair, bringing with it the scent of grass and old grease. I'm confused for a moment until I remember our backyard wall is adjacent to a Pep Boys. I shake my head, clear my thoughts. I'd never tried to kill myself before. This is a first for me. And with death still a few hours away, I'm not sure how best to pass the time. Maybe I should do a final load of laundry. That would sure help Danny. Maybe clean the bathroom a little more. My mid-dinner wipe-down hardly seemed enough. Maybe I should send emails to all my loved ones and tell them I'll miss them. That sounds like a nice thing to do. What about, you know, going down the list of all the major religions… and making sure I'm good with their gods. Nothing beats covering all your bases. I wouldn't want to end up in Hell, although I suspect I've gotten a taste of it these past few weeks.

Right as I decide to send Mary Lou a long, heartfelt, snarky text about how much I'm going to miss her, and that I will do my best to 'swing by' and say hello—maybe move some stuff around her house—Tammy's fussing gets louder. It sounds like she's trying to say something in her sleep, but can't form words.

I'm sorry, Tam Tam. I can't risk harming you. If what I'm afraid might be true *is* true, having me anywhere near you is going to complicate your life in ways I can't even imagine. You don't deserve to be saddled with me. You deserve a normal life, a happy life. I'm sure Daddy will protect and love you and—

"Mommy," mutters Tammy, her voice slurred with the fog of deep sleep.

My hands clench into fists. I shiver, but not from cold. Guilt hits me in the gut. What am I doing? Giving up? Really? Is that the best I can come up with? Just give up and kill myself? Come on, Sam. Hold it together. They need you.

I can't walk away from my family.

Tammy's restless mumbling continues, drawing me back into the house.

After locking the patio door, I pad down the hall to the bedroom and pull my nightgown on before rushing into Tammy's room. By the time I get there, she's stopped tossing, but still fidgets with a worried expression.

It makes absolutely no sense to think that she somehow knew what I almost did, but to see her starting to calm down right as I snap out of that bleak spiral of despair is too coincidental to ignore. I crouch beside her bed, brushing a hand over her head. Watching her fills me with guilt at ever thinking I could simply surrender. The pain I'd cause them by killing myself isn't worth it. Mary Lou always called me 'willful.' I can do this. I can control myself, even if the unbelievable has become truth.

I won't abandon them.

I *can't.*

Tammy smiles at me in her sleep. At least, I think she's directing it at me.

I keep brushing her hair with my hand. So many insecurities whirl around my head about what's happening to me, but no matter what, I will protect Tammy and Anthony. This disease, or whatever I have, will not come between us. I won't surrender. Never.

After a while, Tammy's resumed sleeping soundly. I cross the hall to check on Anthony, who also appears to be having a pleasant dream. He grins when I run my hand over his head. I don't know what the future holds, kiddo, but I'm not going to make you grow up without a mommy.

The night is quiet, save for two cars somewhere outside going by. A dog bark and coyote howl follow some time later. I kiss Anthony once more on the head and walk into the hall, traipsing aimlessly back and forth from the kitchen to my bedroom door.

When last I had this much excess energy, I went jogging. Stupid. Though, perhaps not. If whatever attacked me had been coming for me specifically, my idiocy might've worked out for the better. At least, for my family. If he'd broken into the house to get me, I'm sure at least Danny would've been killed trying to protect me.

I'm half-tempted to go for a jog again, but it bothers me that I'm not the least bit hesitant about the idea. Like, you'd think after what happened, I'd have developed a phobia of the dark or some PTSD type reaction to the idea of a late-night/early morning jog again. Yet, for reasons I don't fully understand, I feel untouchable. It's the middle of the night and nothing can hope to threaten me.

Maybe because I really am a vampire.

I sigh at the ceiling. Or maybe at God.

Yeah, right. Vampire? More like a head case.

And I'm a head case that has to be awake in about three hours for work. I trudge to my room and crawl into bed next to Danny, determined to fall asleep.

Except, one hour of staring at the ceiling drags into the next.

Chapter Sixteen
Fraying

Wednesday at the office, I'm working on my fourth qwerty sandwich.

I'm particularly tired and listless, and more than a little bit hungry. My body reacts with all the nimbleness of a supertanker, requiring great effort to initiate motion, and even more to stop. Anyone looking at me would think I'd smoked enough weed to transcend time itself.

Yeah, insomnia sucks.

One uncoordinated swing of my arm knocks a plastic cup across my desk, a cup I'd been using to hold pens and thumbtacks. I know, an odd combination. Anyway, I reach for a cluster of thumbtacks on the floor and promptly impale my finger on one. Not just impale but, damn, the sucker's embedded all the way to the flat plastic part against my skin. I yelp and pluck the minuscule dagger out of my flesh. The hole closes right in a second. Like, right before my eyes.

Well, that's not normal.

I stab myself again, this time in the thumb, and muffle a cry of pain. A second later, I pull the tack out and watch the hole close again. I can't help but do it a few more times. Okay, this is psychotic… and mesmerizing.

"Sam?" asks Nico.

"Gah." I jump.

Nico flinches back. "Whoa. Sorry. Didn't mean to sneak up on you."

"It's all right." I throw the pin back in the cup and smile at him. "What can I do for you?"

"Umm, why are you here?"

I raise both eyebrows. "That's kind of deep and metaphorical for eight in the morning isn't it?"

He laughs. "I mean right here, right now. You're supposed to be testifying at the grand jury in an hour."

"Crap." I rub the bridge of my nose. "It slipped my mind."

"Everything all right?" Nico steps into the cube and lowers his voice from boss to big brother. "I'm a little worried."

"Other than going through an industrial quantity of sunblock, I'm okay."

He nods, as if he knows what the hell I'm talking about. "What about sleep?" he asks.

"What is this thing called sleep of which you speak?"

"That bad?"

"I felt like running again at two in the morning."

"At two in the morning, I'd already gotten up twice to go to the bathroom," said Nico, rubbing his chin, then snaps his head at me. "That was too much information, wasn't it?"

"Yeah, maybe. Who cares? I just need sleep."

"Well, I'm going to insist you see someone if it continues past the end of this week."

"Fine," I say, grabbing my purse, too tired to argue, but appreciating his concern. "Where's Chad?"

"You haven't checked your email? He had car issues and plans to go straight from the mechanic to the courthouse."

I glance at the screen. The email's right there. Looking at words and comprehending them are apparently two different things. "Right. Email."

Nico flares his eyebrows at me, but doesn't say anything. Lucky for me, I started off with high scores and a reputation for being meticulous. If I'd been a slacker, I think I'd already be suspended.

"On the way," I mutter, darting past him and rushing down the hall to the bathroom.

I duck into the ladies' room and use the giant mirror to check my foundation make up for holes. It's so damn eerie to see openings where my eyes should be, since I've obviously not put makeup on them. Still, my forehead, cheeks, and neck look solid enough—if somewhat plastic.

Our department-issue sedan is still in the lot

since Chad went straight to the courthouse, so I hop in that and hit the road. I'm freaking out enough about being late to the grand jury that I avoid blacking out on the drive to the federal courthouse in LA.

Good news: There's a covered parking deck.

Bad news: It's full and I wind up having to park across the street in a private one that charges $18.

It's not the money I'm moaning about, though. I can't exactly walk into the courthouse wearing that stupid hat and sunglasses. If I look like an insane woman, the grand jury's going to laugh me off and ignore everything I say. So, I leave the hat and oversized sunglasses in the car and walk to the end of the parking deck, standing for a moment at the edge of shade to psych myself up.

Fortunately, I'm not wearing heels.

And I'm already late. Gotta do this.

Fists clenched, I sprint out from the cover of the parking garage, dart across the road, fly up a flight of stairs, and leap through the doors of the federal courthouse building. By the time I'm inside, I feel like an extra-rare steak. Once I'm in the shade, I stop, standing motionless in shock, barely suppressing the urge to whimper and whine at how much that hurt.

"Hey, miss," says a man in a U.S. Marshal's uniform. "There's no smoking in the courthouse."

I look down at myself. A haze of smoke surrounds me, seeping out of my pantsuit blazer and shirt. Waves of pain ripple over my arms and legs, fading away as my hunger grows. He couldn't possibly be referring to what really happened, but I get annoyed nonetheless. Out of nowhere, I picture myself thrusting my arm into his chest, tearing out his heart, and devouring it. The imagery stuns me blank-faced. "Right, sorry." I pretend to put out an imaginary cigarette.

The marshal nods, satisfied. Little does he know what went through my mind.

Jesus.

A weak whisper filters out from the shadows of my mind. *You are foolish, Sssamantha. Dancing in the sunlight? Mingling with mortals. You are damaging yourself, forcing your body to mend, and starving yourself of what you know you need most. Ssstop denying what you have become... and feed.*

I pinch the bridge of my nose, eyes closed. I am not schizophrenic. I am not hearing voices.

Deep in the recesses of my mind, the raspy feminine whisper emits a condescending laugh and goes quiet once again.

Confused, in pain, and, yes, hungry as hell, I head over to the security desk, show my ID and check my gun in before continuing down a hall, deeper into the building toward the elevators.

The walls inside are mirrors from the midpoint up, so after hitting the button for the third floor, I tuck all the way in back and keep my head down. A pair of tall men in gray suits get in on the second floor, standing in front of me. I try my best to ignore them until one sniffs at the air.

"Smells like someone's grilling burgers."

His friend sniffs around. "Yeah. Damn, now I'm hungry."

Grr. Wonderful. My clothes have soaked up the fragrance of broiled Sam.

I push past them when the doors open on the third floor, and make my way down the hall to the courtroom mentioned on my subpoena. The grand jury is seated already, and the prosecutor is questioning the bottle-blonde Marissa, Marty Brauerman's former receptionist.

Chad's in a bank of seats off to the right where a few spectators and some other people who are probably here to testify wait their turn. One middle-aged woman, who's in tears, has got to be Marissa's mother. I hurry around the outer wall and take a seat by Chad while the young woman tearfully explains how she had no clue that Marty was running a scam.

"Close one, Sam. You're next," whispers Chad.

I nod. "Sorry."

Hunger and fatigue get into a fistfight inside me. In what feels like a second, Chad is shaking me awake.

"You're on, Sam," he whispers.

I look up to find the prosecutor, a fiftyish man in a dark suit with short black hair, and the judge, an older Latina, both staring expectantly at me. Oh, great. Fell asleep in court. That looks wonderful.

"Sorry," I mumble, and make my way over to the witness chair.

A clerk approaches with a Bible. I half expect it to burn my hand, but it doesn't. She swears me in and walks away.

"Please state your name and title for the record," says the prosecutor.

"Samantha Moon. I'm an agent with the Federal Department of Housing and Urban Development."

He nods, glances at the grand jury pool, and faces me again. "Would you please explain to the court your involvement in the investigation of Mr. Martin Brauerman?"

I've testified to grand juries as well as trial juries before, but never while feeling like I've gone two weeks without sleeping. Within a minute of me starting, I refer to Brauerman as Kondapalli, the fake name he'd used on his VOIP account.

"Umm. Sorry, I mean Brauerman…" I take a deep breath, trying to wake up, and continue explaining about the 'Call Marty' business cards, the raid on the one property, Rosa (who, by the way, is still in the hospital recuperating from her gunshot, but expected to recover). My grogginess thickens, so I slow down and think every sentence over before speaking. Right around the time I get to explaining my going undercover as Lorelei Duke, the prosecutor raises a hand to stop me.

"I'm sorry, Agent Moon. Are you feeling unwell?"

The grand jurors are whispering amongst themselves and giving me odd looks.

I glance at the judge, feeling helpless and

confused for a second. She's got an eyebrow up. When I look back at the prosecutor, he folds his hands in front of himself, clasping a leather-bound notepad. "Is something wrong?" I ask.

The prosecutor smiles. "You've just strayed off topic, Agent Moon. The past few minutes, you've been explaining to the court how much your daughter Tammy loves finger-painting."

My face burns with shame. "Umm. I'm sorry. I had a medical issue a few weeks ago. I was attacked and nearly killed in the park at night, and I've been having some problems sleeping."

His eyebrows go up. "Oh, dear. I'm sorry to hear that. Do you need a moment?"

The judge's expression shifts from bewildered to sympathetic.

"Thank you. I'm okay." I adjust my sleeves, sit up straight, and look the prosecutor in the eye. "Where did I leave off?"

"You were telling us about the skimming."

"Oh, yes. My investigation of the financial records of several HUD recipients showed that they were making payments to MBM, Inc. in excess of their monthly mortgage amounts. This excess varied from $150 to $300 in one case. Our investigation led us to determine that Mr. Brauerman had deceived these people into believing they were *renting*, and he pocketed the difference in the payments."

The prosecutor nods. "Did you bring any documentation for this?"

My jaw opens.

Chad stands and waves a bunch of papers.

"My partner, Chad Helling, has the documentation." I gesture at him while giving him a *Thank you for saving my ass* stare.

The prosecutor collects the printouts, gives them a look-over, and hands one to the judge. At a nod from her, the papers make their rounds among the jurors. I nearly drift off while sitting there in the silent courtroom listening to the soporific rustle of papers, but manage to keep myself from blacking out.

When the jury is done reading over the financial notes, I run them through an explanation of our sting operation that included me going undercover.

"I'm sorry, what?" asks the prosecutor.

I blink at him.

"Agent Moon, I'm not sure you understood the question. I was asking you what Mr. Brauerman quoted you as your 'rent payment,' but you responded with… 'spaghetti sauce.'"

Oh damn… I really am out of it. "I'm sorry. It was $550. Mr. Brauerman quoted me a rent payment of $550 a month. When the paperwork came through HUD, we saw the property mortgage at $880 per month, of which the assistance program would've covered $600. Lorelei's mortgage responsibility should have been $280 per month, not $550."

"I see. Thank you. What, if any, determination did you make as to why none of the victims came forward?"

Chad holds up a tape cassette and wags it back and forth.

"Mr. Brauerman preyed on immigrants and the poor, people who had an innate distrust or fear of government. He convinced them that his 'special discount' was legal, but the government would do whatever they could to shut it down. If you review the recording from my undercover investigation, you'll hear him making the same claims to me."

The prosecutor collects the tape from Chad, and hands over to a U.S. Marshal who pops it in a machine. I'm pretty sure I pass out at least twice during the half-hour long recording, but no one seems to notice. I hope.

A few questions from the jurors keep me on the stand a little longer. One wanted to know what made me suspect the defendant in the first place. I explain that I initially thought the 'Marty' on those business cards had drug involvement given the raid on the one property, but when we started finding them at multiple HUD properties that had nothing to do with narcotics trafficking, I got suspicious. Mostly because the residents acted evasive when I asked about them.

That done, I'm excused from the stand. I wobble back over to the seating gallery and fall into the chair next to Chad. He pats my shoulder.

"Could've been smoother, but you did good. Well, good enough."

For now, I'll take good enough. I chuckle to

myself. Wow, I feel like a train ran me over. And I'm so damn hungry.

"Did I really say spaghetti sauce?"

"You did."

The prosecutor calls Chad up. As his testimony begins to sound like a duplication of mine—though spoken in a much faster, more coherent voice—I fade out again. Chad prods me awake in what feels like a split second.

"Hey, Sam. We're done. Meet you back at the office?"

I fidget. "I think I might take the rest of the day off… would you mind telling Nico I feel like death and can't focus?"

"Yeah, sure, Sam. You should go get checked out."

"Starting to sound more and more like you're right." I stand, holding onto the barrier at the front of the seating box to keep my balance. "If Nico really wants me to come in, just call me and I'll be there."

Chad pats me on the shoulder. "You look pretty rough, Sam. I'll vouch that you're sick."

"Thanks." I give him a halfhearted chuckle.

He walks me out to the front lobby, where we retrieve our sidearms from the security desk. Since his car is in the attached parking deck and mine's across the street, we split up. I head out the front door while he veers off down a corridor inside, safe from the damn sun.

Grr.

Nothing for it but to run like hell.

The pain wakes me right up as soon as I run into the light. I dash across the street so fast it doesn't feel possible, and skid to a stop as soon as I'm in the shade again.

"Ow. Ow. Ow." I hold my arms up from my sides, shivering on my feet until the agony stops a few seconds later. "Oh, this is really getting annoying now. How am I supposed to function if it hurts to go outside?"

With the absence of solar fire, Morpheus' dreamy embrace returns. Falling right where I am and going to sleep doesn't sound like a bad idea, except for knowing I'd get run over since I'm on the entrance ramp of a parking garage. Plus, if I spend another hour here, that's an extra $18, even if the government is paying it.

While staggering down the row toward the car, a man pounces on me from behind. I'm so out of it, I flop like a ragdoll in his arms as he drags me between a pair of SUVs and throws me to the ground. The edge of a knife presses against my neck soon after his weight lands on top of me.

"Scream and you're dead," rasps the man.

He reaches around in front of me and fumbles at my belt, trying to get my pants off. It takes a moment for the idea that he means to rape me to drill through the cement shell of delirium around my brain. As soon as he starts pulling my pants down, the full realization of what's happening finally registers.

Pure anger explodes inside me.

I shove at the cement, hurling us both upright while emitting an inhumanly deep growl. A nip of steel at my throat annoys me more than hurts. In a fluid move, I spin to the right, grab him, and hurl him head-first at a column fifteen feet away.

The man flies like a missile, crashing into the concrete. With a *crunch*, a spray of crimson paints the grey stone, and he falls limp and unconscious at the base. Cool air on my bare legs reminds me my pants are around my ankles. Not taking my eyes off the limp figure in a navy wool coat, I stoop and pull them up, re-securing my belt. My attention crawls upward, onto the gleaming red stain.

Hunger rises to a raging boil.

A too-familiar ache spreads across my face, into my jaw. It's much worse this time, painful enough to make me gasp. Something sharp pokes me in the tongue. I can't stop staring at the blood dripping down the cement column.

It's so… so… beautiful.

Chapter Seventeen
In Sickness and in Health

I awake on my sofa at home.

It's dark out. Tammy's curled up on top of my chest, possibly napping, possibly staring sideways at the television. The scent of spaghetti sauce hangs in the air. Sloshing and plate-clattering emanates from the kitchen. Plastic clicks come from my left at the floor level, along with Anthony making voices for his toys.

The last thing I remember is staring at the creep who jumped me in the parking garage. Dark pants, dark-blue wool long-coat, wool cap. He looked like high-end homeless or low-end scumbag. A faint hint of beer lingers in my mouth, but I don't remember drinking anything. In fact, I'm pretty sure if I attempted to drink beer, it wouldn't stay down long.

I reach up with one arm and stroke Tammy's

hair.

She stirs and peers up at me. "Hi, Mommy! Daddy said you were sick again, so you had to sleep. That's why you didn't get us from Aunt Mary Lou's."

"Long day, sweetie. I feel much better now." I do actually… I'm not even hungry anymore. At the memory of the two sharp points poking me in the tongue, my eyes shoot open.

"Daddy made sketti. He said you already had dinner."

Oh, no! Was that an excuse or does Danny know something I don't? Did I… *eat* that guy in the parking garage? I feel around my mouth with my tongue, but none of my teeth are, well, *long*. My canines *do* feel a little sharper than they ought to be, but they're certainly not, like, fangs.

Jesus, the words coming out of my mind… utter nonsense.

"All right, you two… it's time," says Danny. He swoops around the end of the couch and plucks Anthony from the floor, swinging him into the air like a tiny Superman. "Time to fly off to bed, little man."

Anthony waves his arms and cheers.

I stand, cradling Tammy, and carry her down the hall behind Danny. Everything feels awkwardly normal as we put the kids to bed. Not until both bedroom lights are out and the doors pulled shut, does Danny give me the 'okay, what happened?' stare.

"Sorry," I mutter.

"No 'sorry.'" He grasps my arms. "I'm worried about you, Sam. What happened? You don't have to apologize."

I bite my lip. "Things are getting weird. I'm sorry for not telling you sooner."

"Telling me what?" Danny lifts my chin with one finger, forcing eye contact. "Did something happen?"

Possibly, I want to say. Maybe I did to that rapist what some mysterious creature had done to me a few weeks ago. Or, I might've just left him there, injured and bleeding. I can't remember what happened, but I know I'm not hungry anymore. I feel better than I have in days. Alert, strong… I can even *feel* Danny's worry radiating.

"I'm not sure," I finally say. "I… I might've hurt someone, but… there's something else."

"Hurt someone?" asks Danny. "What something else?"

I pull him into the bathroom and explain as much as I can remember of being grabbed, thrown to the ground, and assaulted. He goes from concerned to livid in an instant.

"What? Someone attacked you *again*?" He looks me over like a worried parent checking for scratches. "At a goddamn courthouse?"

"I'm fine, Danny. He didn't do anything but unbuckle my belt. I threw him off. I don't remember what happened after that. Not really. What I *do* remember makes no sense."

He folds his arms. "All right…"

"I think I have fangs."

"You're right. That doesn't make any sense."

"Danny." I tug him closer and take a step back so we're both in front of the mirror. "I'm sorry for not telling you this right away, but something is *really* messed up with me."

"You're not sleeping, the blood… yeah. You're right." He puts a hand on my cheek, flinches and removes it again. My cold, cold cheek. "We'll get to the bottom of it somehow. Whatever it takes, we'll fix it."

Tears brimming in my eyes, I pluck a washcloth from the towel rack and wet it. "Look at the mirror."

He stares at the hollows of my eyes in the reflection, a little color draining from his cheeks. My painted visage disappears as I wash away the foundation makeup. Soon, I'm an empty blouse.

"I don't have a reflection anymore." I drop the cloth in the sink.

"Uhh…" he says. Whatever word he was about to form dissolves into nothing.

Danny looks from me to the mirror, then back at me. He opens his mouth to speak, then closes it again. He tries one more time, but gives up. I know the feeling. He leans in close to the mirror, his breath fogging it. He taps the glass. He looks at the rag in the sink. Picks it up, rubs some of the makeup between his thumb and finger. He smells the rag for reasons unknown to me. My hubby is analytical and clever. He's also stumped, and he hates that. I know that much about him. My husband the attorney would make a clever investigator. He opens the glass cupboard, looks at both sides. Taps both sides. He asks me to lean close to the mirror and I do so, right along with him. I can't help but note that there are twin barrels of dogged breath on the glass before him. My reflection, not so much.

"A trick?" he asks.

"No trick," I say.

"Am I asleep?"

"Maybe," I say, and pinch his arm, harder than I'd intended.

"Okay, not asleep. And ouch."

He goes through the motions again, this time really studying me. He touches the skin of my face carefully, running a hand over my cheeks and chin. In the mirror, his hand makes a Samantha-Moon-shaped caress over empty air.

"How am I able to see the wall behind you?"

"You do and you don't," I say. "Look again."

He does, squinting. "Ah, a diffraction effect. The light bends around you, like it would around a corner."

"Except I'm not a corner," I say. "And we're not talking about light. We're talking about my reflection."

"Why you're not showing up, but I can see the point where the light bends around you… yes, there. If you move a little, there is a shift in the mirror, like a glitch in the matrix, so to speak."

"Great," I say. "I'm big, fat honkin' glitch."

"Not big or fat, but definitely honkin'," he says, and puts a shaking hand on my shoulder, his eyes still shifted left at the mirror. "We'll figure something out."

"Figure what out?" I ask.

"What's happened to you and why."

"You mean that?" I lean against him.

He wraps me in his arms. Fear is quite evident in his voice, but he doesn't hesitate in embracing me. "Samantha Moon, you're still everything to me. Even if you've… got a condition I don't understand. When I agreed to that whole 'until death do us part' thing, I meant it."

I become acutely aware of my overly sluggish heartbeat. Though, it's quite peppier than it has been, a little slower than one beat per second. If I'm really a vampire, and I'm dead, does that mean our marriage is legally over? Here I go again, off the deep end.

"I meant it, Sam." He kisses me. "If you'd been hit by a car and wound up in a wheelchair for the rest of your life, I'd still be there. This is no different."

"Except I can still walk," I smirk.

He chuckles. "Remember when you had a little too much wine at the Christmas party in '92? I thought you were going to break your neck when you fell down that escalator."

"Oof." I cringe into a giggle. "I didn't feel anything until the next morning. Hey, I'm not the only one accident-prone! How about when you tried surfing and smashed your face on the board? Your nose gushed for an hour. Sharks for miles turned in your direction."

"That hurt *so* much. I'm just glad I didn't lose any teeth."

"Or get eaten alive."

He brushes hair away from my eyes. "Can we stop talking about injuries? I'd much rather remember when we first met."

I grin. "That still involved minor injuries."

"Only to my pride." He grins. "I shouldn't have been running down the hallway."

In college, I'd been in a rush to my next class and shoved the library door open, straight into Danny who had been running down the hallway. Papers went everywhere. I lose myself in the memory of the first time we looked at each other, almost eleven years ago. It took him three weeks to track me down after that collision.

We stand there reminiscing about that year, before Danny transferred to Gould School of Law at USC. Somehow, both of us managed to juggle dating and coursework. We relocate to the bedroom and relax, continuing to reminisce about good times, funny moments, and even some frustrating ones involving our yearlong project to restore this house.

The obvious unease that gripped him at seeing the mirror settles, and though nothing sexual happens between us, we share an intimate evening.

It's not too common that a married couple is also the best of friends. Despite everything going on with me right now, I still feel fortunate to have him.

I smile to myself, knowing that no matter how screwed up my life has become, Danny's got my back.

Chapter Eighteen
Rare Condition

A soft knock at the front door reaches my ears.

I glance at the clock. "Who's knocking on the door at 11:49 at night?"

"Really?" asks Danny. "I didn't hear anything."

"I've been hearing, seeing, and smelling things I shouldn't be able to."

He taps me on the head. "Are you sure you're not imagining it?"

"Funny question coming from a husband who *didn't* see his wife in a mirror."

"Maybe we're both bonkers."

I scoot off the bed. "At this point, I'm all for it."

"Better than the alternative?"

"Whatever the alternative is," I said. Except, of course, we *did* know what the alternative is… and we both kept it to ourselves. For now.

Danny follows me to the front door. Finding

Mary Lou standing on the porch is a mixture of surprise, comfort, and (at least for my husband) worry.

She hurries inside. "Sorry for showing up so late." She looks furtively from Danny to me. "But I figured you'd be more awake now." Mary Lou goes straight to the kitchen, not waiting for a response.

I ease the door closed and walk after her.

"I've been thinking about your issue." Mary Lou spins to face me. "And I think you're a vampire."

I tilt my head. "Don't beat around the bush, Mary Lou. Give it to me straight."

"I just did…" She blinks, then smiles. "Oh, you're messing with me."

I look at Danny. "Well, at least I'm not the only crazy person in my family."

"No, think about it…" She grabs my hand. "You've developed an allergy to the sun… although movies usually show vampires exploding into a cloud of ashes instantly."

"Oh, yeah. And Hollywood is such a font of factual information," I say, deadpan. Truth is, had I not been wearing sunscreen, hats and extra clothing… I might have come damn near exploding in the sun or dissolving into ashy nothingness, like in my dreams. Which, by the way, I was certain was given to me as a sort of prophetic what-if scenario. No, whatever I have become, or whatever had been triggered within my cells, or whatever I had contracted, had given me the dream as a warning.

Sun equals death. Trust me, I get it.

"Did you just use the word 'fact' in the context of vampires?" asks Danny, half-chuckling.

Mary Lou's hair dances from her quick back-and-forth stare between us. "Think about it, Danny. Sunlight. She's alert at night, sleepy all day. The wound was on her neck, and it got better in days. Her *neck*, mind you. At first, they said the damage was so extensive she'd never talk again. Do you remember that, lest we all forget? Now? Not a mark on her! She's pale. Her fingers are always cold. Maybe the rest of her too. Can't eat food. Drinks only blood. I mean… how could she *not* be a vampire?"

"You know about that?" asks Danny.

"I saw the filthy bottle." Mary Lou gestures at the fridge. "And Tammy said you threw up the other night while eating."

Crap. I make a mental note to myself to be more careful about my eating habits. How hard is to say that Mommy's not hungry? Sooner or later, I'm going to have to appear normal, at least to my kids. Even if Mary Lou's theory turns out to be true, I can't let the kids think things are anything other than normal. Both for their own sake in terms of sanity, as well as because kids blurt. I don't want them getting teased for thinking their mother's a vampire. Even if I am one.

What am I saying?

"But, of course, I can't be." I rake my hands up over my hair. "Like, that's impossible, right?"

"No reflection," adds Mary Lou, although it felt more like piling on.

"You know about that too?" asks Danny.

"I'm sorry." I face him and sigh. "I had to tell someone, and you were so stressed out… I just didn't want to make things any worse."

He frowns, but nods a moment later. "Well, you did decide to let me in on the little secret without being caught, so there's that. No more secrets?"

"No more secrets," I say.

"Good. Now, can we address the fanged elephant in the room? Supernatural stuff like this doesn't exist."

"Doesn't it?" asks Mary Lou. "There have been legends about vampires for centuries."

"Folklore only," says Danny. "Myths and legends about real people with real diseases like anemia, porphyria, XP."

"Or maybe vampires are using *the* diseases as excuses," I smirk.

"Could be both." Mary Lou bounces on her toes. "This is kind of exciting."

I blink at her. "Did you just say *exciting*?"

"Well, if it's all true." She nods. "I mean, you would have like superpowers and… Sam, they say you'll live forever."

Her words hang in the air, and I'm the first to snort. Followed by Danny. Soon, we are doubled over. Danny holds onto the wall. Tears stream down my face, which, lately, is always exciting. Anything that resembles normal bodily functions is always exciting to me now. It takes a few minutes, but soon, Mary Lou joins in. Laughter, after all, is infectious. Unlike xeroderma pigmentosum… which most certainly is *not.*

"…sleep in coffins…" Danny rasps between giggles, which strikes me as so damn funny that I nearly have to pee, which I almost secretly wish I would… but I don't.

"I vant to suck your blooood," I say, except, well, I actually mean it, and with that thought, my laughter dies down.

"Did you two get that out of your system?" asks Mary Lou. "Can we have a real talk now?"

"A real talk about vampires?" asks Danny, wiping his eyes.

"Yes, dammit. There's something going on here, and it's something we need to address."

I shake my head. "No, Mary Lou. I've somehow activated a dormant gene that's triggered the xeroderma pigmentosum mutation or something." Through it all, my rational mind still refuses to let in the supernatural.

Mary Lou grins. "That's a perfect cover story."

"Well, other than it being a genetic disorder that *should* start at birth." Danny rubs his chin, once his laughter has died down to a few random, hiccuppy chuckles. "But I doubt many people have even heard of it, to begin with, much less would know it's congenital."

We both stare blankly at him.

"Means since birth," he adds, shaking his head.

"Oh, right," I say.

"Do you have fangs?" asks Mary Lou.

"No." I bite my lip. "At least… I don't think so."

"Don't think so?" asks Danny.

"Well, maybe I had a dream that I had fangs. I'm not sure it really happened."

"Lemme see." Mary Lou leans close to me.

I open my mouth.

"Your canines are kinda pointy. Can you make them longer?"

"No."

"Try?" asks Mary Lou.

I think about making 'my fangs' grow, but nothing (as I expected) happens, other than my emitting some stupid noises. "See? No fangs. You should be wearing a tinfoil hat."

She laughs.

But Danny eyes me warily. Wow, really? Does he seriously think this is possibly real? Okay, so maybe I am on the colder side, pale, allergic to sunlight, drinking blood, up all night/groggy all day, healing wounds stupid fast… but a vampire?

Okay, he might have a point. But… c'mon, right? There has to be a medical explanation for this. There just freakin' has to be.

"You don't think I'm a vampire, do you?" I ask, staring at my husband, but I know it's not a fair question to ask him. At this point, who wouldn't jump to that conclusion? But Danny wasn't just anyone. He was my husband.

He fidgets. "The mirror thing is really damn hard to explain otherwise."

"Look." I take his hand. He's tense all over again. Standoffish, even. Like, he doesn't really accept my hand, my touch, only tolerates it. "Even if by some freaky chance this *is* real—and I don't because I don't believe in fairy tales—I will *never* harm you or the kids. Or Mary Lou, or anyone who isn't a direct threat. I'm not a monster, Danny. I'm still me."

He keeps staring at me, though his worry has ratcheted down a tick. His fingers tentatively curl around my hand. I'll take tentative for now.

"All right," he says.

"I mean it. If I ever so much as suspect I *might* be dangerous to anyone I love, I'll hurl myself straight into the sun and end it all."

A distinct sense of displeasure coils like a serpent around the back of my brain.

Well, whatever, I think. *If you don't like that idea, then don't touch my family.*

Mary Lou pulls a small thermos out of her giant purse, and hands it to me. "Sniff that and tell me what you think it is."

I open the cap and give the contents a whiff. It smells… off, but appetizing. Like a beef connoisseur expecting filet and being given cube steak. Reacting on reflex, I tilt it back and drain the warm blood down my throat.

"Umm…" Danny glances between us. "What am I watching?"

"It's sheep's blood," says Mary Lou. "You remember Loretta and Hank?" I shake my head, totally lost. She goes on. "You met them at my house a few years ago. Hank works with Rick."

"Still lost."

"Anyway, they have property in Chino Hills, with pigs, chicken, sheep, you name it. Well, she mentioned they were slaughtering one for food—a sheep, that is—so I asked if I could have some of the blood. I told her it was for a garden project. I'd read somewhere that blood meal makes for a great fertilizer."

Eww, I want to say. And also *yum*. Instead, I pinch the bridge of my nose and try to process the concept of my sister bringing me a blood meal. With a sigh, I ask, "And they just handed you a thermos of sheep blood without thinking it weird?"

"Well, it's not like it's any kinda regular thing." Mary Lou gives me a strange look: half fangirl, half freaked out. "I was right, though. You just drank it." She takes the thermos from me and looks inside. "Like, every drop."

"Every drop?" I ask.

Mary Lou looks at me. "You want to lick the inside of the thermos."

"Don't be ridiculous."

"I won't judge you, Sam."

"Well, let's make sure it's clean before we give it back to them."

"Oh, they said we can keep it, Sam."

But she hands it to me anyway, and I turn my

back to them and run my finger inside the thermos. It comes out glistening reddish-pink, and I lick it like the ghoul I just might be. I swipe my finger around the inside, lick again, and turn to face my husband and sister, who are both clearly staring at me.

"Sam... what's happening?" asks Danny.

I open my mouth to speak, but Mary Lou grabs me in a tight hug. "I know you're still Sammy. I'll always be there for you, no matter what happens."

Danny, meanwhile, stares at me from behind my sister. I give him a weak smile. His is even weaker.

When Mary Lou pulls away, I say, "I think Ruby Grace noticed something odd about me."

Mary Lou nods. "She told me that you felt 'different.'"

"Well, at least she didn't hiss and growl." I fold my arms.

Danny's nervousness breaks into a chuckle. "What? Where'd that come from?"

"Property inspection for work. The resident's cat did *not* like me."

"Kids and animals can sometimes sense the paranormal." Mary Lou squeezes my hand. "Look, I need to run home before Rick flips out with worry. You call me if you need *anything*, okay?"

"All right. I will." I hug her back and walk her out. Standing in the open door, I watch her drive away. Once her taillights are out of view, I close it and sigh.

Danny surprises the hell out of me by hugging

me tight from behind. “Vampire, huh?”

“Please. It’s gotta be a disease or something rational.”

He kisses the side of my neck. “Explain the reflection thing.”

“I can’t.”

“So…” He sways us side to side. “We tell the world you have XP, but we should open our minds to the possibility that you might’ve caught something a little less scientifically explainable.”

“Yes to the first part and no to the second.”

“What do you mean?”

“I can’t accept that vampires are real.” I squirm around to face him, touching foreheads.

“And if they are?”

I open my mouth to speak, close it. I try again. “I’m scared, Danny.”

“Of what?”

“Of what that could mean for us. When I was lying there bleeding in the park, I knew I was going to die. I mean, I had no doubt. This was it. I was a goner. I felt every second slipping away, and all I wanted was to be with my family again. You and the kids are everything to me. I’m horrified at the thought that *this* happened because I refused to die. What if this is my fault? What if I asked for this?”

“You didn’t ask for any of this.” He crushes me into a hug and surprises me again by breaking into tears. “It’s not your fault.”

Him crying gets me crying. “Thank you for saying that. I’ll figure something out. We’ll be okay."

"Absolutely, Samantha Moon." Danny leans back and wipes at his cheeks. "We still have each other. We can do anything."

I hug him, my chin resting on his shoulder. "Just put our minds to it."

"Hey," he says. "We fixed this house up. We can do anything"

Yeah, I think. *Anything... except have Starbucks.*

I sigh. "This might be bigger than rehabbing a house, Danny."

"Then we'll just have to be bigger than it."

"This isn't real, Danny."

"Probably not."

"One or the other of us is probably dreaming."

"Probably."

"I'm scared," I say, and nestle deeper into his arms.

"I am, too, sweetie. I am, too."

Chapter Nineteen
Stakeout

Thursday morning, I evidently decide to eat another qwerty sandwich.

However, I'm alert enough to sit up when I hear Chad's chair squeak. He doesn't catch me sleeping again, but I'm sure my face hit the desk hard enough that he heard the thud. The grogginess is still there, but it's not as bad as it has been. Did I really 'feed' from a guy? Nothing's been in the news about a murder in an LA parking garage, but I could've sworn that ache in my face had something to do with my teeth mutating into fangs or extending or something. The sight of blood had mesmerized me and when I woke up at home, the hunger had abated.

The only logical conclusion is that I drank his blood. Human blood. If that's true, then it invigorated me far more than the beef blood Danny brought home. I wonder how often I need to feed. Every day? Every other day? Every week? Three square meals of blood a day? And, most important, am I going to have to attack people to sustain myself? As in, do I *have* to kill someone to feed or can I just drink, say, a little and move on?

And did I really just ask myself that steady stream of crazy questions?

Crazy, so damn crazy. I'm a federal agent. A mom. A sister. A wife…

I pause, noticing where Danny landed on that list, then shake my head. Coincidence. We'd had a nice night together. No lovemaking, but some serious snuggling.

Still...

I can't shake that look he gave me, and his standoffishness, which is totally a word.

Well, if the tables had been turned, I would be standoffish too, I suppose. And weirded out, too, I suppose. And all the emotions that Danny is going through.

Even crazier is the notion of vampirism. No, not necessarily vampirism, per se, but the inherent supernaturalism surrounding it. Since when did ghosts exist, or UFOs, or disappearing from mirrors actually, you know, become a thing?

I drum my fingers on the desk. Dammit. If it wasn't for the whole disappearing from the mirror thing, I could explain this away, somewhat easily. Well, the blood thing was getting harder and harder, and that's where I just might want to get tested by a real doctor. Maybe I contracted a disease from whoever attacked me. What disease, I didn't know, but it totally could have happened.

Except…

Except, did I really want a doctor poking and prodding me and looking deep into what might very well be something unexplainable? Did I really want that on the table, in the light, so to speak? And what if the results came back conclusive? "Ma'am, I'm sorry to say, you are a vampire. There's a government agency that wants to talk to you. And it's not HUD."

No, I think. I do not want that. Nope, not at all. Whatever was happening, I would find answers myself. And with the help of Danny and Mary Lou. Well, definitely Mary Lou.

And if it is a rare, exotic blood disease I'd contracted?

Then bring it on, I think.

Jesus, am I seriously sitting here debating being a vampire? As if that's some kind of real thing that exists and not lifted straight from Hollywood? Yes, I think. I really am. I've gone down the rabbit hole, hook, line, and sinker. And now, I'm also mixing metaphors—

"Hey, Moon. Ready?" asks Chad.

"Ready?" I look up at him, startled.

"You wanted to observe Mr. Bell, remember? A good, old-fashioned stakeout."

At the word *stake*, I shiver. Chad couldn't possibly have meant that on purpose, right? Huh… I wonder if the whole 'wood-through-the-heart' thing works? Of course not. Vampires aren't real. They don't exist. Only in Hollywood. Definitely only in Hollywood. And where did they get their idea for vampires? Where did anyone get their ideas of vampires? Books and movies, of course. And before that, the folklore of frightened peasants who had to invent myths to explain things they couldn't understand. Cow drops dead for no reason? Vampire got it. No, dammit, I'm sick. With what, I have no idea, but I'm sick. That's all. Period. A frickin' medical problem that science will eventually figure out. Someday.

Again, that would require going to a doctor. Ugh. Sadly, I think I'm well past the stage of 'just hoping it goes away.'

It's not going away. Whatever has me… has me completely and totally, down to my very soul, and I hate whatever it is so much. So damn much.

"Right," I say, getting my head back in the HUD game, no matter hard it might be to tear myself away from my 'issues.' I blink, try to get my brain moving again, rub my temples. Right, the stakeout. Okay, based on a pattern of deposits in Joey's bank account, we suspect that whatever undocumented employment he's involved with takes place on Thursday or Friday. Okay. Head in game. Ready to investigate.

"Let's do this," I say.

"Let's do what?" asks Chad.

"This," I say. "Let's do this."

"Uhh, are you okay, Sam?"

"No," I say. "I'm most definitely not okay. Let's go."

I let Chad drive since the world is still painfully bright to my eyes. We roll up to Joey Bell's house and park an inconspicuous distance away. After a few hours of watching, Chad fidgets. His restlessness grows, and a few minutes later, he opens the door.

"Be right back, gonna go water a bush."

That, of course, reminds me I'm well into my third week of not peeing or doing the other thing. I have quite a bit more trouble explaining that away as a 'medical condition.' Mary Lou had been almost excited at the idea of vampires being real. I guess it *could* be somewhat cool, assuming I'm not a mindless killer, don't *have* to kill to exist, and well, if such things even existed for real.

The sun thing is kinda annoying, though.

A few-year-old blue Ford pickup rumbles by and swings into the driveway at Joey's house. I grab the camera and line up a shot. Three rough-looking biker types hop out of the Ford and move around back to the tailgate. Joey, and two older men emerge from the house. The oldest has short black hair and a bit of a beer gut. He's close to fifty but probably not there yet, dressed in white/grey camo and combat boots. The man behind him is somewhat younger, brown hair, wearing green fatigues and a black T-shirt.

I zoom in and take multiple photos of everyone.

They flip down the tailgate and drag a large, olive-drab crate out. It's coffin-shaped, but only about three quarters as big. Joey and the 'bikers' shake hands. I snap more pictures of an envelope exchange, and keep clicking as the men who emerged from Joey's house carry the crate inside. The almost-fifty-year-old gets in the Ford with the biker types after shaking Joey's hand.

Chad opening the door makes me jump. He flops in and lets out a long moan of relief. "Sorry about that. Some things can't wait."

"Your timing is amazing as always." I nod at the windshield.

He leans forward. "Crap. What happened?"

I give him a quick rundown and pat the camera. "That crate looked like military hardware. I'm thinking guns. Probably rifles, or maybe worse."

"Wanna move on it?" asks Chad.

"Let's call it in first."

He nods and whips out his cell phone.

While he's explaining our theory to Nico that Joey's running illegal firearms, I sneak a few more photos of the Ford as it goes by.

***

Three minutes after Chad hangs up, another pickup truck—a Chevy, red, and battered—comes down the street from the other direction and pulls into Joey's driveway.

Two thirtysomething men hop out and go inside.

Both are rocking the same T-shirt and camo pants couture. They look like rejects from Army boot camp, discharged for failure to maintain their uniforms. And for well, moonlighting as illegal arms dealers. That last part, of course, being an educated guess.

"You think these guys in the red truck are the buyers?" I ask.

"Could be." Chad wrings his hand at the wheel. "And the ones in the blue truck are selling. Joey's the middleman."

One duck, two duck, red truck, blue truck. Ugh. Where did that come from? I've been listening to *far* too much television aimed at toddlers.

"Let's go create a delay. ATF's on the way. I'd rather there be something here for them to find."

Chad nods as he starts the car. "What are you thinking?"

"Property inspections are random, aren't they?"

He chuckles. "Right."

We drive the hundred feet or so to the house and park behind the beat-up Chevy. The walk to the front door covers me in burning hell. I double-time it past the truck to the shelter of the porch, and seethe in pain, which mutates into anger. Rattling, like guns being examined, comes from behind the door.

"That's badass as hell," says a man.

"M249 squad support weapon," replies Joey, sounding proud. "800 rounds-per-minute cyclic."

Say what?!

I grab the knob with my left hand while my right settles on my Glock. Without even thinking, I twist and push. The knob comes off in my grip and the door crunches inward, the still-locked latch gouging the wooden doorjamb like taffy.

Chad catches up and gives me a look.

"What?" I whisper. "Rotten door frame."

I chuck the knob aside into the bushes and shove the door open. Joey and three other men stand around in the living room (in front of the super-expensive TV that is now the least of our problems) holding military-style weapons. The oldest guy with brown hair's hefting the M249, everyone else has an M16 rifle, one even has a grenade launcher attachment. My Glock feels like a pea-shooter.

All four men stare at me like Mom just caught them masturbating.

"Federal agent!" I say, raising my puny weapon. "Drop the weapons and get on the floor!"

Chad edges in behind me.

The men lower the weapons to the rug and stand back up with their hands in the air.

I wag the Glock to the right. "Over there. Away from the hardware. Get down with your arms out where I can see them."

"Jesus effing Christ," mutters Chad. "Is that a grenade launcher?"

"I got a Class III dealer permit," says the fortysomething man with brown hair.

I shift my attention as best I can among the men, watching for sudden motion. "Well, if that's true, then you boys have nothing to worry about. It'll just take us a little bit to sort everything out."

Joey's shaking and white in the face. His hands twitch, so I shift to point my Glock at him.

"Get down, Joey. Don't do anything stupid," I say.

Chad looks over the hardware and whistles. "What the hell is this all about?"

The brown-haired guy gets down and flattens himself out on the rug. As Joey starts to lower himself, I hear an odd ringing in my head, almost as if it's an… alarm or something. What the hell? Out of the corner of my eye, I spot one of the Army rejects pulling a handgun from behind his back. It's bad. He shouldn't be doing that, but all I can do is watch as he raises the weapon.

The *bang* barely registers to me, along with a mild impact near the middle of my chest. Another *bang* goes off before I can force my uncooperative body to move. Truth punctures the fog walling off my consciousness. The skinny rat with long, oily hair has a silver Beretta pointed at Chad, who's collapsing over sideways. I draw a bead on him and fire twice. The Glock bucks in my hands, two empty shell casings flying off to the right.

My arms are sluggish; my shots hit in the thigh and shoulder, too far away from anything vital to kill, but still, the Axl Rose wannabe crumples to his knees.

Chad hits the floor with a *thud.* His gun goes off, and a gout of crimson sprays from the suspect's neck. I want to look away, but I can't. A part of me *feels* his life depart.

Joey's pulled a 1911, but he hasn't quite aimed it at me.

I swivel, pointing my Glock at him. "Drop it, Joey! Now!"

Chad gasps and groans.

Joey gawks at me, all the color in his face gone. I think he's too terrified to move.

The man to the left of the dead guy reaches behind his back.

"That goes for you, too," I say, aiming at him instead.

"Do it, Joey," rasps the man I'm aiming at.

"Fuck you, Dale," says Joey. "Ted, what do we do?"

The fortyish man who's still on the ground in a compliant posture replies in an eerily calm tone, "Well, you've already shot at feds. Either you go to prison or you finish killin' them and head on up to the compound."

"B-but…" Joey points at me with his left hand. "S-she…"

I glance down at myself. There's a bullet hole right in the middle of my chest; clean, undamaged skin peeks out from a bloody circle of fabric. The son of a bitch shot me and I barely felt it. Adrenaline's wonderful. Damn. That means I've only got a few seconds left to live.

Dale starts to draw his weapon.

I pivot to aim, but Chad's weapon discharges

before I can pull the trigger. The sudden *bang* startles me into firing, but my shot strikes a standing corpse. My partner's hit him right in the heart. Dale staggers back into the wall and slumps to the ground, leaving a blood smear on the white paint. My hands shake, the Glock in my grip wobbling. I stare over it at Dale's body. The sight of blood welling out the holes in his chest pulls at something inside me.

Odd tightness spreads across my face. Fangs extend, all four of my canines, both lower and upper jaws. Before I can even think *no!*, I leap at Dale, shredding at his shirt with my claw-like fingernails so I can get my mouth over the wound, suckling on the blood pouring straight out of his heart.

I'm distantly aware of Joey screaming like a schoolgirl.

When rational sense returns to me, I find myself crouching over Dale like some kind of ghoul, my face smeared with warm blood. I think my nails have even gotten longer…

Chad moans, and rolls flat on his back. His arm, and gun, hit the floor. I'm appalled at myself for being more grateful that he'd slumped away from me and hadn't witnessed what I just did than worried for his life.

Argh!

I wipe my face off on Dale's shirt and scramble over to my partner. He's been hit in the side, probably punctured his left lung. Oh, no! This is my fault. We should've waited. If my reflexes weren't in the toilet… I should've been able to react fast enough. Why did I just stand there watching the Axl Rose wannabe shoot us? I couldn't make myself move. That whole four seconds replays in my head like a waking nightmare.

After ripping Chad's jacket and shirt away, I clamp a hand over the entry wound. He tries to mumble something, but only blood comes out his mouth. "Hang on, big guy. Backup's already coming." I flip my cell phone with my free hand and fire off 911.

"Nine-one-one, what's your emergency?" asks a woman.

"My name's Samantha Moon. I'm a federal agent. My partner's been shot. Agent down. Repeat, agent down." I rattle off the address and my badge number. "Two suspects down; two others have fled the scene, likely armed. My partner's been hit in the side. I think he's got a breached lung."

Chad gurgles as if on cue. More blood seeps out between his lips. I spare a fleeting second of gratitude at Dale for being dead. Or, who knows what I might've done to Chad at the sight of all this blood.

"All right, Agent Moon. Stay calm. We received a heads-up a few minutes ago of an ATF team already en route to your location. I'll send an ambulance right away."

"Thank you." I flick the phone to speaker and drop it on the rug so I can clamp both hands over Chad's side, blood oozing between my fingers.

"Stay with me, Helling. It's just a little 9mm to the lung. No big deal, right?"

He gurgles, but, amazingly, smiles. Tough guy. Air wheezes in and out his nose. He's working so hard to breathe, I start shaking with worry.

My partner's going to be okay. I keep pressure on the wound while chanting that over and over in my mind.

He's going to be fine.

And dammit!

I think I am a vampire.

Chapter Twenty
Absolution

I hate hospitals.

Not for their existence, mind you. I mean I hate them because the only time I wind up inside one, something awful has happened to someone I care about. Or to me. Though, technically, me winding up in the hospital was something awful happening to my friends and family, so the first statement is still true. Chad's still in surgery as far as I know, and my butt is planted on a bench in the hallway as close as they'll let me get to the OR, which isn't all that close.

A passing nurse skids to an abrupt stop in front of me. "Ma'am, are you hurt?"

I sit up. "What? Me? No."

"There's blood on your shirt." She leans closer, gesturing at the spot where the bullet hit me. "You… appear to have been shot."

"Oh, that." I shake my head. "It's my partner's blood. Must've smeared on me when I was trying to stop him from, you know, bleeding to death."

"I'm sorry." She grimaces. "Can I get you anything?"

"No thanks. I'm just worried about Chad. But, thank you." I look down at my bloody chest, and fidget at the fabric to conceal the hole. "On second thought, I'm kind of cold."

She smiles warmly. "I'll get you a blanket."

And she does, returning with a surprisingly warm, hospital-issued blanket. She wraps it around my shoulders, nods and walks off. At least I no longer look like a human bull's-eye.

Seconds later, Ernie, Michelle, Bryce, and Nico arrive in a group from the elevator at the far right end of the hallway. They hurry over and crowd around me.

"Sam… what happened?" asks Nico.

"You okay?" Ernie sits beside me.

Michelle stares at me imploringly. Bryce paces around.

"Rattled, but not hurt."

"And Chad?" asks Nico.

"In surgery… I should've been quicker." My lip quivers as I peer up at Nico. My sitting to his standing makes me feel as small as I deserve to be. "I should've seen that coming. I should've been ready."

Nico bows his head, shaking it. "It's not your fault, Sam. Blame the son of a bitch who pulled the trigger."

"We shouldn't have gone in," I mutter.

"Why did you?" asks Ernie, in a soft, non-accusing tone.

I fidget my fingers in my lap. "Another vehicle arrived, a truck. We thought the suspects were going to transport the weapons off-site before the ATF arrived. All we wanted to do was delay them… another routine inspection. But when we went inside, they all had rifles and a friggin' machine gun out. I… just reacted. Ordered them down."

Nico nods. "Sounds relatively reasonable. Of course, there's going to be an investigation."

I nod. I'd expect nothing less. I stare at the glaringly white polished floor. "If I'd have been faster…"

"He's gonna be fine, Sam." Ernie pats me on the back.

Michelle plops down at my right. "Yeah. Chad's tough. Stop blaming yourself, hey, *chica*?"

"*Fui demasiado lento*," I mutter. "*Demasiado lento*."

She holds my hand. "*Él estará bien*."

"Hey." Bryce snaps his fingers a few times in the air. "English, please."

Nico eases himself into a chair on the other side of the hall, bracing his head in his hand.

"I should've stopped that guy from shooting Chad. I… I haven't been right since the attack. My reaction time is too slow."

What am I even doing? I think. *I'm in no condition to be out in the field.*

"Stop blaming yourself already." Ernie nudges my shoulder. "Any one of us could've done the same… or worse. It could've been the two of you *dead*."

"Yeah, girl." Michelle winks. "You walked off without a scratch. Reactions can't be *that* bad."

What she doesn't know is that I stood there like a target dummy and got shot clear through the heart. Yet somehow, I'm still here. And somehow, I'm not even hurt. Guilt and disbelief get into a swordfight in my thoughts. The group of us sit in silence, broken only by the occasional reassurance from the others, or a hospital staffer walking by. Chad's parents still aren't here, but they moved to Oregon a few years ago. It's going to take them a while to show up. I *really* hope I don't have to give them bad news.

I'm not even sure how long we wait before a doctor in scrubs approaches. He's got an upbeat look, so I stop clenching my fists hard enough to make diamonds and stand. "How is he?"

"Mr. Helling is out of surgery and in recovery. The bullet went clear through him. Nicked a rib on the way out. He'll be on an intercostal drain for a few days to alleviate fluid buildup in the pleural space. The puncture resulted in a pneumothorax, but we expect he'll make a full recovery. He's looking at about a week in the hospital at least, depending on how he responds to treatment."

Relief floods me. “When can we see him?”

“Probably not until tomorrow. He’s in a post-op recovery suite now. By the time the anesthesia wears off and we’re safe moving him to a standard room, it’ll be well after visiting hours are over.”

I look down at the floor, mentally willing the doctor to let us see him.

A pause, then the doctor sighs. “All right. You folks can see him for a few minutes if you like, but don’t expect him to be responsive.”

I blink, smile. Wow. “Thank you,” I say.

We follow in a group down the hall, around a corner, and past two pairs of double flapping doors. The doctor leads us into a room with eight beds, two of which have privacy curtains around them. He approaches the occupied one on the right and tugs the curtain back enough for the five of us to duck in and surround the bed.

Other than the tube coming out of his side, Chad looks okay, and quite deeply out cold.

“Hey, man,” says Ernie. “Duck next time, okay?”

“Helling, you really ought to stop going to such extreme lengths to get time off.” Nico pats the bed rail twice. “Next time, just ask.”

“Sleep well, *amigo*.” Michelle wipes a tear. “Moon got the sons of bitches.”

“You get better, right?” Bryce nudges the footboard. “Your first day back, Nick’s Super Burger on me. In fact, that goes for everyone.”

“You got five witnesses, Anders,” says

Michelle. "No take backies."

Bryce grins. "Not planning to take it back. Or backies, or whatever the hell you said."

I ignore them and edge up to the bed, grasping Chad's hand and holding it as gingerly as I can without compressing the pair of IV needles. *I'm sorry, Chad. For suggesting we go in. For not being fast enough. For being suspicious of that TV.*

Where I got the dream to become a federal agent from, I can't remember. Somewhere between senior year of high school and my first year in college, a random idea turned into a driving obsession.

I shake my head now. That was back when daylight was my friend. And normal working hours, too. But now…

Now, I'm going to get someone hurt. In fact, I *did* get Chad hurt. This isn't working. Me and daylight aren't on speaking terms anymore. I'm going to get someone killed.

Dammit! I'm a freakin' vampire.

Mary Lou and Danny were the only two people I'd ever confided in about the true depth of my drive to become a federal agent. When I'd mentioned to my parents that I was considering becoming a HUD agent, they weren't too impressed. Dad thought I sold out to 'The Man.' So did my brother, Clayton. He takes straight after my father, down to the hippie lifestyle and weed.

My dreams are crumbling around me…

I wanted this job, and I fought for it through a

whole mess of crap. Late nights of studying, grueling physical courses, sexism, Quantico… but it's not worth Chad's life. Or anyone else's life. Only the presence of my entire squad being in the room stops me from breaking down. Truth is, I couldn't feel guiltier if I'd shot Chad myself.

How could I live with myself if he'd died? A lifetime of guilt, and, if the mounting evidence was true, an *eternity* of guilt.

That moment replays over and over again in my head. Shot in the chest, I'd stood there helpless and entranced, and only reacted three seconds after Chad had been hit. By all rights, I should be dead.

Maybe I already am.

Or, more accurately, dead again.

Someone'sss learning, rasps a voice in the back of my head.

I squeeze his hand again. "I'm sorry, buddy," I whisper. "I shouldn't have come back."

Not your fault, whispers Chad's voice in my thoughts.

My head snaps up to stare at his face. He hasn't moved. There's no way he spoke out loud. Except I don't have time to wonder if it's wishful thinking or supernatural BS, because the doctor steps in.

"All right, everyone. Mr. Helling needs to rest now," he says.

I squeeze my partner's hand, let go, and trudge out behind the rest of my team. The badge and gun hanging on my belt weigh me down with guilt. At the curtain, I peer back at Chad.

"Get better fast, 'kay?"

Not your fault, whispers Chad's voice again, and this time I clearly see that his lips never moved.

I rub my eyes. Insomnia's a real bitch.

Chapter Twenty-One
Danger

I stop the Momvan in my driveway at close to ten at night, after a marathon gauntlet of statements and reports.

Perhaps I got lucky in that most of the interviews didn't come until after sunset. Once it got dark, I went back to being my old self—no grogginess or hesitation, perfect clarity of mind. I still lamented my slow reaction time to the investigators, but considering they believe (wrongly) that I didn't suffer a fatal gunshot wound, they regarded that as 'survivor's guilt' or something. Chad was shot and I wasn't—or so they thought—so I'm normal for feeling as if it's my fault.

Not like I'm going to admit I took a bullet that should've killed me and didn't.

I'm still not sure I've totally admitted it to myself.

Danny's at the dining room table working on the laptop. He looks up as I shut the front door. "Crap, Sam. How you holding up?" I nod and give him a smile. Truth is, I'm holding up damn fine, physically; after all, the hole in my chest is healed. Psychologically, I'm a total mess. I'd filled Danny in on the situation via a slew of texts, so I'm not surprised when he springs from the chair and jogs over, meeting me near the middle of the living room. "How's Chad doing?"

I hold on to him for a few minutes of silence, trying to decompress my thoughts before giving him a rundown of my partner's condition. My partner who I'd nearly killed.

"Glad to hear he's going to be okay." Danny smiles at me when I finish. "Now, what about you, babe?"

"I had to shoot two men." I want to shrug, but I don't. Shrugging isn't the right response here. Not when I almost killed two men today. I *did* watch two men die, but, even wounded and lying on the floor, Chad had better aim and reaction time. Something is *really* wrong with me during the day. So, I don't mention that having shot them didn't affect me much. For years, I've dreaded that moment and how I'd handle it if I ever had to take someone's life. Now that it almost happened, I'm horrified at myself for being so blasé about it. I should care that I nearly took a human life. I should care that two men died right in front of me. I should care a lot…

But I don't. Something deep within my brain makes me think, *they're only humans.*

He cringes. "Sam…"

"There's something else, and I'm not sure if it's worse."

Danny blinks. "Worse than you shooting someone?"

"First off, I'm sorry for not telling you about the mirror right away. That said, you're the first person to know this next bit."

He tenses. "What next bit?"

I raise both hands to my chest and flatten my shirt so the neat, round hole in the fabric is obvious. "The bastard didn't miss me."

Danny puts his finger on the spot, the tip warm against my skin. "You were shot. Here?"

"Yes." I hold eye contact. "It didn't even hurt. No, that's not true. Felt more like a sharp thump." I knock on his chest about as hard as I'd hit a door. It probably *should* have hurt a lot more, but being barely awake plus adrenaline… or whatever I have now. "Like that."

"Is… the bullet still inside you?"

In response, I pull the malformed lump of lead out of my pants pocket. "I found it on the floor after they loaded Chad on a stretcher."

"Sam… you removed evidence from a crime scene?" He gawks at it.

"I removed evidence of something that didn't happen. If they found this bullet that looks like it hit someone, but there's no wound to go along with it…"

"Right." He paces back and forth, running his hands over his head in a repetitive, nervous motion.

"There's something else."

"Oh? There's *more,*" he says, a little too loud, and swivels to face me, arms out to the sides. "Great. Hit me."

"I think my sister was right." I fidget and look down while describing the sensation of fangs growing in my mouth, and how I couldn't help but pounce on the geyser of blood coming out of Dale's chest.

Danny takes a step back, both his eyebrows climbing. "I don't like the sound of that. You couldn't *help yourself*?"

"Well." I pull my blazer off and drape it over the back of a chair. "I *had* just been shot, and that kinda pissed me off, and blood was everywhere. The guy was already dead."

"Mmm," says Danny.

For some reason, memories of the year we spent working on this house come on strong. Me in underwear and one of Danny's old flannel shirts painting the hallway, him sneaking up on me and carrying me to the bedroom, paint roller still in my hand. The madness of re-tiling the bathroom. Danny wasting three days on the kitchen sink before caving in and calling a real plumber. Our first night here, sitting on the floor with no furniture while eating fast food. Wine at night, cuddling with Danny on the couch, realizing our dreams were gradually coming to fruition.

And now, I'm a monster.

Is my family safe? *Could* I possibly lose control and go after them? What if Danny cuts himself in the kitchen and I see blood or one of the kids falls off a bike in a couple years and skins their knee? How crazy would I get at the sight of blood?

Tears gather at the corners of my eyes. I run down the hall and stand in the space between the kids' rooms, twisting left and right to watch them both sleep. Part of me wants to go far, far away from them where I couldn't possibly be a threat.

Tammy squirms and fidgets, another bad dream coming on.

The look on her face twists my heart into pieces. Even Anthony fusses, grunting.

Damn, it's as if they can sense my thoughts.

Come on, Sam. Don't be silly.

I hear Danny coming up behind me, but he pauses, seeming afraid to get too close. That could just be my imagination. After all, I can't really see him behind me, but I sense him and almost… almost sense his thoughts too.

Crazy, just crazy.

All of it.

Lord help me. Like, seriously help me.

The uneasy, sinister thing that's been shadowing my thoughts wells up ever so slightly. I'm not sure why or how, but the understanding that the children are safe—at least from me—settles firmly in my consciousness. With that inexplicable security, I let go of the idea of abandoning my family. Last month, when that strange darkness manifested in the hallway trying to keep me away from Tammy's room, I gathered my courage and forced my way past it. I know, no matter what happens to me, I will draw upon that same determination to protect my children.

Even if the shadowy monster threatening them is me.

I spin to face Danny—evidently too fast as he leaps back with a gasp.

"S-Sam?" He starts to raise his hands like he's talking down a madwoman with a gun.

"I will never hurt you or the children, Danny. Do you understand that?"

He lets his arms fall. "Yes, I do. I really do." He pauses, his eyebrows rising. "But we don't know much about your… condition, do we?"

"No, we don't. And, quite frankly, we may never know. It's not like there's a how-to manual out there about being a vampire… or whatever the hell I am."

"The funny thing… I bet there is. Maybe all these novels by Anne Rice, Bram Stoker? Maybe they're on to something the rest of us are just catching up to."

"Maybe." I start to chuckle, but it melts into a sigh. "Well, you don't have to worry about me not coming home from work anymore." My fingertip teases around the hole in the fabric. "If this didn't do it…"

"But it should have," he says. "I mean, that shot should have killed you."

I hear the tremor in his voice, and nod. There's no denying it. "Yeah, I think so. It would have killed Andre the Giant, I think."

Danny nods, turns away, swoons into the wall. He keeps nodding and shaking. He slides to the floor, and I'm pretty sure my husband is having his first mental breakdown. I want to break down right along with him, but I can't, not now. I stand there for a second feeling helpless as he sits on the floor, shaking with sobs. When I snap out of the fugue, I swoop down beside him and wrap my arms around him.

"I'm still here, Danny. You haven't lost me. I'm not going anywhere."

At first, his embrace is hesitant, but he clings tighter as his grief belts out in gasping breaths and huge tears. This is how my worst-case scenario nightmare pictured him reacting to the police showing up to tell him I'd been killed. But I hadn't been—at least, not today.

I hold him tight, even as I feel him slipping away, which is a terrible, terrible feeling. And all because of that night three weeks ago. So much of it is a blur, but… in light of recent events, it's starting to seem more and more like I *did* die in the woods of Hillcrest Park.

Did some power beyond understanding hear me begging not to be taken from my family and grant my wish, or would this have been my fate, regardless?

Danny's grief wanes in maybe half an hour, and he sits there in the hall, staring blankly into space.

"Look on the bright side," I say. "If it is true that I am what we think I am, I'm going to look young for the rest of my life. Eventually, people will think I'm your daughter. You're a lucky man. Your wife will never grow old."

He glances at me, his face a mask of loss. It takes him a second to react to my words; finally, he chuckles. "That's only a *little* creepy. There's got to be a way to fix you, Sam. I will find it."

I lean against him, my head on his shoulder. "If we can fix it, I promise I'll do something safer so I don't get shot again."

He shrugs. "Like you said, I don't have to worry anymore. You're basically bulletproof now."

"Technically not, since the bullet went through me, but functionally… I suppose."

"Don't be semantic, sugar butt."

"Sorry."

He reaches across his chest and cradles the back of my head, stroking my hair. "Where are we headed, Sam?"

"I'm not sure. I've never been down this road before. But, we're together. That's what matters."

"How are you handling it?"

"As well as can be expected, I guess. Still feeling guilty over Chad being shot."

He keeps running his hand over my head, petting me like a cat. "How is that possibly your fault?"

"I could've objected to going in. We should've waited for the ATF to get there. But… my reaction time. I'm so groggy during the day. I don't belong in the field like this. I can't function, at least not during the day. Hell, I keep falling asleep at my desk. I think my time at HUD is over."

He slips his right arm around my back and pulls me close. "I can't say I haven't been hoping you'd eventually say those words. All I've ever wanted is for you to be safe, but I'm worried it's too late now."

"I'm still here… and I'm evidently a lot harder to kill. Hell, I might be safer now than I ever was."

"We'll find some way to fix you." Danny kisses the top of my head. "I won't stop trying."

I grin, poking him in the ribs. "That day I smacked you in the face with a door was the best day of my life."

He chuckles. "Except I didn't ask you out until a few weeks later."

"Yeah, but you never would have if I hadn't sent your biology report flying all over the place."

Danny groans. "It took me over an hour to put all the pages back in the right order."

I examine my fingernails. Jesus, do I have claws? I tuck them back into my palms. "So… what sort of job do you think a vampire could possibly do for a living?"

"Something on the night shift?" He leans his head against mine. "They never really bother showing that in any of the movies, do they? Vampires always seem to be, you know, wealthy and live in huge castles in the middle of nowhere. Or run through graveyards and whatnot."

I laugh. "I'm not really the castle-dwelling type, and if this transformation is supposed to come with a Transylvanian estate, I haven't gotten the paperwork yet."

"What about being a private investigator? You could set your own hours with that." He shrugs. "Or maybe you could try writing books!"

"Writing books?" I peer up at him. "Don't be ridiculous. I'm trying to come up with something we can live on, bub. And yeah, right… me, a PI?"

"Well, you'd be good at it. You're a hell of an investigator already. It's not *so* different from what you've been trained to do. Plus, I wouldn't have to worry so much about you."

I pick at the bullet hole in my shirt. I'm not in danger anymore… everyone around me is.

"Moon Investigations," says Danny. "Has a nice ring to it."

"Yeah," I say. "I'll think about it."

Chapter Twenty-Two
Dream in Ashes

Friday morning, I drag myself out of bed after a mere hour of sleep.

The sunblock and makeup process is becoming routine, and I breeze through it before helping Danny get the kids dressed and fed. The whole time I'm watching them eat, I debate my need for sleep versus it being some kind of aspect of being a vampire that demands my body be idle during daylight hours. Do I actually require rest, or is it merely a way to pass time when the sun's out there waiting to burn the crap out of me?

I figure after weeks of forcing myself to be active during the day while being unable to rest at night, if it was a requirement that I rest, I'd have already cracked and gone insane by now. Or suffered some kind of malady. As it is, I've got the usual grogginess, but nothing worse than that. And even the leaden feeling is less than normal. I suspect it may have something to do with my feeding on Dale. His blood sure tasted a damn sight better than beef or sheep.

Danny offers to take the kids to Mary Lou's on his way to the law firm. Sounds like a decent idea since my eyes are still sensitive. No sense I insist on doing it out of clinginess when it puts them at risk. Protecting my children includes not exposing them to a car accident because I have crappy reaction time and poor eyesight during the day.

Since I won't be with them for the ride, I spend the last ten minutes before Danny leaves, holding both of my children and telling them over and over again how much I love them. I carry them out to Danny's old-but-perfect-looking Beemer… which lacks child car seats.

"Hang on. You don't have car seats."

He grumbles. "They're in the garage."

"I know, I know. It doesn't look 'professional' to the clients."

"Sam, it'll take too long to move the car seats right now."

"Then I'll take them… or you drive the van."

"You take them, and I'll reinstall my car seats tonight."

He sounds begrudging about that, but I know it's not any resentment toward the kids. He's afraid car seats won't look professional.

"People like a lawyer who shows a little humanity."

Danny chuckles. "All right, that's a good point."

I move around the car and kiss Danny quick before darting over to the van and pulling the side door open. Argh, this sunlight burns like a bastard. The kids climb up and I buckle them in place.

So, I drive like a little old grandmother, but I'm super-extra-careful. After dropping Tammy off at preschool and Anthony at Mary Lou's, I head to the hospital. Chad's somewhat awake, but on painkillers to the point of being high. And, for once, funny.

He's lucid enough to recognize me, but starts babbling about banana fudge cake when I ask him how he's doing. It's good to see him conscious, at least. I step out into the hallway and give Nico a quick call to let him know I'm going to be late, due to visiting Chad. He's perfectly okay with it. For about an hour, I sit by the bed, telling him over and over again how sorry I am that I didn't see the gun coming out in time to react.

Chad mutters and waves dismissively.

Around nine, I leave and head to the office. The mood is somber, though I get back-patted and 'it's not your faulted' by everyone. Once at my cube, I hang the stupid hat and scarf on a peg and sit, tucking up to my workstation. Might as well get started on the reports of the shooting. There's going to be another round of interviews coming up after the investigation's done.

I'm noticeably less groggy today, a fact I again attribute to consuming Dale's blood. Believing that

I'm an actual honest-to-goodness vampire is still a bit much for me to accept. The memory of sucking at his chest is simultaneously repulsive and fond. Daydreaming about still-hot blood gushing down my throat should *not* make me salivate, but my mouth tingles anyway. That achy pressure in my facial bones returns, and my fangs extend.

Oh, crap.

I probe around my teeth with my tongue. Sure enough, I've got a pair of elongated canines, top and bottom, with painfully sharp tips. Makes sense to me now how a man could've done so much damage to my throat so fast. Human teeth wouldn't be capable of that… at least not in the few seconds he had to chew on me.

That makes me shiver. A vampire attacked me and drank so much blood from me that I died. Or nearly died. Or something.

Still, it's an indescribably bizarre feeling to have fangs, much less retractable ones. Out of curiosity, I pick up a sheet of scrap paper and bite it. My teeth puncture it with ease, barely hesitating. Wow. Four holes, the inner two a touch smaller than the outer ones.

I find myself wondering if some higher power does exist. Did some manner of intelligence design vampires? The retractable teeth probably happened because it would be awkward to talk with these sabers in my mouth. Or maybe they retract for stealth. Hard to prey on peasants when you're obviously a visible danger. Better to save the weapons for the best moment when the unsuspecting victim has been lulled into a state of complacency. Ooh. I need to go check these bad boys out in the mirror.

Or not. Damn.

If I'm a vampire, and I'm dead, that means… I rub my stomach. I can't have kids anymore. My emotions start to run haywire at that thought, but I catch myself. If I'm honest, I hadn't been planning on any more additions to the family anyway. Tammy and Anthony are here already and they're perfect. Okay, crisis averted.

"Sam?" asks Nico.

Eep! I look to my right, hiding my (probably visible) fangs. "Hmm?"

"Got a minute?"

"Mmm. One thec. Be right there."

Nico chuckles. "Sorry, didn't realize you were eating. Whenever you finish, pop in my office, okay?"

I nod. "Mmm'kay."

Retract! Damn you.

As soon as Nico walks off, I grab my right top fang and try to push it up. Away! Put thyself away! I try to concentrate on how it feels to have fangs, picture their position in my skull, and focus on the concept of relaxing. Evidently, I've also developed a new set of muscles to move them, muscles no normal human has. It takes me about ten minutes of focused trying, but I finally manage to work out the controls, so to speak.

I wonder if their initial extension as a reaction to the thought or sight of blood is a bit like a man's reaction to the sight of a beautiful woman… as in, gets longer without any conscious control. Well, experimenting with the teeth can wait.

Once I'm sure they're safely back to unassuming size, I hop out of my chair and hurry to Nico's office.

"Come in," he says, after I knock.

Nervous, I ease past the door, half-expecting a group of investigators, but it's only my boss. "What's up?"

"How's Helling doing?"

"He was awake. High as a kite so we didn't get much communication done, but he looks better. We'll need to get him a banana fudge cake when he's back."

"That's good." Nico smiles, not really hearing me. His voice turns somber. "Please, sit. Tell me how it all went down."

"The shooting?" I ask, while sitting.

"Yes."

I nod and try to clear my mind from the fatigue of being awake during the day.

Minutes later, I hear myself saying, "…and when we made entry on the premises, we observed the four individuals holding military hardware. I drew my Glock and ordered them to drop the weapons and get on the ground. One man complied right away, the two on the far left and dropped the M16s but made no move to get down. The homeowner tossed the M16 but also remained on his feet and appeared to be reaching for a weapon. I pointed my Glock at him and again ordered him down. The next thing I know, the man on my left, the one with long hair, is shooting at us. He fired twice, one bullet striking Agent Helling. We returned fire and neutralized the suspect. I should've been watching them all, but Joey had me too distracted. I should've been faster."

Nico nods.

I blink, focus my thoughts, willing myself to stay awake. "The man on the far left also went for a weapon. Somehow, Chad noticed him, despite being hit, and shot him before he could fire on me. When I engaged him, Joey and the other suspect bolted out the back door. Since Agent Helling had been wounded, I stayed with him and called for medical assistance."

"Well, that doesn't sound like you two did anything glaringly incorrect. I probably would've waited for the ATF to arrive unless you saw them taking the box of suspected weapons back outside."

"Yes, sir."

Nico leans back in his chair, steeples his fingers together. "So, Moon… still wearing the hat?"

"It's looking more and more like I've developed that condition I was telling you about, xeroderma pigmentosum."

"The one that causes your skin to blister after only brief exposure to sunlight?"

I nod, let out a long, slow sigh. "I'm starting to

have doubts that it's going to improve, boss. It's possible that it could interfere with my functions here at HUD… unless you stick me on a desk job where I don't have to go outside. I just don't want something like this to happen again. Chad's hurt because I couldn't react fast enough."

"Moon…" Nico raises a hand. "The investigation's barely started yet. Don't hang it all on yourself. But, that skin condition might be an issue. I'd like you to get a medical evaluation, and see what the doctors have to say about it."

I nod, holding back the tears.

Nico leans forward, his expression comforting. "Give it more time, though, Agent Moon. I don't want you reacting on emotion, based on what happened to Chad. I don't say this lightly, but I consider you one of our better investigators. We'd had the Brauerman thing going on for years, and you're the only one who caught on."

I shrug. "I got lucky. Noticed the business cards. Any of the other agents could've done that. I just happened to be in the right place."

He chuckles. "And humble, too. I suppose people who want glory go to the FBI."

I grin. It's an old HUD joke, the FBI glory hounds. My smile doesn't last, though, and I sit there looking at fingernails that are, in all likelihood, growing sharper and thicker. Like, seriously? As if I needed *more* strangeness.

Quitting is probably the best thing I can do for everyone concerned, but it feels so damn wrong to just walk away from all the ass-busting work I've put into this. Maybe Nico's right. I could be overreacting with emotion after what happened with Chad. Like any other situation, it takes acclimation. Feeding appears to reduce the grogginess, so my problem could be simply that I've been resistant to accepting what I am and not taking proper care of my new self. I need blood. If I stay nourished, I might not be so useless during the day.

"You're right. Maybe I am reacting too emotionally."

Nico smiles. "Just keep your head on. Get checked out, and let me know what the doctor says."

"Sure thing."

Ugh. What the heck am I going to tell a doctor?

He asks more about the current case, so I talk for a little about Joey and the other unidentified man who fled the property. We've had local cops watching the place since then, but Joey hasn't returned. Odds are quite low he will. The ATF took possession of the weapons, which they traced back to a theft from the National Guard armory at San Bruno that occurred two months ago.

Nico excuses himself to call his buddy at the FBI and prod them about finding Joey and the other man.

Speaking of…I have pictures to develop. Unease at my staying with HUD hounds me all the way back to my desk. Excuses and justifications flow like water, leaving me more confused than ever. I have no idea what I am or where I belong, but I do know at least one thing.

I open and close my hand, staring down at my unnaturally sharp nails. Sharp, thick, and ghoulish. Yes, I know at least one thing…

The sons of bitches responsible for Chad being hurt will pay.

Chapter Twenty-Three
Handoff

Bryce goes by my cube offering donuts. Tempting, but, I think I'll pass on the feeling that my shoes are about to come flying out of my mouth in a few minutes.

"Your loss. More for me." He wags his eyebrows and roams off.

Electronic digging on Joey Bell doesn't turn up much useful information but there's no way his job as a security guard's covering a $4,000 TV. Somewhere in the notes I took during the crime scene investigation after the shootout is the serial number. Once I find it, I call Sony corporate and try to get someone to tell me what retailer received this particular serial number.

Forty minutes later, I'm on the phone with another vampire in a Circuit City store in LA. At least, I think she's a vampire because she sounds about as awake as I feel.

"…so you can't look up a sale record by serial number?" I ask.

"Umm." Computer keys click. Bubblegum snaps. More keys click. "I'm not sure how."

"What about model number? Looks like an XBR 52."

She snaps her gum again. "Umm. Maybe. When was it purchased?"

I sigh mentally. "I'm not sure. How many giant $4,000 televisions does your store sell?"

"One sec."

Of course, 'one sec' is retail clerk speak for 'oh, why won't you hang up already and go away.' And sometimes, it means 'there's someone else I can dump this bitch on.'

Sure enough, after I sit on hold for a little over a minute, a guy picks up the line.

"Circuit City, this is Marc with a C."

"Hi, Marc with a C. I'm Agent Samantha Moon from HUD. I'm trying to track down a television that a suspect involved in a federal crime may have purchased at your store. Do you have a record of sale for a Sony XBR 52 television, probably within the past few months?" I read off the serial number.

Vanita from the mailroom swings by and drops an interoffice folder on my desk. I mouth 'thank you' without lending it voice. She grins at me and walks off with her cart.

"Oh, sure, hang on. Sorry about Trinity." Marc lowers his voice to a near-whisper. "She's the manager's kid." He types a bit and hums. Must be holding the phone with his cheek since his nostril-breaths blast the receiver every few seconds. "Got it. Looks like it was a cash sale. Sorry, Agent Moon. There's not much of a paper trail. The customer declined the warranty, too. All I've got's a delivery confirmation." He reads off Joey Bell's address, which I already had.

I ask Marc to fax me a copy of the sales receipt, thank him, and hang up.

Well, that's something at least. I now know Joey paid cash, and there's nothing even close to a withdrawal big enough to cover the TV, tax, and delivery. Whatever he's doing on the side is paying in cash, and he's not depositing it in the bank. It's not true evidence of anything, more like the smoke I need to see in order to justify hunting for the fire.

The envelope Vanita dropped off contains the photos I took of the men arriving at Joey's house. I scan them into the system and email them over to Agent Whitaker with the ATF. He's the guy that took over the firearms part of the investigation. I also send copies over to the FBI. Until someone gets back to me with information—assuming anyone *can* get back to me with information—I continue staring at endless lines of boring financial information, backtracking Joey's life as much as I can from a computer.

Wham.

My face hits the keyboard hard enough to knock me back awake.

"The hell was that?" asks Michelle through the cube wall.

"Whacked my elbow on the desk. Son of a bitch," I say.

"Ooh." She sucks in a sharp breath. "I hate that."

Grr. This 'you need to sleep when the sun's out' thing is a royal pain in the ass. Sooner or later, I'm going to pass out at a rather inconvenient moment and get someone hurt. Losing an hour or so at the office in the blink of an eye isn't *so* bad, but… what if this happens to me out in the field? I'm clearly not operating under the laws of nature anymore. Can willpower alone override a vampire's need to be inert during the day? Good grief. Even thinking the word *vampire* makes me want to cringe, like I've gone into serious padded cell territory.

I tease my tongue around my fangs again. That, of course, makes me think of the would-be rapist back in the parking garage. Fair bet, I fed from him. Better question is: did I kill him? I don't remember a bit of it. My eyes widen at a sudden realization. When I was in the hospital, an old man down the hall went into cardiac arrest. He had two puncture wounds on his neck and had lost a lot of blood… and I didn't remember if I was involved in that either.

Crap.

No, 'crap' isn't strong enough.

Shit!

I set my elbows on the desk and hold my head

in my hands. That's twice I totally lost control and harmed people without wanting to. Well, once. True, I feel bad about the old guy, but the parking garage rapist? Not so much. Ugh. Wait, I've blacked out *three* times… the guy, Dale, at Joey's house. I don't feel bad about him either. He tried to shoot me. Okay, two out of three were bad people.

However…what if the next time I lose it, someone innocent suffers? Reasonable certainty that the dark thing that's moved into my soul understands what I will do if it hurts my children or Danny, so I've got somewhat of a sense of security that I won't attack them. Do I *have* to kill to feed? Perhaps not as evidenced by my three victims. Two survived, I think. Dale was already dead to Chad's shot before I touched him, and I still have no clue about the rapist in the garage. I'm hesitant to look him up. I'm not eager to see if he was, in fact, found dead. That, plus, if someone notices me looking into that situation, it could trigger some awkward questions.

Better not to know, I think.

Well, I have been denying the (however unlikely) truth of my being a vampire and not been consuming blood. Maybe I'm prone to having hunger-induced blackouts if I go too long without a snack? One way to test that. I'll ask Danny if he can get more beef blood from his butcher client. A week or two of regular blood 'meals,' and if I don't pounce someone like a pregnant lady spotting a tub of dark chocolate Häagen-Dazs after a long, crummy day at the office, I'll know I'm good.

Or at least under control.

An email comes in with a *ping.*

Score one for the FBI.

Looks like the older man I photographed is Mitch Gallagher. The FBI's got a file on him due to his involvement with an anti-government militia group that's been operating in the area for about fifteen years. They call themselves the Brothers of the Republic. He's also buddy-buddy with some Klan types. Ugh. His record's got a bunch of simple assault charges, but the pattern of them is weird. About half occurred in bars frequented by members of the Armed Forces. Never *on* a base, but always close to one where soldiers hang out. I bet Mitch is going in there looking to recruit like-minded idiots, and every so often, he runs into a real patriot who doesn't take kindly to wackos.

Anyway, the other incidents are scattered around geographically, and all those victims have one thing in common: they're not white. Ooh, I really wanna nail this guy if I can. A picture is starting to form in my day-fogged brain. Joey probably fell in with these idiots. He strikes me as the wannabe-cop washout who wound up working security while his repeated attempts to apply for law enforcement failed.

A whim, and a few phone calls later, I get confirmation. Joey's been applying for the LAPD every time the test comes up. His affiliation with Gallagher's group, along with pitiful test scores, has been keeping him back. I wonder if he realizes that or not?

The other guy, the one who hit the floor at Joey's house and *didn't* try to shoot us, is Ted Clarke. He's also a member of Gallagher's little group. He, too, has a police record. Domestic battery is the most severe charge. There's a restraining order against him from his ex-wife. I'm happy to read there are no kids involved. He's also been investigated for making threatening calls to a federal judge who ruled on a land dispute in a case involving Mitch, but they couldn't prove he'd been the one on the phone.

Wow. I've found a little nest of happiness.

Or hornets.

Smashing a hornet's nest with a stick isn't usually a wise course of action, but I'm pissed. And, apparently, I can't die, either. Which makes me the perfect candidate to do all the smashing. And if the smashing occurred at night…

Well then, it could actually be a little fun, too. I am, after all, a different woman at night.

Very, very different.

I spend about a half hour cobbling together as much information as I can from the reports at the house, the FBI files on the two men, and everything I can dig up on the Internet related to Mitch's group, the 'Brothers of the Republic.' Oy.

With my bundle of information, I head down the hall to Nico's office and knock.

"Come in."

I enter with as confident an expression as my mind and body are willing to generate at three in the afternoon. Having bones of lead and muscles of rubber is getting old *fast.* "I think I've got something."

He leans back. "Flu?"

"Ha. Ha. No, I mean something on the Joey Bell case." I set the papers on his desk, sit in the facing chair, and explain my theory that Joey is working for Gallagher—probably selling arms—and that accounts for the undocumented income.

Nico reads for a moment or three more, then peers at me over the top of the file. "Undocumented income? You're still chasing that?"

"No… I mean." I rub my forehead in frustration. "They took Al Capone down on tax evasion, right? The undeclared money is a technicality to get him in custody."

"Sam… the man shot at you and Helling."

I cringe. "Technically, the other two did. Joey just ran."

"He's still a party to felony attempted murder of two federal agents." Nico chuckles. "Not declaring his extra cash to HUD isn't even the cherry on the top of a 'you're screwed' sundae."

My back stiffens. "But I—"

"I know exactly what you're doing, Sam." He gives me the kindly/worried Dad smile. "You're fishing for an excuse to be personally involved in going after the bastards."

Dammit. He's right, but is that a bad thing? "I

can't just sit here crunching numbers while he's still out there."

"It's already ballooned out of our reach, I'm afraid. This is HUD, Sam. Those guys are trading in weapons stolen from a US National Guard armory. I can run a note up the flagpole that we're offering some extra hands if they need us on a raid, but this is FBI/ATF territory now, Sam. Out of our hands." He sinks back in his chair, drumming his fingers on the desk.

I feel like the kid who thought she had an awesome science project, but got a D. For a second, I start to feel the nip of depression coming on, but I wind up angry instead.

"Nothing against your investigation, Sam. Solid work."

My barely-awake brain isn't prepared for a debate with my boss. If I try it now, he'll run rings around me and I'll probably only piss him off to the point of being ordered to stay far away from anything to do with this case. Besides, I'm technically stuck in the office for at least two weeks while they continue to investigate the shooting… and I've got a meeting with Dr. Burdine coming up next week. Not sure if I'm looking forward to or dreading my post I-just-shot-two-people fireside chat with a shrink.

I slouch and rub my face. "Thanks… Hey, I'm feeling a little out of it. Maybe you're right about that flu thing, and about me not thinking clearly over Chad. My queue's caught up. Think I could head home early today?"

Nico nods. "Yeah, sure. You look like death warmed over."

Or death chilled. Heh. If he only knew. I don't know why I find that funny. If I'm dead, I shouldn't be laughing about that. But I don't *feel* dead—if you discount the cold skin, slow heartbeat, and not breathing or peeing thing.

"Thanks. Sorry to bother you with all this crap." I stand and collect the papers. "Just *had* to do something for Chad. At least feel like I was trying."

"Understandable." Nico leans forward, his expression going concerned. "How are you holding up?"

"All right, I guess about as well as can be expected. Maybe not so all right… I mean, I'm more upset that Chad got hurt than I shot two men."

He purses his lips, nodding. "Heat of the moment. The reality of it still hasn't hit you yet."

Heh. The reality of a lot of things haven't hit me at the moment, and shooting two guys has nothing on the mess that my life (or lack thereof) has become. Really, the only thing *bothering* me is the nagging fear that the shitstorm I've been swept up in is going to spatter all over my family too. Maybe I am going crazy, since the shootings hardly registered as an event to me. What kind of psychopath has no reaction to almost taking life?

Hi, Sam, you're a vampire now.

Maybe, just maybe, I am a killer, too.

Chapter Twenty-Four
The Unclean

Tugging at my hair wakes me up.

My eyes creep open to a close-up view of my sofa cushion. I'm face down with the weight of a four-year-old girl kneeling on my back, the scent of mac-and-cheese still in the air. Tammy's pulling a brush through my hair in reasonably gentle strokes for a kid.

"Come on, sweetie," says Danny from above and behind me. He emits a soft grunt, and Tammy rises off me. "Mommy's not feeling well."

"Why not?"

"Well, she's got a rare sickness that makes her tired during the day. So, if she's sleeping, you should try not to wake her up unless it's important."

"What's rare?"

"Means not everybody has it."

"Oh. But why does she have it?"

Why indeed? I think.

"Sometimes bad things happen to good people," says Danny, although I am not sure that is a smart thing to say to a four-year-old, but I'm too groggy to protest.

"Mommy's a good people," says Tammy.

"Yes, Mommy is good people." Danny laughs.

I push myself off the cushions and sit up. Dark orange shimmers in the windows from a just-completed sunset. I feel good. Maybe better than I ever have. Like, ever. "It's all right. I'm up." I twist around and tickle at Tammy's feet, making her squeal.

Danny smiles at me, but the hint of sadness underneath it is quite obvious. He's taken on a mournful affect ever since that night he broke down sobbing. I try to ask if he's upset with me for sleeping through dinner or if the sorrow's coming from him thinking me 'dead.' Interestingly, I try to ask all of that with my eyes, but there is a small chance I tried to ask it telepathically, too. *Really, Sam? Telepathically? Is that even a thing?* At any rate, he doesn't react. So much for that.

He sets Tammy back down on the cushion beside me, then folds his arms on the sofa back. "So, how was work? Still groggy?"

"Yeah. Not quite as bad today, though." Which is true.

Tammy retrieves the hairbrush and holds it up with a 'can I?' face.

"You were doing such a good job. Of course." I

kiss her on the forehead and shift sideways so she's standing behind me. While she resumes brushing my hair, I ramble to Danny about the investigation I think should be mine being handed off to the FBI/ATF.

"You're not going to drop it, are you?" asks Danny. "I know that look."

I sigh. "Had certain unforeseen circumstances not come to pass, I'd probably be a good little obedient agent."

He nods, understanding what I mean. I'm facing the frustratingly intractable truth that my present 'condition' makes functioning in any sort of formal day job a massive pain in the ass at best, and a lethal hazard at worst (to other people). Bending rules doesn't bother me much when I'm already giving serious thought to resigning. Not like I've got any realistic expectation of another twenty years of career to protect anymore.

A spike of sadness hits me out of the blue at that realization, that everything I'd worked so hard for is gone. I grab Danny's arm and pull it down from the sofa back, hugging it like a doll.

"I'm sorry," he whispers. "It's not fair. None of it. You worked harder than anyone to get where you are. I'm sorry I ever wanted you to find a less dangerous job."

"Thank you." I rest my head against his arm. "It's hardly your fault, and you only wanted me to be safe."

A sad chuckle escapes him. "Maybe I prayed

you'd do something else?"

"You? Pray? Since when?" His parents had been very religious, but as what often happens with overbearing parents, Danny had gone far in the other direction as soon as he got out from under their roof. That said, I suspect he still wanted to believe in something greater, something beyond himself. Truth is, maybe I do too. I think. I wonder what it's like… to have faith?

Danny leans down and kisses me. "My dad always used to say there are no atheists in foxholes. Since you got shot and broke a rib, I guess a brush with losing you was enough to make me reach out to the Big Guy."

I laugh. "Big Guy?"

"Big Woman?"

"Okay, that only makes it sound worse." I pause. "If there *is* a God, I'm pretty sure he had nothing to do with"—I glance out of the corner of my eye at Tammy's reflection in the window working a hairbrush over empty air—"me getting sick."

Danny shrugs. "Well. Certain things I thought to be stories turned out to be not stories, so who knows. All I'm saying is, if it'll help you, I'll believe in anything. Well, you know what I mean."

"In God," I say.

"Sure," he says.

This coming from the same man who once, in his darkest hour, questioned why a supreme being who demanded worship couldn't be bothered to show evidence of its existence. Of course, I'm the girl who begged the universe, God, and anything else who'd listen for help while bleeding out in the woods three weeks ago. Welcome to the foxhole. I suppose maybe there aren't any atheists bleeding out in the woods at one in the morning either.

"Sorry for missing dinner," I say. "I was exhausted from work."

Danny winks. "It's all right. The kids understand. And I saved you some, umm, food. You know what I mean."

I nod. Liquid food, of course. "Where's Anthony?"

"Asleep early. He's got a cold. Your sister said he's going to be one of *those* kids."

I raise an eyebrow. Mary Lou's probably thinking of Clayton, our youngest brother. Some kids are just *always* sick. Fortunately, Clay grew out of it around fifteen or so, but for most of his early life, he had a cold, flu, or something. In hindsight, it probably had to do with his aversion to clothes.

"Ugh. I really hope Anthony's not going to be 'that kid who's always sick."

Danny nods. "I should go check his temperature again… In the fridge whenever you're ready."

"Thanks."

Tammy and I spend a little while talking about her day at preschool before Danny returns with Anthony, who's apparently feeling better.

"He wanted to see you," says Danny past a big smile.

I take Anthony and hug him. "How's my big little man?"

"Fick." He scrunches up his nose. "I'm gotta code."

"Ruby Grace threw up *five* times today," says Tammy, wide-eyed with awe. "An' Billy Joe pooped on the floor."

"What?" I ask, half-laughing. "On the floor?"

Anthony giggles, making a snot bubble.

Tammy nods. "Yeah, Mommy. He was sittin' on the floor, an' he sneezing, and poop flied out his pants legs. It got on Ellie Mae's dress and she screamed."

Danny and I wince at the same time. The runs plus four-year-old equals epic mess. Oh, poor Mary Lou. That at least explains where Anthony got his cold from. Most likely, one of the older kids brought it home from school.

The four of us sneak in a little family time, and maybe we let the kids stay up a smidge late. After we get them settled in for the night, we walk down the hall together. I head to the kitchen while Danny breaks off to the right and goes into the living room. Sure enough, there's a hidden bottle in the back of the fridge full of the red stuff.

Hmm. If this becomes routine, two things need to happen. One: an opaque bottle. Two: Maybe a second fridge in the garage. The last thing I want is one of the kids trying to have cereal and dumping gore on it.

Though I'm not particularly hungry, I drink half

the bottle, cap it, and put it back in the fridge. It tastes a little different from last time. Kinda watery, and it had a few bits of flesh floating in it. Maybe even a hair or three.

I stash the bottle again and wander into the living room, where Danny looks *too* innocent.

"What did you do?" I ask.

He wags his eyebrows at me in a 'wanna' gesture while holding up a DVD. I can't make out the whole title, but the big word is 'vampire.' Oh boy. I start laughing. We snuggle on the couch watching the cheesiest thing I've ever seen. I can't tell if it's intended as comedy or a serious horror and it's just *that* overacted. The story's told from the point of view of a vampire hunter, a doddering fifty-ish guy who's part Dick Van Dyke and part Inspector Clouseau. I can't say I've ever seen the actor in anything else, and if this movie was his first, it's easy to see why.

A small village in some fictional European country is, naturally, under attack by fiendish vampires. The hunter's survived thus far (the first thirty minutes) by sheer dumb luck and slapstick nonsense like how he stoops to pick up a coin right when a vampire leaps out of the shadows, so the creature sails over him.

Danny and I hold hands and chuckle through most of it.

"Oh gawd," I moan in an overdone accent when the female lead winds up rising from the dead with an enormous coiffed hairdo and a nearly see-through gown. "They didn't tell me vampirism requires that much Aqua Net. And hey, my boobs didn't double in size, either. Not fair."

"Tell me about it!"

I jab him in the ribs with my elbow, maybe a little too hard. He oofs and rubs the spot.

The hunter, and his merry band of three local idiots (one of whom is the former fiancé of the now-vampiric big-busted, big-haired princess of the undead), line up to break into the master vampire's home. Naturally, a house that big in a small village in fictional Europe has a secret underground catacomb with a convenient tunnel entrance at the side of a hill.

Apparently, all the locks in this village suck. Every door opens when subjected to 'vigorous shaking.' The hunter leads the group into the basement with a bunch of obligatory jump scares from spiders and rats.

"How bad do you think this is going to be?" I tuck my feet under my rear end and lean into Danny. "Caskets?"

"Oh, definitely." He chuckles. "They've spared no cheese here."

I snort, laughing.

Sure enough, the group enters a chamber with cobwebs and four fancy coffins. One's white. Gee, I wonder which one holds Fiona of the Huge Hair. Also, predictably, Romeo beelines for the woman's casket and throws himself over the lid, wailing and gnashing his teeth. The addled hunter pulls him off.

"Get a hold of yourself, man! What's under that lid is no longer Fiona," says the hunter, gazing off into the distance. "The girl you fell in love with was gone the instant the master vampire's fangs pierced her neck."

A squirm of self-consciousness runs through me. I hope Danny doesn't take that line to heart.

"Okay, Doctor, okay." Romeo clutches a stake. "I can do this. Please, let me be the one to put Fiona to rest."

The hunter nods and pats Romeo on the back. "You can do it, boy. Remember, the fiends are weak during the day."

Fiend. Great.

Idiot One and Idiot Two take positions by two other caskets while the hunter steps back, away from danger. Romeo faces the white casket. The men simultaneously open the lids, revealing the woman, and two foppish men in wigs even more ludicrous than her hair. All three exposed vampires are sleeping with their hands clasped like corpses at a wake.

Even Danny rolls his eyes.

"On three," whispers the hunter.

Danny leans close and mutters, "I bet they all die except Doctor Galloway."

Romeo raises the stake in both hands. Fiona's eyes snap open.

"Now!" rasps the hunter.

Idiots one and two plunge their stakes down into the chests of their respective vampires, but Romeo hesitates. Fiona starts to sit up, looking groggy and out of it. Gee, I can sympathize with that. She's doing her best, 'you couldn't hurt *me*, could you, Ethan?' routine.

"It's not her!" rasps the hunter. "Do it, boy, before it's too late!"

'It's not her' resonates with me. *Am I still me?*

The other casket opens, revealing the master vampire: a man in his late fifties with overly grey skin and a helmet of Brylcreem hair. Despite his fancy black suit, he staggers about like a wooden-legged mannequin, barely able to move as he totters toward Idiot Two, raking his arms at the air. Idiot Two fumbles at his belt for another stake he just can't seem to get out of its little holder. He screams as the master vampire totters closer and closer.

Sobbing, Romeo lowers his stake and embraces Fiona, who promptly bites him on the throat.

"Fools!" shouts the hunter.

The master vampire swats the head off Idiot Two's shoulders with an arm as stiff as a baseball bat, and claws as sharp as, well, mine, and pounces on Idiot One while the hunter wails in terror and runs for his life. Evidently overcome by 'daytime,' once the imminent threat to their unlife is passed, the master vampire collapses asleep in the middle of the room. Yup, I can relate. Fiona slumps back in her casket, pulling Romeo with her.

"You were right," I mumble. "All dead except for the coward."

Danny laughs.

"I'm nowhere *near* that bad during the day." Speech appeared to be out of the question for those made-up fiends, and their motions had the herky-jerky awfulness of B-movie zombies.

"And your hair doesn't need its own bed." Danny strokes his fingers down my chestnut-brown mane. "It's still as beautiful as the first day I saw you. All lustrous and perfect."

Can I blush anymore? I cling to his arm. "This movie is really bad." And wait—I haven't put anything in my hair in days. It looks like I've been spending hours a day maintaining it, but…

"So bad it's funny," says Danny. "I don't think they meant it as a comedy. Maybe real vampires made it to give hunters a false sense of security. You know, get them to think daytime means they'd be sluggish and easy prey."

I laugh. "I am *not* sleeping in a box."

Danny's joviality fades in an instant. Uh oh. Mixing thoughts of me in his head with a coffin was a mistake.

"I mean, how stereotypical can you get? It's just Hollywood nonsense. Besides. I'm not dead."

He recovers a nervous smile.

Damn.

Well, any hope I had of getting frisky or cute with him is shot to hell. Still, we do cuddle for the rest of the movie (the hunter rallies some villagers for a grand attack on the vampires, but Fiona and Vampire-Romeo return). Danny expects the hapless hunter will run off and leave the village to its grisly fate, but the movie pulls a surprise. The 'hunter' inexplicably goes from clueless to badass, and takes out three lesser vampires before getting into an overacted showdown with the master vampire, ultimately killing him by impaling him on the broken strut of an old windmill. The dead master vampire goes around and around on the creaking wood, with such a silly look on his face, I have to laugh.

He thinks he's won, but Fiona and Romeo sneak off unnoticed before the credits roll.

"Wow, that was… special." I whistle.

"I was hoping you'd find it funny," says Danny.

"Yeah. That was pretty funny." I glance at him. "Hope you didn't find it realistic."

"Pff." He waves dismissively. "It's a movie. I already know you don't *have* to kill when you eat."

I blink, stunned. This is information that I am only starting to grasp. Danny already knew? He accurately reads my expression.

He says, "The man in the hospital a few rooms down the hall from you." Danny fidgets, rolling a bit of his shirt back and forth between his thumb and finger. "Some things are making more sense now."

"Danny?" I reach over and grasp his chin, pulling his head around so I can stare into his eyes. "I will never, ever, hurt you or the kids. Please believe that."

"Of course I believe that." False lawyer smile leaps onto his face. "Besides, I'm going to find a cure. You're going to be back to your old self in no time. Mark my words."

"Wow. Did you just say 'mark my words' and mean it?"

"I did, yes. But I'm not proud of it."

"Take heed!" I shout, raising my finger.

"Sam, the kids…"

"Heareth my voice!"

"That's it," he says, rolling on top of me, covering my mouth with his hand.

"Take notice!" I mumble between his fingers.

In the past, such playfulness usually ended up in the bedroom. Now, it ends up with giggling and tickles… and a sense that Danny and I might, just might, be getting through this together. That he feels more like a friend than a lover is something I squash down and hide in the deepest recesses of my mind, back where that thing has taken up residence inside my head.

***

The worst part about being a vampire is boredom.

I feel like some poor bastard on swing shift who's home when all their friends are at work. Roaming a house full of sleeping people is about as fun as… well, roaming a house where everyone's sleeping. Can't watch TV too loud, can't eat… I suppose I could take up reading or writing. Maybe there is a book in me. How many vampire mamas are there out there in the world? Can't be too many. Or, hell, maybe I'll see what the deal is with World of Warcraft. Maybe I can be a secret gamer. I shake my head at the thought, suddenly depressed. I catch crooks in real life, not in games. True, I have been bored these past few weeks, but tonight I have a mission.

I fire up Danny's laptop and start hunting online.

The Brothers of the Republic have an AOL presence, but it's super basic and appears to be a membership application form. I get the feeling the extent of their entry criteria is making sure any potential recruits believe 'guns are good, government and minorities are bad.'

Grr. After reading the website, my drive to take this guy down gets even stronger.

I run a couple searches, hunting for 'Brothers of the Republic,' then the names of the men I've identified. Eventually, I get a hit from a small local news station about a reporter, Terrell Summerlin, who disappeared four days ago in the middle of doing a series on 'homegrown hate.' A small transcript teasing the as-yet-unaired segment mentions the Gallaghers rallying against 'unclean outsiders.'

Ugh. Fair bet that guy's dead. Probably buried in a shallow grave somewhere on Gallagher's property… wherever that is. There's no mention of the address anywhere I can find on AOL or *Yahoo!,* nor on their membership form. Only a P.O. box to which people are supposed to mail the form to after printing it out. I even try out a new search engine called Google, but even that turns up nothing.

The FBI did have quite a case file on Mitch. He's been seen frequenting a Walmart in Corona, buying large quantities of nonperishables. That makes me think he's got a compound somewhere within driving distance. Duh. Of course, he does. The one guy said he could go to jail, or 'kill us and hide at the compound.' More than likely, Joey is doing just that. Since we haven't heard anything come down the hall about a raid, I'm betting the FBI hasn't pieced together where this guy is yet. I'd bet money they've got people staking out that Walmart, waiting to tail him.

An odd nagging suspicion that Terrell Summerlin is still alive strikes me with no explanation. Dammit. I have to do something. Nico didn't specifically tell me *not* to get involved, only that he couldn't call in a raid or officially pursue the investigation.

Under normal circumstances, I'd go make a pot of coffee and get ready for an all-nighter. However, my circumstances are far from normal and it's not as if I have any problem staying awake at night anymore.

With Danny and the kids sound asleep in their beds, I sprawl over the dining room table in a mess of pictures, papers, manila folders, and stapled bundles: all the evidence I managed to photocopy or print out concerning Mitch and his moron brigade.

A small black-and-white booking photo of a man by the name of Renton Chase catches my eye maybe twenty minutes into my hunt. Early forties, thinning hair, no neck, and a biker-type beard. Hmm. He looks like a fun sort. The photo's stapled to some papers that detail his involvement in an assault-and-battery arrest where he and Mitch Gallagher got picked up after a bar fight. I leaf through the packet, growing more disgusted with each page. Three Hispanic men and a black guy pressed charges, claiming that Gallagher and Chase, plus six others, targeted them as a hate crime. It appears that the others ran off before the police showed up. Mitch had been knocked out during the fight and Renton suffered a stab wound to the thigh that I guess kept him from running.

Considering their militia manifesto refers to non-whites as 'unclean,' this sure feels to me like Mitch and his boys got into far worse than a simple bar fight… Alas, the indictment didn't include a hate crime, so either a plea happened or someone has friends in high places. I cross-check the FBI's files on the Brothers of the Republic, looking for references to this Chase guy, and he turns up fairly often. At least nine photos show him hanging out with Mitch and company, the pair acting like best buds. Lots of guns and beer involved in being a militia, apparently. Hmm. Ol' Renton's address is east of here, past Corona. The probation officer's got an address for him south of Lake Mathews. Probably a trailer on a giant lot of dirt.

I bet he knows where Mitch hides out. Guess I'm going to do a little running around tonight.

The last time I went out for a late-night jog, something bad happened. Still, I can't shake that feeling that Terrell is still alive… and in deep trouble.

I think something bad *is* going to happen if I go out for a run tonight.

But not to me.

Chapter Twenty-Five
Tall Tales

Danny doesn't stir out of his sleep while I change clothes.

I throw on as stealthy an outfit as I can find: black jeans, black shirt, brown hiking sneakers. Hey, the only black *shoes* I have are heels, and who in their right mind wears heels out to the sticks? Once dressed, I spend a moment watching my husband breathe. He's kind of edged into my half of the bed as if he's getting used to sleeping alone. Ouch.

Okay, now, I'm feeling sorry for myself.

Or maybe, he's only trying to cuddle me in his sleep and doesn't realize I'm not there.

Damn, now I'm feeling guilty all over again.

What I'm about to do could go quite wrong in a myriad of ways, and it's probably foolish of me, but…that reporter must've found the compound and

I don't like the results when my brain tries to come up with what men like that would do to him.

Oh, hell. In all probability, Terrell Summerlin's dead already, but hoping he isn't is the excuse I need to get myself out the door. Not to mention, I'm confident Joey Bell is hiding out where he thinks the law can't touch him. Maybe they're planning for another Waco Massacre type event. Based on what I read about them on their page, these guys sound like real wingnuts fully willing to martyr themselves in the hopes it sets off another American Revolution.

Great.

Well, good thing there's only about a dozen of them.

I wave at Danny and whisper, "Back in a few hours."

After checking on Tammy and Anthony, I head out the door and hop in the Momvan. I check my *Thomas Guide* maps, plot a route, and start driving. For a little more than a half an hour of driving, the 'should I/shouldn't I' argument goes back and forth in my head. At present, the 'shouldn't I' argument is winning. After all, this is way out of my comfort zone, probably because I'm planning to break a bunch of agency policies and I don't have any kind of official sanction to do this.

Still, it's becoming clear that my days at HUD are numbered, and before I am responsible for someone else getting hurt, I owe it to Chad to make sure these bastards go down. Though I get no closer to feeling confident, I keep going out to Cajalco

Road, and almost miss the right turn into the barren nothingness south of the lake.

My thoughts drift to my kids. No matter what happens tonight, HUD or no HUD, they're all that matters. Hell, I'll work night security if I have to. And with that thought, the idea of working as a private eye sounds just that much better; after all, as a PI, I would be my own boss and work the kind of cases I want to work. Okay, that suddenly doesn't sound so horrible. Better than working a night security shift.

I let that thought play out for a few minutes, and find myself smiling at calling myself a private dick… and later find myself wondering if Terrell had a family.

A heavy sigh slides out my nose as a beat-up one-story building comes into the glare of my headlights. Dust clouds swirl around over head-sized green scrub in front of me. A small corrugated steel awning over a well on the left clatters in the wind. I'd call the place a house, but it's not. More like an elaborate shack, or a house trailer with an extra room built onto it. Three motorcycles and a beat-up green pickup truck with a lift and giant tires sit out front. Only one of the bikes looks capable of actually running.

A flimsy front door swings open, striking the wall with a *thwap*. Renton Chase steps out onto the concrete block serving as a stair, bare-chested in jeans, with a metal bat. Hmm. Well, that's not too neighborly of him. He's still got the horseshoe of brown hair around his otherwise bald head, and a puffy beard down to his gut. He's also quite thick in the chest and arms, so despite his general beer-bellied couch potato look, he's probably quite strong.

As soon as I open the van's door, he yells, "Don't want none. Get on gone."

"Oh, shoot," I say, in a raised voice so he can hear me from the distance. "But I just got in a new batch of Thin Mints. And Samoas!"

Evidently, Renton wasn't expecting a woman. At the sound of my voice, his aggressive stance slackens to merely unfriendly. "Hell you want?"

I suppose full sentences is going to be too much to ask. "Okay, you caught me. We're auditioning a backup singer for ZZ Top."

Renton glowers at me as I walk up to stand in front of him. He's a big guy. More than a full head taller than me and I guess he didn't take advantage of the prison gym. But I shouldn't underestimate natural strength; his biceps are bigger than my thighs. I've heard it said that vampirism is a curse, and at this moment, I would tend to agree. The fragrance of feet, fishy bellybutton lint, and beer fart is making my eyes water. Sometimes amped-up senses are *not* helpful. Luckily, I can see easily in the night, and note that we are alone, with no one sneaking around. Curiously, I note a light ringing just inside my ear again. Almost… yeah, almost as if it's some kind of warning. Am I the only one who can hear it?

"You funny, lady." Renton spits to the side.

I don't hear anyone else moving around inside the house. Whatever happens between us is going to stay between us. "I was hoping you could help me out."

"You a cop?"

Right, because undercover cops aren't allowed to lie. "No, I'm not a police officer."

"You sure?" He squints and points the bat at me.

"I think I'd know if I was a cop or not." I smile. "Can you tell me where I can find the Brothers of the Republic?"

He leans to the left, presses a thumb to one nostril, and huffs out his nose, sending a streamer of snot flying. "You ain't the type."

I step into the glow of the light above the door. "What? I don't think it's possible to get much whiter than I already am."

"You's askin' wrong."

"Oh." Hmm. Never heard that before. I hesitate for a second before asking, "How exactly does someone ask wrong?"

"Only cops walk up an' ask. There' a process, and it don't involve no talkin' to no one."

I blink at him. Wow. Was that a triple negative? I'm not even entirely sure what he tried to say there. "What?"

He growls and edges closer. "You best get gone, lady."

"I'd be happy to leave. As soon as you tell me where I can find Mitch."

Renton pokes me in the chest with the end of the bat twice. "I ain't gon' warn you 'gain. Git off mah property."

"Look, Renton. I know you just got out, and you're still on probation for knocking around a couple of those 'unclean' people. I might be able to make things go a little smoother for you if you help me here."

"How you know all that? Never mind." He raises the bat in both hands. "Get outta here."

"What would your mother say if she saw you threatening a woman with a bat?"

Renton snarls and takes a half-step at me, raising the bat higher. I see the feint coming and don't move an inch. He eyes the Glock on my hip, and the badge hanging next to it. "You lied! You is a cop."

"I'm not a police officer, Renton. I'm a federal agent."

"Aww, shit," he mutters, then swings for real.

I duck and sidestep left. Renton puts power behind his attack like he's hoping for a grand slam. So much so, he can't recover from hitting nothing. From the *woof* of the bat passing by my ear, I think it might've decapitated me. Somehow, this guy mashing me in the face with a bat becomes more of a frightening thought than being shot again. He spins around in a pirouette and staggers a few steps away from the house.

"And that's somewhere between assault and attempted murder of a federal agent, Renton."

He makes a noise like a hog jabbed in the backside with a branding iron and charges at me, swinging the bat down in a wild overhead chop. My nighttime reflexes are *much* better than they are in the day—heck, they're better than human. Far, far better than human. Certainly faster than I ever was. I dart to the right, letting the bat sail past me. Before he can raise it, I grab on with my left hand and hold it down.

"Now, Renton, I believe we got off on the wrong foot. Why don't you tell me where your buddy Mitch is, and I'll forget we ever met?"

The man grunts, trying to pull the bat out of my grip, but he's not moving me much. His eyebrows convey the surprise we both feel, but I manage to keep a straight face.

"The hell?" he asks.

"Renton…" I say in the tone of a scolding mom, and jerk the aluminum bat straight out of his grip. "I'm afraid I need to take your toy away."

He stares awestruck as I hurl it off into the dark. It lands too far away to see, though the soft *clank* of it hitting the dirt is obvious—five seconds later. "The hell?" he asks again.

"Your record's skipping." I lean toward him. "Where's Mitch?"

"I ain't snitchin'!" He lunges at me.

I grab his right arm, twisting it in a pain-compliance hold. Renton yowls, stooped over sideways due to our height differential as I wheel him around and hurl him staggering at the house.

The whole place shakes with his impact; it's flimsy and he's… well, not.

He collects himself, goes wide-eyed like he got an idea, and runs for the beat-to-hell pickup—which no doubt has an AR15 or something similar hidden inside. I bet his probation officer would *love* to hear about that. The warning bell in my head blips a little louder. Yup, he's definitely going for a gun. No, it may not kill me, but a shotgun blast sure could do a lot of damage to the side of my head.

I catch up to him just as he gets his fingers on the door handle, grabbing his shoulder and yanking him around in a spin. Before he knows it—maybe even before I know it—I have him pinned to his truck. I haul him off his feet and carry him away from the vehicle.

"You're on probation, Renton. You're not supposed to have firearms anymore."

"What makes you think I got firearms?" he gasps, gurgling; after all, his collar is certainly cutting off his air supply. The thing is, he had a good question. How *did* I know there was a gun in his truck? I am struck, once again, with the possibility that I could have… no, just too crazy. No way I read his mind. No, his intent was obvious. Right? A few steps later, he seems to realize that his feet aren't in contact with the ground. "What the hell?"

Another good question. I literally had no idea I was carrying the man.

Sweet Jesus...Well, at least I have his attention

now.

Remarkably, I carry a full-grown man back to his house before dropping him on his feet. Okay, I might have shoved him a little, too. He totters backward, crashing against the wall with a hollow *thud.* Faster than I ever expected from a man of his size, a combat knife appears in his hand. I lunge in, slap the knife away and clamp a hand around his throat, pushing him up on his tiptoes. He grabs my forearm with both hands, going red-faced from the strain as he tries to pull my grip off his neck.

Ugh. Having a greasy beard covering my entire arm is making me want to hop in the shower.

I'm definitely crossing a policy line here. Roughing up potential witnesses is unethical. But hey, he swung a knife at me so I could've shot him. Too much paperwork, plus dead men don't talk.

Renton gurgles.

"Let me guess… what the hell?" I tilt my head.

His eyes bug out.

I push a little harder so he's almost off the ground again. "I'm going to ask you one more time. Where. Is. Mitch Gallagher?"

Renton attempts to nod rapidly.

Happy for the opportunity to stop touching him, I let his weight back down and lower my arm. Resisting the temptation to wipe my hand on something takes a lot of willpower.

He coughs and wheezes. "Jesus…"

"Not exactly. Come on, Renton. Where's Mitch?"

"Lookit all this land. Ain't no one gon' find your grave." With a grunt, he swings his ham-sized fist at my face. I almost admire the man's resolve, perhaps the only thing I could admire about him. Though, I suppose there's a fine line between determination and stupidity sometimes.

I catch his fist, stalling his attack cold, and squeeze until he screams, but stop before any bones crunch. "You raise a good point. No one will find *you* or your stupid beard. I don't have all night, and I'm starting to think you're not useful. Plus, I'm pretty sure I need to shower now."

He lunges again, this time trying to grab the Glock on my hip. I sidestep and stomp on the back of his right leg. Renton's shout of surprise at me moving so fast mutates into a howl of agony. Oh, I probably dislocated his knee. Whoopsie.

The big man crashes down on his chest like the giant falling off a beanstalk. I twist his right arm up behind his back and land on top of him, giving his wrist enough torque that he whimpers.

"Mitch. Now."

"Okay, okay!" he shouts. "He's got a compound by Corona. East of the reservoir."

I add a smidge more pressure to his wrist. "That's a lot of area."

"Gah! Head on up past Stagecoach Park. Keep goin' on Stagecoach Drive alla way 'til it turns into dirt, an' follow that down 'round to the woods."

"Now, there. See? That wasn't so hard." I let go and back up.

He rolls onto his side, cradling his arm and giving me a malicious stare.

I head over to the pickup. The door's unlocked, so I reach in and pluck an M16 assault rifle out from behind the seat. Now, how did I know that was there? "I appreciate your assistance. So much so that I probably won't include finding this little bit of probation violation in my report."

"They're gonna kill you, bitch," mutters Renton.

"Aww. And I thought we had established at least a professional rapport." I frown at him and check the weapon. Sure enough, loaded with one in the pipe. I drop the mag out and rack the slide to send the chambered round flying, and catch it out of midair. "This is an instant ticket straight back to jail, Renton. You're not allowed to have these anymore."

"You can't just come out and take my shit, break my arm. Damn government sellout. You gotta play by the rules. Gonna be your ass in jail this time," shouts Renton from the ground.

I drape the M16 over my shoulder, one hand on the barrel, and saunter over to him. "And you'll tell them what exactly? That I found a loaded firearm on the premises of a felon on probation, or that little old me threw six-foot-seven you around like a small boy? Are you honestly going to admit to anyone that you got beat up by a woman on the small end of average? And cute, to boot?"

He stares at me, no readable expression on his face.

Grinning, I bend forward over him like Tinkerbell. “Something tells me, they won’t believe you.” I stand straight. “Now. Go back inside and do whatever you were doing before I got here. If I see you again tonight, or I think Mitch has received a heads-up that he’s going to have a visitor tonight, this rifle’s going to land on your probation officer’s desk. Do we understand each other? Oh, and I will be back.”

Renton keeps staring at me.

“Good. Have a pleasant night.”

I spin on my heel and walk back to the Momvan. Light scuffing in the dirt and a soft *whump* tells me he gets up and limps back inside. Here’s hoping he’s afraid of jail enough not to warn his buddies. Still, I should probably move fast.

The rifle lands on the mid-row bench between the kids’ car seats. The loaded magazine winds up in Anthony’s spot. Crap. Don’t let me forget that. I gotta turn it in when I go back to the office. Or not. Maybe this whole side trip will stay hush-hush.

I grab the *Thomas Guide* from under the driver’s seat and flip pages until I’ve got one showing Corona, California. There’s a nice little spot of green northwest of the city. It starts at Prado Regional Park and follows the hills south to a dense-looking patch of green around the reservoir. A thinner swath of trees cuts northeast, running between Eastvale and Norco.

Hmm. Militia guys like this love their woodlands. Lots of cover to hide in.

Of course, the green spot in the southwest corner is the Prado Reservoir, restricted government land. It's unlikely they're inside there or even too close to it. I find Stagecoach Drive and trace it up to the edge of 'civilization.' Or, in this case, a dirt road. I can find that. And a square mile or so shouldn't be that difficult to search on foot, considering I have excellent night vision and don't get tired from running.

I briefly stare at my hollow shirt in the rearview mirror. You know what else is creepy? My middle finger, two inches from the mirror, has no reflection either.

I shake my head, put my van in gear, and get moving.

Chapter Twenty-Six
Patrol Boat Alpha

My Momvan isn't quite made for stealth, but I suppose dull brown isn't the worst possible color to be inconspicuous with.

A thought hits me after a while of driving back west to Corona, that I don't really need the headlights on. I guess it would be a pile of evolutionary fail if a nocturnal hunter couldn't see in the dark. Though, I'm not convinced evolution had anything to do with what I've become.

Part of me can't believe I'm doing this, but here I am. While my half-baked plan percolates, I wind up racking my brain, trying to understand why going out here feels like a good idea.

It's not as though I've got any hard proof of Mitch Gallagher's location, just a wailed statement from a felon given under duress. For cryin' out loud, the FBI can't even find him. Though, granted, it's only been days. Even if they knew right where he was, putting a raid together takes time. And without the belief there's an imminent crime in need of being stopped, they're going to be slow and methodical. That's one thing about the FBI, they don't even take a dump (as Nico says) unless they've filled out all the required forms and arranged a media blackout.

My head swivels back and forth between the road in front of me and the spiral-bound *Thomas Guide* in the passenger seat. Headlights sail by on my left down the oncoming lanes of the Riverside Freeway, a surprising amount of traffic for after 11 p.m. I make good time on the freeway and cut through Corona's city center before randomly picking a 'this looks good' turn down a street heading north. Eventually, I find West Rincon Street, which I've been hunting for. That'll go straight to Stagecoach. Hmm. There's a nice little patch of trees between this development and the airport. Maybe I should check that out. Who knows if Renton sent me to the right place? That dirt road might not lead anywhere. So, I swing a left onto Stagecoach Drive and another left into a little section of perfect suburbia.

Wow, these houses are super nice. I wind up parking on Big Spring Court, about as far southwest in the development as I can get.

A retaining barrier blocks off a relatively sharp downhill slope into the forest. I check my Glock, tuck my badge into my back pocket so it's not glinting in the moonlight, and crouch to leap the fence.

The house I decided to park by perches at the top of a hill, with a long, flat slope descending toward the woods. Other than being unpaved, it looks like someone made a nice road down to the trees… for all of about a hundred feet.

Well, since I threw a rock a couple city blocks and had a doorknob break off in my hand, I have a feeling this vampire deal might come with some perks—at least, at night. I vault the barrier with far more grace than I expected. And far higher, too. So much so that all that grace goes clear out the window and I land like a blind, drunk ostrich on the other side, and fall into a tumble. After I stop rolling at the base of the hill, I lay there for a moment, staring up at the trees and stars, feeling like a jackass.

Next time I try to jump a fence, I will be ready for superhuman legs that can bounce me three times my height straight up.

Right. Time to get serious.

I stand… and spend about twenty minutes roaming around before I'm convinced there's nothing here. Maybe the racist bastard did give me the right directions.

Back up the hill I go.

The second time I leap the barrier they put up to stop random children and drunks from falling down the hill, I'm way better on the landing part, and don't even break stride. One light comes on in a nearby house, but no one appears in any window before I hop in the Momvan and drive away. Following Renton's directions, I turn left again on Stagecoach, and roll to where the road comes to an end. A 'somewhat paved' spur to the left leads past a sign welcoming me to Starlight Kennels. That route bends up into a parking lot. No crazy militia idiots there, I bet. Straight ahead, I spot a pair of wheel ruts. Not so much a 'road' as it's where people have been driving in the dirt.

I steer down that way, but stop by a chain-link gate. Following a brief delay to break open a padlock, I'm underway again. Lordy, it was nice to snap that lock open. With my bare freakin' hands. Sure, it took a little muscle and some serious twisting, but snap open it did. I grin again at the thought and continue on.

A horribly uneven trail rambles downhill, curving to the left and running along the base of the ridge below where that blue sign pointed. Soon, the suburban paradise is out of sight above me, and my Momvan is bouncing and rattling around on a route that probably sees one or two vehicles a month—if that. She's *so* not designed for going off-road.

"Sorry, Mama," I whisper to the van.

The dirt road follows the contour of the raised plateau to the south, heading around to the east past the tip and straight into the woods. I can't explain why, but this feels like the right place. It also feels like I ought to start being *much* quieter than a two-ton van.

Hmm.

I slow to a stop, pulling as far off the road as I can without putting the Momvan somewhere it'll never get out of on its own power. Engine off. Lights off. Okay. Infiltration take two.

This time without tumbling down a hill.

Intuition pulls me into the trees. Moonlight filters down between the leaves, illuminating the wilderness to my eyes. Cracks in tree bark, small rocks, even a creeping rattlesnake stand out as obvious as high noon. The sky isn't overly clear, so I have a strong suspicion normal people probably couldn't see much out here—at least not without night-vision equipment. Hmm. There's a thought. What do I look like on thermal cameras now? I suppose I'd blend into the background temperature.

Before any depressive thoughts can seep into my mind, I focus on how pissed off I am that Chad got shot… because of me trying to cling too hard to something I can't have anymore. Me trying to function during the day is like asking an ambulance chaser lawyer to get through a whole trial without lying once. Sometimes, it happens, but it's a clumsy, flailing mess. And, yeah, I recognize now that I might, just might, be talking about my own attorney hubby.

Focus, Sam.

Chad's in a hospital bed because of me. And I've got to set this right. I also don't want anyone in the FBI or ATF getting hurt, either. Not if I can take these scumbags out myself. After all, since I seem to have rearranged my relationship with the laws of physics—and bullets—I'm in a unique position to prevent further ruination of lives.

Of course, Gallagher and his people might have some ruining coming their way, but that's a sacrifice I'm willing to make.

I creep through the woods about twenty paces left of the dirt road, generally following it. About fifteen minutes after I'd left my van behind, I catch a whiff of man on the air. The smell is one that I would never have noticed before my change, likely something akin to how dogs can scent people. Essence of cheap beer mixes with a fleshy smell, and a bit of sour cheese. Ugh. Dude needs a shower.

My gaze zeroes in on a small bit of motion up ahead, so I freeze in place. At the range course in Quantico, I went through a watered-down version of Army basic training. There, I learned that humans are predators, and our eyesight tracks motion. It's better to stand still in the open than run to cover when a magnesium flare goes off overhead, turning night into day for a few seconds. Fair bet the man I'm smelling probably doesn't have flares.

He does, however, have a rifle.

Twenty-ish yards ahead of where I stand statue-still, a potbellied guy in a wife-beater and camo pants appears to have drawn the short straw and got guard duty.

His M16, however, worries me more than the bored/sleepy look on his face.

After observing his pattern for a few minutes

(he mostly stands in place scratching himself or spitting) I creep to my right and circle around. The closer I get to him, the stronger this weird feeling of being a hunter comes out of nowhere. Instincts I never had before kick in, guiding me in for a kill. My feet find purchase on ground that doesn't rustle. I leap from dirt patch to rock to dirt patch with little effort, stealing up behind this guy like a cat on a blind mouse. When I get within four feet of him, I edge into hiding behind a tree and watch, waiting for his right hand to release the pistol grip of his M16 and plunge into his pants for another scratch.

A brief vision of leaping out and sinking my fangs into the side of his neck comes and goes.

Stop it. That's not why I'm here.

The instant he lets go of the rifle grip, I swoop up behind him and clamp my left hand over his mouth. He doesn't even manage to get his hand out of his belt before I swing him around and drive him forehead-first into a tree hard enough to leave a pat of blood on the bark and knock him clean out.

After easing him to the ground, I squat beside him and unload the rifle, also ejecting a round from the chamber. Unlike Renton, this guy's got a full-on M16 with three-round-burst on the fire selector. I'm quite sure none of these guys have a Class III weapons permit. Oh, the ATF is going to have a field day with them once I'm done here.

The magazine and stray bullet, I keep. His rifle is now little more than a glorified club without ammo. A quick search turns up a 1911 .45 pistol on a belt holster, which I also unload and clear. I'm not worried about the knives along his belt; those won't make noise. Besides, he won't be doing much moving anytime soon, especially after I break the strap off the M16 and use it to bind his arms behind his back. I doubt it'll hold him for too long, but with that hit to the head, well, he's going to be dazed enough that it'll buy me some time.

While I'm securing the nylon strap into a knot, it hits me that I just rushed up on and took out a sentry. It feels like I'm playing that game Danny likes… *Patrol Boat Alpha*—some Vietnam War thing he's got on the laptop. He cheered like a little boy the first time he pulled off a 'silent takedown' of a sentry. Then again, this guy is hardly a trained enemy soldier, but hey, I gotta start small, right?

My ears prick at a distant sound—voices.

Leaving tall, bald, and sleepy behind, I start off at a fast walk to the south. About a minute later, I spot a natural wall formed by a pair of fallen trees, which seems like a decent place to take cover for a look around. It's also got a convenient hole to stash the magazines I'd confiscated. From where I'm crouching, I catch sight of electric lights shimmering in the distance. They're probably not *too* bright and obvious, but my eyes aren't exactly normal anymore. Hell, *I'm* not exactly normal anymore. Any lingering doubts I have about what I am are in serious jeopardy after manhandling Renton, plus that sentry. Sigh. Well, that does explain how my attacker threw me thirty feet into a tree and broke my ribs. Maybe he *did* break my spine and it healed the same way my neck did?

I shudder.

Six steps from my temporary hiding place, something gleams near the ground. Ooh, they've set up tripwires! Wow, I've found a bunch of paranoid bastards. Or big little boys playing fort. A thin metal wire runs from a tree, crosses a six-foot span a few inches off the ground, and connects to a black box a little larger than a soda can duct-taped to a tree.

Unfortunately, I have about as much training with this sort of thing as Tammy has at being a sushi chef. This could be a noisemaker alarm, a smoke grenade, a nail bomb, or an *actual* grenade hidden inside a can. I don't bother attempting to disarm it, or even touch it. I'll leave that to the ATF for later. For now, I step over it and pay extra attention to the ground. Over the next thirty or so yards, I avoid three more tripwires and a couple of pit traps.

At least these guys suck at rigging traps. They're *so* easy to spot.

Or… maybe I'm cheating. I don't think many people have eyes this sharp at night.

Crap. What's wrong with me? Am I actually starting to entertain the idea of *enjoying* what I've become? I admit, it is kinda cool to feel super-powered (though night vision is kind of a wimpy power if I'm honest with myself. Give me flying or laser beam eyes, right?), but… my family. I still don't know for sure what effect my change is going to have on my kids. No superpower, no matter how cool, is worth losing my family.

And I can't have Starbucks anymore.

At least not without puking it. Hmm. Maybe I can make an exception and order the tall size to enjoy the flavor. Or maybe just swish it around my mouth and spit. For mocha, I'll tolerate the occasional prayer to the porcelain god. Maybe I can train myself to hold food down longer than a few minutes.

Anyway, I creep around traps and holes, as well as any spot of ground that doesn't look *completely* normal. Hell, these morons might be stupid enough to use actual land mines. After all, they stole a machine gun from a military armory. I bet the CID guys are having a field day trying to figure out which Guardsman is working with them. Nothing like that happens without an inside guy.

Again, I take cover behind a tree and peer out at the Brothers of the Republic compound. From my position north of the property, I've got a clear view of the grounds. A ramshackle fence of chain link, corrugated metal panels, and wood surrounds it on all sides except where the dirt road I'd been driving on enters at the northwest corner. The leftmost building, a huge, one-story rectangle, appears somewhere between horse stable and warehouse as far as design goes. Its north wall has a garage door with plenty of dents. Directly in front of me, a smaller, square building appears hand-made from cinder blocks. It's got no windows or doors on the side facing me, so that's got to either be an armory or where they plan to shelter when 'The Man' comes for them. The rightmost building at the west end looks like an ordinary one-story ranch house, albeit small. It's L-shaped, with the long part going to my right and the short end pointing at me.

Three vehicles, two pickup trucks and a cargo van, stand in a cluster near the front of the house where the dirt road ends. A glint to the right of the house draws my eye to a squat metal shed barely two feet tall, the roof of which is a pair of doors secured shut by a chain wound through the handles and padlocked.

That looks like a root cellar or underground bunker entrance.

Hmm. If Terrell *is* still alive, he'd likely be in the reinforced cinder block structure or maybe in the root cellar. Those doors appeal to me more, both due to their being easier to access plus, well, the large padlocked chain securing them.

Something or someone is in there...

I stand and dart over to the fence. Climbing it would make noise, and the gate by the road is only about sixty feet away to my right. Of course, if these people are watching anywhere at all, they'll be watching the road. Still, I am a lot quieter and darker than a car with headlights. Aww, hell with it. With slow, deliberate strides, I make for the road and duck inside, veering hard left as soon as I'm past the gate so I can keep to the shadows.

All the buildings have exterior lights, but only garden-variety 110-watt bulbs. This isn't exactly Fort Knox. No halogen lamps, infrared cameras, or motion sensors here. The blue Ford I saw at Joey's is one of the vehicles parked in front of the house. Score! Hmm. On a whim, I change course and hurry due south to the trucks.

I'm intending to disconnect the batteries to keep any suspects from fleeing, but when I reach the front of the van, I notice keys hanging from the sun visor. Wow, how dumb are these guys? After swiping the keys and pocketing them, I ease the van door closed and move over to the blue Ford.

Footsteps crunch behind the house, getting closer.

I drop to the ground and scoot under the pickup a few seconds before a set of black boots and jean-covered legs walks into view around the corner. He (most likely a he) heads over to the root cellar. Once Boots gets far enough away and I can see more than just legs, I recognize the fortyish guy from Joey's, Ted Clarke, the one who hit the floor and didn't try to shoot us.

He kicks the door twice. "Hey, reporter man, you sleepin' good?"

My eyes narrow. Okay, first of all… bingo. And second of all… yay. The reporter's alive.

Yet, somehow I knew this. Hmm.

Anyway, there's no reaction from beneath the doors. Ted chuckles and walks off to his right, apparently meandering around for a not-too-urgent patrol. I lay there in the dirt under the Ford, inhaling the reek of motor oil and tire rubber for a few minutes until he's way off by the 'barn' at the opposite end of the compound.

After crawling out away from him, I open the passenger door and check the sun visor for keys. Sure enough, these guys *are* that predictable. The other pickup, a red Chevy, has its keys there too. Awesome. All three vehicles hopefully disabled.

My over-tuned ears pick up a moan of pain, echoey like a stone-walled room, from the direction of the root cellar.

Yes! The reporter *is* alive.

I peer up over the bed of the Chevy and look around for any signs of motion. The house is dark, the 'stable/garage' is dark as well. Way off to the east, the *crunch-crunch-crunch* of Ted walking continues. He's probably about as far away from the root cellar as he can get without leaving the fenced-in area. Perfect.

A sprint covers the thirty or so feet to the root cellar in seconds. I grab the padlock in both hands and lean backward until I've taken up all the slack in the chain.

Okay vampire-ness, let's see what you can do.

And what I have to do is break open this lock *silently*. I lean backward some more, my shoes at first finding purchase in the dirt, but then slipping. I next brace one shoe against the metal door… feeling sort of badass in the process. The lock starts to slip out of my hand, so I squeeze harder. My quick gasps of breath are purely out of habit, since air is evidently not important for me anymore.

The twin doors creak and groan from the chain pulling at the handles. A subdued *thump* from bending metal startles me motionless for a second. Once I'm sure no one heard or reacted to that, I resume increasing force. Grunting, I grab on with my other hand, and pull with all the strength I can pour into it.

Pank!

The shackle snaps, sending me flying over backward. I have no damn idea where the padlock's loop went; I'm holding only the case. Chains fall with a loud *clatter*—well, at least loud to me—on the cellar doors, so I decide to stay down.

Ted doesn't come running, so perhaps my enhanced senses have scared me again and he couldn't, you know, actually hear it from so far away. That, or he thinks it's just Terrell kicking the doors again. Right. Kidnapped reporter. On it.

I spring to my feet and pull the chain away from the handles, slinging it clear and tossing it over the fence into the woods. The moaning continues from down below, along with gasping, grunting, and the scuff of a shoe on concrete. Sounds like Terrell is preparing himself for another close encounter of the redneck kind. Little does he know…

"Terrell," I whisper, before easing the door up an inch. "Relax. I'm a friend."

He moans.

Damn. That sounds bad. I pull the door up

higher, revealing a steep stairway down to a concrete-floored room full of narrow support columns and steel shelves packed with canned goods and brown MRE packets. Semi-dry bloodstains on the floor cause a mixture of angry and hungry. Great. Most people see a man being tortured and get furious.

I get hangry.

Grumbling to myself, I climb down and lower the door closed over my head. “Relax, Terrell. I’m here to help.”

Chapter Twenty-Seven
The Root Cellar

I'm sure it's pitch dark down here with the door closed, but I can still see as if the space had dim lighting.

Perhaps even more interesting is the means by which I can see; indeed, the air is filled with fine filaments of glowing light, filament that seems to show down in waves from an unknown source, filaments that I had never known existed before. The light particles illuminated everything around them, and I paused briefly, in awe of this ability to see further than I had ever seen before. What the light source was, I didn't know, but it was everywhere, and it flowed, flowed… endlessly.

Terrell Summerlin lays slumped against the rear wall between two shelves about thirty feet away. Bloodstains saturate the fabric of his tank top undershirt, and his dark pants have multiple rips and tears. His hands are cuffed behind his back and linked by padlocked chain to one of the shelves. The stink of piss and blood is overwhelming.

Sons of bitches. My knuckles creak from clenching my fists.

“Hey,” I whisper, hoping he’s got enough coherence to understand me. “I’m a federal agent. I’m here to help.”

Terrell lifts his head. Goopy blood trails from his lower lip, still swollen from a recent pummeling. “What? Where?”

“Don’t yell. Keep quiet, please. I’m a friend.” I hurry over to him and take a knee.

He startles when I put a hand on his shoulder. His skin is burning hot. At least my complete horror at how people could be this cruel to another human being is so strong I don’t feel the least bit of temptation to suckle straight from one of his many open wounds.

Eww. Did I really just think that?

I reach around behind him, grasp the cuffs, and snap the chain (flimsy as hell compared to the one on the doors). He makes no attempt to move. I ease his arms around and drape them in his lap.

“Can you walk?” I whisper.

“You’re really here?” He looks toward me, almost. “I can’t see.” His lips quiver like he’s about to start crying.

“Relax. It’s dark in here. You shouldn’t be able to see.”

His emotion levels off to confusion. “How are

you seeing?"

"Never mind that," I say, knowing intuitively that my suggestion will somehow be heeded. Really, mind control? "Come on. Let's get you out of here."

Right when I grab his arm to pull it over my shoulder and help him up, the lights come on.

For a second or two, I feel like I'm at ground zero of a nuclear test. *Everything* goes white. I can't see a darn thing.

"Ugh!" moans Terrell.

"Well, well, well," says a thick voice with a hint of phlegm. "What have we got here?"

My eyes adjust to the rapid change from total dark to having six naked lightbulbs blaring. A pattern of irregular scuffing tells me I've got three men walking up behind me.

"Stay down," I whisper to the journalist.

He nods.

I stand into a turn, facing Mitch Gallagher, Ted Clarke, and Joey Bell. All three carry M16s, but in a casual sideways manner, likely not thinking a little woman's any real threat. Mitch, sporting a goatee he didn't have in any of the pictures, leads the pack.

The instant we lock eyes, the front of Joey's jeans darkens with piss.

"Federal agent," I say, putting a hand on my Glock. "Put the weapons down and take three steps back."

Ted snaps his M16 up, pointing it at me.

Mitch chuckles. "And I'm Elvis Presley."

"Oh, she's the real deal," says Ted, nodding toward Joey. "She's the one from numbnut's house."

"Don't matter." Mitch grins in a way that makes my skin crawl. I can practically picture him peeling my clothes off with his eyes, thinking he's going to keep me down in this cellar like Terrell for who knows how long. "She ain't got no authority out here. Damn fool thing you did, girlie. Comin' out to visit us all alone. Not quite sure what you threatened my good friend Renton with, but your fine little ass ain't gonna stir up no shit on him. Or be heard from again. Yeah, we found your minivan. You're alone. God knows why you're alone, but you are. And now, your ass is mine."

That's almost funny. Mitch thinks this is a horror movie where a woman gets chained up and abused. He might be right about horror—my claws tingle—but he's got the wrong movie script.

"Just yours?" I ask. "You won't share? You hear that, boys? He's taking my ass all for himself. What a douche."

Mitch frowns. "You think you're funny, girl? Eh? I think you're as unclean as that reporter man."

"Really?" I blink, holding my arm up. "*This* isn't white enough for you?"

Ted scoffs. "It ain't *all* about blood purity. You sold out to the government. You're one of them now."

"Them?" I quirk an eyebrow at him. "What, like lizard men or the grey aliens? Which particular conspiracy LSD are you guys on? Help me out here."

Mitch spits to the side.

"You let 'er leave, an' she's gonna bring whole heap o' trouble," yells a woman from the stairs. "The whole damn government's been taken over by the damn unclean ones. They're all like her."

Wait. Like *me?* Crap! Joey saw me take a bullet and not die. His soaked jeans are proof he knows that my life has gone into two-plus-two-equals-six territory. But the other two don't appear worried. No stakes. Nothing out of the—oh, she's talking about unclean in the way their little group uses it. Anyone who works for the government is with the opposition team.

Well, for however much longer my status as a government employee lasts.

Mitch shakes his head and raises his rifle. "Damn shame. Awful damn pretty thing ta waste."

"Thank you for trying," whispers Terrell behind me, before continuing to mutter prayers.

"I saw your website," I say, leaning toward the men. "I realize you three aren't exactly on speaking terms with rational thought, but it's in your best interest to stand the hell down."

"Just shoot her," mutters Mitch.

I let off a snarl far too deep for the register of human vocal cords and fling myself at Mitch. Ted's rifle barks with a brilliant orange flash, but he misses, due to my supernatural speed. I plow into Mitch, grabbing his M16 in both hands and ramming it up into his face. The hit knocks him reeling backward, staggering him enough to lose his grip on the weapon.

Joey lets off a scream and bolts for the exit. His rifle clatters to the concrete at the base of the stairs.

Ted swivels to aim at me, still firing, pumping two bullets into a shelf full of paint cans to my left. Seeing muzzle flare coming for my face still triggers a normal human '*oh shit!*' reaction. I hurl myself straight down onto my side so his third and fourth shots go over me, and reach out with a stomping kick that crushes his right knee inward.

The woman outside shouts something angry while Joey keeps screaming.

"Bitch!" howls Ted, then lands flat on his back, still shooting wildly around the room.

Before he can correct aim, I flip the rifle I grabbed from Mitch around and pull the trigger, lighting off a three-round burst. Blood sprays from his shoulder and arm; his screaming goes from anger to agony.

Bang!

A bullet whistles past my face, inches from my nose, close enough that I can perceive the smear of copper in the air. I pivot to my right while springing upright. Mitch has a handgun out, trying to get a bead on me. I spring into a leap the same instant he squeezes another shot off at the ground where I no longer am. He doesn't have time to process me moving; I bring the M16 around like a baseball bat and crown him with it. He goes sliding across the floor, alive, but *very* unconscious. Things will go better for me—and the investigation—if I don't leave a trail of bodies behind.

Mitch lets off a gurgling wheeze and crashes into a metal shelf, knocking stacks of MREs to the ground on top of him. My ears ring from gunfire in such an enclosed space. Blood trickles down his face from a likely-broken nose. With luck, he'll survive. If not… meh.

A fortyish woman in a nauseating coral-colored dress rushes into the light, pointing Joey's M16 at me. The sight of the two men unconscious on the ground stuns her. Clearly, she wasn't expecting one woman to take these guys out. I point my rifle at her.

"Drop the weapon, ma'am," I say, far calmer than I should sound. "Don't make me shoot."

She glances at me, the blood draining from her face, perhaps due to my blasé reaction to her having a rifle trained on my heart. Her face is kinda familiar, so I assume she's Mrs. Gallagher, and the little bit of recognition I'm getting is from the case file photos I spent a day looking over.

"Mitch?" she asks.

"Mitch was stupid. Don't be like Mitch. Drop. The. Rifle."

She stares at me.

Oh, hell with this. I'll take a bullet to avoid having to kill someone tonight. I start walking toward her, reaching for her weapon. She leaps back and swivels to take aim at, of all people, Terrell.

Shit!

I charge at her, pushing the gun to the side a second before she squeezes the trigger. Her bullet pings off the stone a few feet over Terrell's head, and pings around the root cellar. It's trivial to wrench the weapon from her grip. After disarming her, I spin into a backhand strike that launches her at the metal shelves. She lands draped over one, out cold, blood dripping from her mouth, neither arms or legs reaching the floor. There's a chance I might have hit her harder than necessary. Either way, it felt damn good.

"What is *wrong* with you?" I rasp at her, while hurling the rifle contemptuously to the ground.

"Mother of God," mutters Terrell. He crawls out from his hiding place among the shelves and gazes up at me in awe.

I bow my head, rubbing the bridge of my nose. "No… not even close."

Chapter Twenty-Eight
One Small Complication

I help Terrell over to the narrow stairs leading out of the cellar.

For now, the others will have to deal with their injuries, although I did my best to staunch the bleeding. Ya know, this root cellar is one scary-as-hell place. They have an entire *box* of handcuffs. Bet these idiots never imagined they'd wind up stuck in them.

Boy, I'm a one-woman wrecking crew.

The woman who tried to shoot Terrell remains draped over the shelf, out cold. Who knows what motivates a person to do something so stupid? I can only feel so sorry for knocking her senseless when she was about to murder an innocent man. It's not as if she tried to shoot *me*. Whether she wanted to silence a possible witness or somehow blamed him for their misfortune, I can't even begin to guess.

"You should've dropped the damn gun Don't be pissed at me for breaking your jaw.," I mutter before turning my attention to Terrell.

"Stay out of sight for now. One suspect is still running around topside, plus I don't know how many others there are."

Terrell holds on to the corner at the base of the steps for support. "I've only ever seen those people, plus two more guys who haven't been around in a couple days."

"Yeah, they contracted lead poisoning." A silent sigh slips out my nose. So far, I've single-handedly hospitalized most of this militia movement, and Chad killed two. It's starting to feel like I should go back to Renton's place and pop a bullet in him, just to be thorough.

No deaths, I think. *Too much damn paperwork.*

"That was… amazing. I don't know who you are, but you've got balls of steel." Terrell sucks in a gasp of air. "They were going to kill me for sure."

I pat him on the shoulder. "Can you hang on a few more minutes until I secure the compound?"

"Yeah." He cradles his side, wincing as he nods. "Go get those bastards."

"Hopefully, only one."

I should probably get away from the cellar before the smell of blood makes me do something I'll regret. Also, calling this in sounds like a good idea. Crap. My cell doesn't have a signal out here. I stuff it back in my pocket and head out.

Had my life not taken a turn for the bizarre, I'd

draw my Glock and creep carefully up the stairs for a cautious peek. Granted, if I hadn't been *changed*, I wouldn't even be here. Normal me would never have even thought to be this reckless and come out here alone in the middle of the night, but more to the point—I'd have been dead in Joey's house.

HUD's the safest choice… right.

I fling the cellar doors open and climb out, only to find a young girl with long, straight blonde hair staring at me. She's maybe eleven or twelve, thin and reedy, the wind pressing the outline of her form into the knee-length T-shirt she must've been sleeping in. Huge blue eyes stare at me over a chrome-finished handgun the little angel has pointed at me in a two-handed grip. Pink-painted toes grip the front of her flip-flops; her whole body trembles.

"Easy, sweetie…" I raise my empty hand into the air in a soothing gesture. "Please put the weapon down and let's talk. I'm a federal agent."

"You hurt my parents!" she shouts, trying to sound angry, but her voice smells like terror.

Oh, no. No. No. No. This kid's gonna shoot me. As I realize this, my brain tortures me with a future image of Tammy at the same age. No, I can't shoot a child. Of course, what would I have done if I hadn't been turned into a vampire? Well, I probably wouldn't be out here now. And I certainly wouldn't have survived the gunshot from Dale earlier. I don't even have my weapon out, and going for it will make her fire for sure, so that's not an option.

Okay, Sam. Relax. You've already been shot in the heart once and it was... annoying. Painful, but annoying.

"What's your name, sweetie?"

"Don't call me sweetie!" The girl scowls and shifts her weight from leg to leg. "What did you do to my parents?"

I'm sure she stood here waiting for me to come out of the cellar, convinced she wanted to kill me, but now that the moment's right in front of her, she's freaking out at the idea. Yay for a good freak-out.

"I didn't want to hurt anyone, but they didn't give me a choice. They're going to be fine. Help is coming. But *you* have a choice right now. You can put your gun down."

Tears roll down her face. If she didn't have a weapon on me, I'd find it hard to resist the urge to hold her and let her cry on my shoulder. "What happened to my parents? Is the unclean reporter still alive?"

Screw those people. I hope some therapist can fix the damage and deprogram her before it's too late.

"Terrell is not unclean, kiddo." I inch closer. "He's a human being, just like you or me." That is, of course, if I was still human, which I'm no longer totally sure of.

"Get away," says the girl, alternately squeezing and relaxing her grip on the gun. Granted, it's the squeezing part that makes me nervous.

I take another small step closer. "No one is going to hurt you, kiddo. You're too young to understand what's going on here, and you've been lied to."

"You're lying to me right now!" shouts the girl. "And *stop* calling me kiddo!"

"What should I call you then?" Another step. "I'm Samantha."

The girl's trembling intensifies to the point that she might actually miss me from only four feet away. "You're a traitor! And you hurt my parents! I hate you!"

Oh, such a charming angel. "Your parents have a lot of things screwed up about how the world works." Another step. Three feet away.

Her mouth closes. A second later, her throat undulates with a gulp. "Go to hell, bitch!"

Blam!

A bullet nails me in the chest, high and right of my heart. Okay, that hurts like hell. Again. Crazy as it sounds, the most noticeable sensation is the aftershock of the slug glancing off my shoulder blade as it exits my back. My whole skeleton rattles.

I wince, gasping for air I don't need. The girl gawks at me. I can't tell if she's more stunned that she actually pulled the trigger or that I didn't react. Taking advantage of her confusion, I pounce, grabbing the weapon away from her and tossing it aside.

"What… happened?" She stares into my eyes, no longer crying, or even trembling.

"You missed."

The girl pokes a finger in the small hole in my shirt, where no wound remains. Hmm. I didn't even bleed much. Maybe being ready for it, I somehow commanded my blood to stay inside? Okay, that sounds weird even to my own ears.

I grasp the girl's wrist. "That was already there. And, yeah, I really need to get new clothes."

A loud *crash* comes from the main house. Probably Joey. Dammit.

Not taking the chance she runs off and gets hurt or goes for another weapon, I drag the girl over to a tree by the root cellar and handcuff her 'hugging' it. I can deal with her later. At the moment, I have another problem.

"Eva," whispers the girl, surprising me. "I'm Eva Gallagher." She starts trembling again and fidgets at the cuffs. "What's gonna happen to me?"

"Right now, you're going to stay here out of trouble and not get hurt. I don't expect you to believe me, but I did not want to hurt your parents. They will be okay… at least physically." With luck, they'll wind up in prison long enough that this kid can grow up normally. "I'll be back in a few minutes to let you out once I'm sure it's safe."

She sinks into a squat, struggling to reach and wipe her eyes.

Another *crash* comes from the house. Crap. What is he doing in there? Eva clings to the tree, still staring at the little hole in my shirt. Ugh. I can't dwell on feeling guilty about scaring this kid and knocking the crap out of her parents. Then again, her parents are real shitheads. Things could be far worse. I *could* have orphaned her. Any normal human agent in my shoes would've shot to kill. Sad to say, that might've been better for her.

"Wait here." I pivot and rush toward the house.

Handcuffs click behind me along with soft grunts. "Please don't leave me tied to a tree!"

"I'll be back in a few minutes," I half-whisper, moving up to a jog.

As she starts crying, I feel like a complete bitch, but hey… the kid shot a federal agent. She's getting off way light. Rummaging and banging continue in the house. I draw the Glock and veer to my right, going around the back of the house, the long side of the L-shaped building. When I reach the first window, I pivot and aim, but it's a kid's room. Judging by all the pink, probably Eva's. It's no paradise. Looks more like a post-apocalyptic settlement than an actual child's bedroom. A pink post-apocalyptic settlement.

How sick am I to think sending this kid's parents to prison is probably the best thing that's happened to her? Something dark in the back of my mind laughs, taunts me with the urge to go finish them off. Ugh. Where did that come from?

Next window's an empty bathroom. I spot the back door up ahead and beeline for it. It's locked, but rickety as hell. A quick tug snaps the door open, sending a little bracket flying.

"Shit! Shit!" yells Joey inside. Another heavy

object slams to the floor.

I glance to my right at the cinder block bunker and the larger building beyond. No sign of activity, so I'm guessing this 'militia' was on the small side. Joey's making quite a bit of noise inside the house, plus all the gunfire in the root cellar. If there had been anyone else in the compound, they would've been on me already.

Speaking of more people in the compound…

I pull out my cell phone and call Nico.

"Moon? Do you have any idea what time it is?" asks my boss, after six rings.

"12:04 a.m., sir."

He sighs. "This better be good."

"I dunno about good, but it's important. I've located Joey Bell, and that militia group that's been dealing in stolen military weapons. They weren't happy to see me. I've also located a missing reporter, Terrell Summerlin. He's banged up pretty bad. Three suspects hurt. I'm about to engage Joey."

"Dammit, Moon! What the hell is wrong with you?"

More than I care to admit, I think. Instead, I say, "Couldn't sleep."

"Yet, you sleep all day."

"I'm a complex person," I say, then switch gears. "Sorry, boss. I had to do this for Chad, and when I found out about that missing reporter, I had a weird feeling he didn't have a lot of time left. Can you send in the cavalry?"

He groans. “All right. Where are you?”

I can picture him sitting up in bed, rubbing his eyes. He’s a widower, so I suspect he’s alone. But who knows. Maybe he has a lady friend over. If so, I can’t hear her. Anyway, I explain my location. During that, the front door of the house slams, so I start moving into the building. Phone in my left hand pressed to my head, Glock out in front of me, I sweep and clear the kitchen and a tiny dining room while explaining to Nico how to get here.

When I reach the living room, I have a clear view of Joey out in front of the house, half-into the Ford. He’s checking the sun visor. Hah!

“All right,” says Nico. “Sit tight, Sam. I gotta send this over to the FBI, you know.”

“Obviously. That’s why I called it in. Oh, and bring the ATF. The woods out here are loaded with booby traps. Tripwires, even. I have no idea what they are. Could be grenades, could just be noisemakers. The dirt road in should be safe enough.”

“Jesus. You keep your ass in one piece. We’ll talk soon.”

“Copy that, sir.” I hang up and stuff the phone back in my pocket as Joey runs over to the van, muttering a steady stream of profanities. I sigh. ‘We’ll talk soon’ sounds a whole lot like ‘you’re going to be suspended, maybe fired.’

Can’t say I wasn’t expecting that when I walked out my house a few hours ago.

I kick the front door open and draw a bead on

Joey. "Joseph Bell. You're under arrest. Back out of the van with your hands in the air and get on the ground."

Forty feet or so isn't a great shot for a pistol, and I think Joey realizes that since he decides to bolt. I clear the wooden porch in two strides, jump down to the dirt in front of it, and sprint after him.

Joey zigzags back and forth like he can't figure out where he should go. His two temptations appear to be the cinder block structure and the gate out to the road. In seconds, he abandons both options and zooms straight to the root cellar.

What the heck does he hope to find down there?

At the last second, he veers to the right and rushes at Eva, who screams, "Help!" at him.

Oh, great. Whatever fantasy he has of some cross-country 'guy and a fugitive kid' movie going on his head ain't gonna happen. Not if I have anything to say about it. I sprint after him, closing distance with ease. Eva leaps to her feet, shaking the handcuffs at him.

"Joey! Help! Get these off me!"

He whines and looks back over his shoulder at me like I'm a 450-pound Kodiak bear who wants him for dinner. Screaming in the voice of a horror movie teenager, he swoops around behind Eva and grabs her into the air with an arm across her chest—and a gun to her head.

"Stay back!" shouts Joey.

Shit. Now *that* I was not expecting. I skid to a stop maybe fifteen feet away. I don't like my odds of skipping a bullet past her head into his face, so I hold my fire.

"Joey! What are you doing!?" Eva squirms at the cuffs, swinging her feet back and forth, off the ground. "Ow! Stop!" It takes her a second to realize she's got a .45 pressed against her skull. The second she does, she goes platter-eyed. One of her flip-flops falls off. Two minutes ago, I was the demon that attacked her family, now she's begging me for help with just her stare.

"Lose the gun!" yells Joey.

I keep pointing it at him. "If you hurt her, you'll need a priest instead of a lawyer."

He cackles maniacally, twitching and sniffling like a coke addict, which he probably is. "You're gonna kill me anyway. Only difference is if you want a kid dead too. Hah! Maybe I should shoot her before you do to her what you did to Dale! Better she dies pure!"

"No!" wails Eva, kicking at him. She screams some more, and lands a heel into his shin.

Grr! He's on the express to Crazy Town, but I can't let him punch that little girl's ticket. Seeing me take a bullet and not die must've been too much for him. "All right. Calm down, Joey." I let the Glock roll back on my finger and lower my arm.

"Toss it," he says, pulling her higher so her head obscures most of his face.

"Ow!" she wails, pedaling her legs in the air and jerking at the handcuffs. "Put me down! Joey! Please stop!"

I toss the Glock into the dirt nearby with a soft *thump*. "Leave the child out of it, Joey."

"Oh, no way, bitch. This kid's the only thing keeping me alive. You took the keys, didn't you? Give me the keys, then it's your turn to hug this tree."

"The FBI is already on the way, Joey. You won't get far. It'll go easier for you if you give up."

Joey pushes her head sideways with the gun and screams, "Keys! Now!"

Eva wails.

Even if I do what he wants, he's probably still going to shoot her. Or kidnap her. Child plus interstate car chase is a worst-case scenario. Guess watching me jump on Dale and suck blood from his chest wound snapped the last shred of sanity he had left.

Eva whimpers and begs him to let go of her, but her protests only make the crazy in his eyes flare brighter.

Well, shit.

Chapter Twenty-Nine
Shattered

Eva strains to stretch her legs toward the ground, toes missing the dirt by inches. Her hands turn red from her struggle to slip out of the cuffs.

Joey keeps staring at me. One good thing about this condition of mine, I can do 'corpse-still' really damn well. He's probably expecting me to leap on him and rip his head off or something; after all, he saw me feed on a dead man, so I don't even twitch an eyelid. He also saw me take a bullet with the best of them.

"What are you doing?" yells Eva. "Stop it! I thought you were my friend!"

"He's not your friend, Eva," I say, in as soothing a tone as I can. "I'm sorry, but these people aren't your friends. All they know is hate. They're only nice to you as long as they think you are a benefit to them."

Shaking with fear and rage, Joey shouts at me, spittle flying from his teeth. “Hurry the hell up. Keys, now, or I’m gonna kill this kid. You wanna live with that?”

My eyes narrow. “Eva is your only ticket out of here, Joey. If you shoot her, there’s nothing stopping me from pulling your arms off, one after the other.”

Motion in my peripheral vision draws my attention. Terrell slips out of the root cellar, eyeing me. He creeps toward Joey, circling around, angling to approach from behind. I knew investigative reporters had balls, and this guy is living proof of that.

“All right, Joey,” I say. “Do you want the keys to the Ford, the Chevy, or the van?”

“Uhh.” He glances past me at the cluster of vehicles.

Terrell edges closer.

“You might want to go with the van,” I say. “It’s enclosed, so you can hide Eva in the back. I mean if you’re going to kidnap a child, better no one can just look in the window and see her, right?”

Joey blinks. “Uhh, yeah, okay. The van… and gimme the keys for these cuffs, too.”

I shrug. “Suit yourself, but you’ll probably need them. Instead of chaining me to that tree, you should probably leave them on Eva so she doesn’t run away. In fact, you guys have a whole box of them down in the cellar. Better chain her ankles, too, just in case.”

Joey twitches, his eyes shifting right and left.

Eva gives me a what-the-hell stare.

"On the other hand," I mutter, my stance going casual as I tap a finger on my chin. "Vans get poor gas mileage. Not that trucks are much better, but if you're going to be eluding the authorities, every time you stop for gas is a chance to get caught. What if Eva makes a run for it and asks the clerk for help?"

Terrell's eyes lock on to Joey's gun arm. He's three steps away.

"Uhh, you're confusing the shit out of me," says Joey. His face goes red. "Keys now or I'm gonna kill all three of us!"

"Well, two of us would die tonight. I'm kind of hard to kill, remember?"

"Give me the goddamned keys right the hell now, or this kid is going splat!"

"All right. I'll give you the keys. Just, do me one little favor?"

"What?" he rasps.

"Please take the gun away from her head, so you don't accidentally destroy your ticket out of here. My gun's way over there. I'll never get to it before you can shoot her, so it's okay to stop pressing the gun to her head. No one wants an accident, right?"

"Uhh."

Eva wails, hanging limply in his arm. "Please, Joey! Please!"

I reach into my jeans pocket and pull out a random set of keys from one of the vehicles behind me. "Here's the keys. Just move the gun away from the side of her head."

Joey relaxes his weapon. The instant the .45 is no longer pointed at Eva, Terrell lunges. At that, I rush forward. Joey and Terrell grunt in a twisting struggle. Terrell pushes him away from Eva, who falls to her knees as he shoves Joey away from her. Joey spins at Terrell; the weapon goes off with a sharp *bang* and a flash.

The men fly apart, Terrell collapsing on his side, clutching his shoulder. Joey spins back to face toward me/Eva, but screams like a schoolgirl at finding me right on top of him. Before his brain can even process how I covered twenty feet in a second, my fist mashes into his nose.

He doesn't make a sound, other than the dull *thud* of flesh and bone colliding. His floppy body flows over backward and lands a good ten feet away, skidding and sliding. He's clearly out cold, blood streaming from both nostrils. The urge to kill him rises up inside me, but… not in front of a child. And… I'm still a federal agent. An unconscious man isn't an imminent threat.

"Terrell!" I run to his side and slide to a stop on my knees. "How bad?"

"Shoulder." He cringes. "Hurts like hell, but I'm still here."

I grab his hand and put it over the wound. "Keep pressure on it. Help is already on the way."

He nods, wincing and gasping.

Eva's simmered down to faint whimpering.

She's scooted around the tree to the other side so she can watch us, and stares at Terrell with an expression of abject shock. Joey's .45 left a red mark on the side of her head behind her right eye.

"Thanks for holding on to these for me," I say while grasping the handcuff chain. "Joey needs them now."

She glances up into my eyes. Her lip quivers, but she neither cries nor speaks. Oh, screw it. This kid's going to have enough problems without me putting it in my report that she fired a weapon at me.

"Make you a deal, 'kay?" I ask, while inserting the handcuff key. "I unlock you, and you behave like a nice normal little girl and don't run off, grab a gun, or do something crazy, all right? And I won't tell anyone you tried to shoot me."

She manages a mute nod, and stares at my chest. "I did shoot you."

"No, sweetie. If you hit me, I'd be hurt, right? And I'm not. You missed." I unlock the cuffs, staring into her eyes, wanting with all the willpower I can summon that she forgets shooting me. Not that I expect anything to happen, but, maybe God is listening. "You're going to have enough challenges ahead of you without having to worry about attempted murder of a federal agent. Behave yourself, and as far as my report will say, you didn't even have a weapon."

Eva shies away from me as soon as I free her, and sits curled in a ball at the base of the tree. She stares over her knees at Terrell. "He helped me. After all that mean stuff I said."

I tromp over and cuff Joey's hands behind his back. "Terrell is not 'unclean,' Eva," I say. "That's just hate talking. Believe what your own eyes tell you."

The crunch of tires on dirt reach my ears. Guess backup's coming in quiet—no sirens. I pull out my cell phone again and call Nico.

Amazingly, Eva crawls over to Terrell. Her parents are injured in the cellar, but she chose to go to Terrell first. He lifts his hand and she grasps it. They have a silent moment. Perhaps understanding, or at least doubt glimmers in her eyes. I don't expect that kid to ever like me. She might never forgive me for sending her parents to prison. Still, I'll call it a win if she can learn to think for herself.

Nico answers. "Talk to me, Moon."

"I'm pretty sure the area is secure. I hear cars approaching. Where's that ambulance?"

"Look up in about two minutes," says Nico. "A medical bird is inbound."

I jog over and collect Joey's .45 as well as retrieve my Glock. "Great. Let them know I'm in here, huh? Don't wanna get shot. Four suspects in custody, one with bullet wounds. Terrell Summerlin, the missing reporter, has a bullet wound to the shoulder. I've got a minor child here as well… Mitch Gallagher's daughter. She's gonna need CPS…and a therapist."

The *whud-whud-whud* of an approaching helicopter drowns out the cars. Headlights wash over the front gate compound a second or two before a convoy of black SUVs roll in. "The king's men are all here. Gotta go."

"Right." Nico lets out a resigned sigh before hanging up.

Yay. This is going to be fun.

I make sure my badge is clearly visible on my belt and walk out toward the approaching trucks.

"I hear a helicopter," says Eva.

"Yep. That's an air ambulance for Terrell and your parents."

Agents in black and body armor spill out of the trucks. A cluster of laser sight dots swarms over my chest for a second until the guys notice my badge.

I smile. "You boys are a little late to the party. All the cake's gone."

Chapter Thirty
Guilty

When I get home at four in the morning, I pluck Anthony from his bed, carry him to Tammy's room, and sit there holding them both while they sleep.

Danny finds me sitting in Tammy's bed at 5:54 a.m. He always wakes up right before the alarm goes off. "Bad night?"

"Yeah… something like that."

He drifts over. "What happened?"

"Busted some bad guys last night."

The color drains out of his cheeks. "Serious? What happened?"

"Tell you later."

"That bad?"

I nod. "Pretty bad."

"Did anyone, ah, get killed?"

"Not that I know of. Still, I'm probably going to get fired today, Danny."

I kiss the kids one after the next atop their heads. The sun's coming up. I can feel it as surely as, well, as surely as anything. The drowsiness is hitting, and it's hitting hard. Despite my exhaustion, I say, "Stayed up late doing research. Found where the guy was hiding out. Maybe I went in without getting approval."

"Cripes, Sam." Danny runs a hand up over his head.

"Well." I half smile. "I wasn't exactly told *not* to go in."

Tammy stirs. "Good morning, Mommy."

I squeeze her. "Good morning, Tam Tam."

Is it fair that my children still have their parents while Eva's are going away for a long time? No, it isn't. But this existence of ours is not based on fairness. Truth be told, if I stretch technicalities, my children have already lost their mother. I'm just too damn stubborn to accept that. And, though I'm sure Eva disagrees, she's better off being away from them.

Eventually, the weight of the rising sun is too much, and I lose about ten minutes. By the time I can force myself to function again, I'm alone in Anthony's room. Clinking spoons tell me they're all in the kitchen having breakfast. All talk of my midnight foray has to wait. I stumble off the bed and trudge down the hall to the kitchen with the closest thing to a smile I can conjure in my current dazed state. We go through the motions of a normal family breakfast, except I drag my barely-conscious butt to the fridge for a 'special milkshake.'

Danny takes the kids in the Beemer, now with car seats, on his way to the office. I stand in the doorway, inches away from sunlight, and I can't figure out what I dread more: going through the sunblock and makeup routine or facing Nico.

Well, whatever I do with my unlife after this, termination for not showing up won't look good. Being late, though, screw it. I take a hot shower to get rid of the smell of gunpowder and blood. There's a little bit of red skin around where Eva shot me. If recent events mean anything, the red skin will be gone in days, if not hours. I nearly fall asleep twice in the bathroom, but force myself to keep going.

Much sooner than preferable, I'm painted up in sunblock and foundation, and out the door.

I don't even make it to my desk before Nico's in the aisle between cubes giving me the look.

As soon as his office door shuts, he almost shouts, "What were you thinking?"

"Sorry." This moment has been the substance of my nightmares for years. In the boss' office getting chewed out for screwing up. Even in training, I'd have bad dreams of my career going down in flames like this. Every single cop movie/TV series has the protagonist butting heads with their boss. I guess I thought real life wouldn't be like that. It hadn't been… until now.

"Jesus, Sam." Nico walks a circle around his desk twice before falling into his chair. "I spent two hours on the phone with Strickland getting reamed out, and then had another half-hour tag-team bitch-out session with ATF Frank and DeLuca from the FBI. My ass has been chewed so much, I'm going to be missing pieces for a month."

"I'm sorry. I… listened to my gut." Strickland is Nico's immediate supervisor. No one really likes him, but no one dislikes him either. The man has raised bland to an art form. He's basically a policy and procedure manual that evolved sentience. "I had a hunch they'd be gone before the FBI found them."

His eyebrows go up. "Your gut." Nico drums his fingers on the desk for a moment. "I've got *five* people in the hospital, the two from the house plus your shooting spree in the cellar. You nearly made an orphan on top of it. At least tell me she didn't watch."

I cringe. "No, sir. She was waiting for me outside. They brainwashed her, too. Kid was ready to kick my ass but, she's still a kid. Didn't do anything. I talked her down."

"And…" Nico tosses a newspaper at the front of his desk. He tried to land it so I could see the headline, but it flopped wrong. Grumbling, he flips it over and points at an article.

Militia Groups Rally—Waco II?

"You've gotta be kidding me," I mutter. "It was hardly a massacre like that. No one even died."

"Still, there are at least six militia groups in the western United States using this raid of yours as a springboard for recruitment, claiming the government has gone tyrannical." His expression softens—a little. "At least you managed to get that reporter out of there alive."

"How is he doing?" I ask.

"He'll live. Be in the hospital longer than Chad, but he'll live." Nico gives me a long, weird stare. "What exactly did you do to the suspect, Sam? The young guy, Joey? He's stark raving mad. Claims you're a demon or something that won't die."

I shrug. "He was already sanity-challenged. I guess he tried to shoot me and missed, but he thinks he hit me. Who knows how this nutjob's mind works?"

"What happened in there, Sam? Off the record. Between me and you. What the hell happened out there?"

Hmm. Just how much should I tell my boss? I decide the poor sucker isn't ready for the truth. Hell, who would be? I say, "I went in there attempting to verify that Joey Bell was at the location. The idea that Terrell Summerlin might still be alive crossed my mind." I explain finding word of his going missing during my investigation. "I observed one of the suspects kick the root cellar and taunt Terrell, so I decided to try and sneak in and get him out. My objective was not to engage any of them, sir. I wanted to slip in and out, but before I could leave with Terrell, I was confronted in the cellar. I identified myself as a federal agent, but Mitch, Ted, and Joey thought that, due to the remoteness of the area, they could kill me and no one would ever find out… when they pointed their weapons at me, I had no choice but to react. Mrs. Gallagher then entered the cellar, observed her husband and his friend wounded, and picked up a weapon."

"Why didn't you stop her from picking up a weapon?" Nico taps his pen against his left hand in a repetitive gesture. The hollow plastic clicking pounds into my brain.

"As soon as he recognized me, Joey ran away and dropped his rifle by the stairs. She was too far for me to get to her, and I didn't want to shoot her. However, she moved to kill Mr. Summerlin, but I'd managed to get close enough to jump on her before she could shoot him."

"This is a giant goddamned mess, Sam." He grumbles to himself for a moment, shaking his head at the desk. "I realize I didn't specifically order you *not* to pursue it, but I thought that implication had been clear when I told you the investigation had been handed off to the FBI and ATF… and I really hope you've got a good explanation for why you had a military-spec M16 in your personal vehicle?"

"I confiscated it from Renton Chase. He's a paroled felon. You know me, sir, I had every intention of turning it in."

"I know you, but it doesn't look great. HUD agent with a Rambo complex. You know how the FBI people are. They think we're all just a bunch of underachievers who couldn't make it in the big leagues."

"That's not who I am, sir. Nor you, or Chad. Or anyone I know here."

He rubs the bridge of his nose. "You don't need to convince *me* of that."

"Those people threatened me. They had Terrell locked up for days, torturing him."

"That's no reason to conduct a solo raid. Even if they are a pack of monosyllabic bigots."

I sit straighter, shaking off a bit of the day-fatigue trying to drag me off to sleep. I'm really starting to hate the smell of sunblock. "They were going to kill me, sir. And Terrell. And, later, Joey was inches from killing the little girl."

"Which wouldn't have been an issue at all if you hadn't gone in alone." He waves a hand around randomly. "It looks like you're somewhere between suicidal or went in there knowing you'd get into a situation that would end in gunfire. We only have your word to go on, and—"

"Beg your pardon, sir, but Terrell witnessed it all. He will corroborate my account of what happened, because my account *is* what happened."

Nico freezes mid-wave, staring through his fingers at me. "Well, that's something at least."

We sit in awkward silence for a minute or so.

"I'm honestly not sure what to do here, Sam. This is a giant mess."

Here it is. The moment I dreaded. Once again, a few seconds can totally destroy dreams I've spent years working for. But, how can I justify being a risk to the people I work with? Even now, sitting in the hot seat, it's taking an extreme amount of focus for me to remain conscious.

I take a breath and let it out.

Nico wobbles his pen between his fingers.

My sharpened fingernails pick at the armrest.

He smirks, frowns, and goes blank-faced.

A paper clip striking the floor would tumble over the room like a cannon blast.

"Maybe it would be best if I resign and save you the headache," I say, barely giving it voice.

There it is. Years of work, hope, and determination dangled over the trash can. No. I can't think that way. This isn't my choice. Something happened to me that I didn't ask for. I don't belong out in the daytime anymore. I can't risk other people's lives for my vanity, my love for being able to say '*I'm a federal agent.*' Even if it is only HUD.

Nico winces. "Sam… I don't think this will get to the point of termination. It *might.* Probably a reprimand, maybe a suspension. It's not like you disobeyed any direct order. Going in alone without any notification is…"

"Reckless. Yes, sir, I know. I've been considering my present situation, and in all honesty, I don't think I'm in any physical shape to continue. As best I understand, I've developed a rare skin condition that causes me to break out with a wicked sunburn in mere seconds. I'm covered in SPF nine million right now, and I still hurt. My reaction time during the day is slow. I can barely stay awake. If I saw a doctor, I'm sure they'd tell me I need to stay out of the sunlight or I run the risk of melanoma or worse. Plus, what happens if I'm out in the field and I can't function due to sunburn, or my slow reaction time gets Helling shot again? Maybe next time, he gets worse than a two-week hospital vacation." I gesture at the paper. "And this brewing political mess is just one more reason."

"Sam…" Nico sighs, steepling his fingers.

"It's nothing I asked for, sir. I busted my ass for years to get here. I love this job. I love the people I work with, but I don't want to give you these kinds of problems."

"I'll keep what you said in mind." He pats the desk twice. "For now, consider yourself on paid suspension until further notice while the investigations progress. They're still working on the shooting at the first house, and now, they've got your midnight raid on top of that."

Yeah. Suspended with pay. That's like saying, here's two months to find a job.

A heavy lump glides up into my throat. I'm not sure I could talk right now if someone put a gun to my head. All I can do is nod.

"It wouldn't look good on you to quit so fast, Sam. Makes you seem like you're guilty of something." Nico attempts his paternal smile.

"I am guilty… for letting all you guys down. For not being fast enough to stop that guy from shooting Chad." I show off my greasy, sunblock-slathered hands. "I didn't ask for this, either. You know I'm happy here."

"And you're one of our sharpest investigators." He tosses the pen onto the middle of his desk. "Maybe you're right about the medical issues. God dammit, it sucks."

"Yeah." I stare down.

"It'll be a damn shame to lose you, but don't give up hope, Sam. Go see a doctor. Perhaps there's some kind of management regimen you could try. If your condition improves, we can always talk reinstatement."

I summon a weak smile, the tip of my tongue circling the point of a retracted fang. Something tells me my condition's going to stay right where it is… probably for quite a long damn time. "Thank you, sir. I appreciate that. I'll let you know if anything changes."

Nico remains stoic as I remove my sidearm and holster from my belt, and leave them on his desk, along with my badge. Standard procedure for being suspended, but I think we both know I won't be taking them back.

I feel like crying, as if a close relative has died. I'm terrified, freaking out, angry (at whatever attacked me that night), and defeated. That monster took more than my life; he took my dreams away, too. But, badge or not, I still have my family, dammit.

I'll find a way to make this work.

Nico stands and offers a hand. "Take care of yourself, Sam."

"Thanks. You too, sir. It was an honor to work with you."

"Don't talk like that, Sam. Suspensions aren't forever."

No, but vampires are. I'm sure he's saying that to be polite. My willingness to resign is no doubt going to weigh on the evaluation process. Hopefully, it'll let HUD sweep me aside and forget the whole thing ever happened without the need to concoct charges and turn me into a sacrifice on the altar of public opinion. I'm not too worried about being charged, since I didn't technically break any laws (other than roughing Renton up a little, but good luck proving that).

"Thanks. You've got my number if you need to reach me."

He nods.

For what I'm sure is the last time, I lower my head and walk out of Nico's office.

Chapter Thirty-One
Acceptance

I spent about two hours at the office having an awkward-as-hell meeting with Ernie Montoya, Michelle Rivera, and Bryce Anders—my former associates.

They all now believe I have xeroderma pigmentosum, a medical condition that prevents me from properly executing my duties as a HUD agent. I'm sure they suspect my solo run on the Brothers of the Republic compound is part of my suspension, but not one of them objected to it. They're all glad I got the bastards who put Chad in the hospital.

Speaking of Chad…I need to visit him soon. Unlike the others, he'll get the whole truth about the raid…except for the part about Eva shooting me. As far as anyone is officially concerned, she never fired—or even had a weapon on her. Luckily, no one ever thought to check her hands for gunpowder residue. Probably because I never mentioned she had pulled a weapon on me. And, like a good daughter of militia wingnuts, she kept her mouth shut about it. Last I heard, she's still with CPS while they try to find her mother's 'filthy lib parents.' How sad is it that she only knows of her maternal grandparents by that term? She's never even met them. Mitch's parents have been dead for a few years. Speaking of Mitch, he and his wife are recovering in a secure room at the hospital. They'll likely be guests of the federal government for a decade or six, between what they did to Terrell, trying to kill a federal agent, and being involved in selling stolen military hardware. It's possible they'll die of old age in prison, assuming nothing else happens to them.

Everyone's recovering, except for me.

Still. It's a damn miracle no one died.

After we'd loaded Terrell on the medevac helicopter, I made sure Eva understood that I wasn't upset with her, and I would not be documenting that she pointed a weapon at me. My report stated that she carried it outside, thinking they had a burglar on the property, in case anyone questions finding her prints on it.

So, that's the official story.

Except for being shot by a twelve-year-old, I told the truth everywhere else.

Anyway, two days have passed since I left the HUD office. No one's called in any official capacity, though I've gotten a few "hey, how's it going" morale-boosting calls from Michelle and Ernie.

Between Danny and Mary Lou, I've tried obeying my body's desires for those days and staying asleep during sunlight hours. My new metabolism is weird. I don't feel any better or worse for 'resting properly.' When I force myself up during the day, I'm merely crummy-tired during the time the sun is up. I guess *they* got vampires wrong in all the movies and stuff where they either cannot wake up at all, or can only force themselves to function when facing an attack, and promptly pass back out once the danger is gone. I'm neither wooden nor forced to sleep, except at the moment of sunrise.

So, yeah. Hi, I'm Samantha Radiance Moon, and I'm a vampire.

I've moved past the point of denying it. How can I? The sun burns me. I drink blood, can't die, groggy in the daytime, wide awake at night. Great night vision too. I have fangs. Oh, and mirrors hate me too. All that's kind of difficult to argue with.

It's not all bad. I mean, I'm strong, fast, can take a bullet without an issue. Sure, I can't go out in the day without a bucket of sunblock cream slathered all over me, but if circumstance demands it, I can cope… just not when people around me are likely to get shot.

Yeah, I'm probably a vampire. As ridiculous as that sounds in my head. But, I will make this work. For my kids. For Danny.

For me.

I can't give up. It's already taken the job I loved. But no more, dammit. My family is where I draw the line. What can I do? They wouldn't let a blind person drive, and if vampires were a 'thing,' I'm sure they wouldn't let us hold day jobs, either. Especially risky ones involving guns, sunlight, and innocent bystanders. I'm going to take this circumstance that happened to me, this being a vampire, and I'm going to turn it into a benefit. I won't let it crush me.

I won't let it define me.

***

On a Wednesday, I force myself out of bed in the morning. Danny's pleasantly surprised to see me up and around, and we have a nice family breakfast. He's okay with me driving Tammy to preschool today, so I drop Anthony at Mary Lou's for a little while since I'm going to visit Chad. Not being in a rush to go to work, I spend some time with my sister.

Her kids are all over me, except Ruby Grace, who's still giving me the suspicious side-stare. I feel like a huge dog that she doesn't quite trust not to be dangerous. Making a big deal out of it will only worsen things, so I pretend it doesn't bother me and act like my old self.

Eventually, I duck out and go to the hospital.

Chad's sitting up in bed, watching *Wheel of*

Fortune. He glances over as I walk in and starts to look away until his brain registers who I am. His head snaps back to smile at me. "Hey, Sam. How's it going?"

"It's going." I flop in the chair next to his bed.

He pats his side. "The drain's coming out tomorrow. My lung's almost fully inflated again."

"That's great."

"You don't sound happy." He quirks an eyebrow.

"Oh, it's not that." I smile. "I'm glad you're feeling better."

Chad pushes a button on the bed, motoring himself upright a little more. "So…"

"I got the bastards," I say. "All of them who were involved."

He rolls his eyes. "Yeah and they'll be back on the street in six months."

"We'll see. Joey, in fact, might wind up in a mental facility."

"What happened?"

"It's complicated." I chuckle. "Well, maybe 'complicated' isn't the right word. I'll substitute 'reckless' or 'stupid.'"

I fill him in on the details. To avoid putting him in an awkward position, I don't mention my throwing Renton around like a rag doll or that Eva shot me. Chad groans when I tell him the kid's middle name is 'Braun.' Yeah, nice parents to do that to her. Of course, not everyone knows that Eva Braun was Hitler's wife, before she popped a cyanide pill. Anyway, I wonder if they would've given her up for adoption if she hadn't turned out blonde. At one point before the CPS woman took her from the compound, I suggested she really ought to change it when she's eighteen, and suggested Marie. Eva Marie sounds much prettier.

Chad shakes his head. "Jesus effing…Nico must've flipped."

"As much as he's capable of flipping." Truth is, our boss is a pretty sedate guy. "So, anyway… I'm suspended until further notice."

He cringes. "With pay, I hope."

I nod. "I'm probably going to resign, Chad."

"What?" He stares at me. "No… Sam, please don't. Not over me. This isn't your fault."

"It's more than that." I shake my head. "I have some medical issues that are getting in the way."

"Damn. What? You busted your ass to get here. It's a shame to walk away."

Having Chad stare at me like we're about to be divorced gets me choked up. "I know. Believe me, I know how hard I had to fight for this. Twice the work of any man and a third the credit. This is not a choice." That damn lump in my throat comes back. It takes me a minute to get my voice back. "If things were different…"

"Maybe it's not that bad? What kind of medical issues are you talking about?"

"The sunlight thing, mostly."

"Sunburn? Really?" He chuckles. "You're going to resign over that?"

"That, plus whatever is wrong with me that I'm barely awake during the day. I should have been able to shoot that man before he got his weapon drawn. You know how when you've been up all night, you bump a glass over and think, 'I should really do something about that' as it's falling, but you just stand there and watch it crash to the floor? That's how I felt. I had my weapon already out and just stood there. I couldn't react."

"Shock?"

"No. I've been on raids before. I don't hesitate. You know that. This is different. Like a really thick brain fog is paralyzing me. Everything during the day happens a few seconds late."

Chad grasps my hand. "The attack. You've got PTSD."

"I've got something. But, there's still the skin thing."

"But it's just a sunburn—"

I hold up a finger and stand. His eyes track me as I walk around his bed to the window, pulling my sleeve up. When I stick my forearm (where I didn't put sunblock) into the light streaming in from the window, my skin reddens instantly to blisters. I jerk it back with a gasp of agony before the smoke starts. Better to show my partner.

"Holy shit," he mutters.

Before he can notice the redness and blisters already healing, I tug the sleeve down and cradle the arm like it's still burning. "I've got industrial-strength sunblock on my face and hands. You know, the kind they make for Irish people?"

He chuckles.

"I can't take the risk that something like that happens out in the field, Chad. What if a suspect rips my shirt and I'm crippled with agony while you get killed because I can't function?" I flop back in the chair, head down. Tears I felt for sure would start as soon as I saw Chad in the hospital bed start now. "I'm sorry, Chad. My pride isn't worth your life. I really can't function that well ever since the attack."

"Wow…" He lets out a long, slow sigh. "That's so messed up. I hope they get the son of a bitch. Think he's got the same thing with the sun? Maybe you caught it from him?"

If he only knew how close to the truth he was. I almost laugh, but can't quite do it.

"Pretty sure he does. I wish I got a decent look at his face, but I still don't even know what he looked like, other than being a man."

Chad motors the bed back a little to recline. "It's going to stink babysitting a new agent, but Jesus, Sam. That arm… You need to stay the hell inside during the day. I'm a believer now."

So am I. "Yeah. Sorry to stick you with new meat. I *hate* having to resign, but I'm too much of a risk."

"Maybe they'll find a cure?"

I chuckle. "That's what Nico said. I really love how much you guys don't want to lose me. Maybe there's a cure, but I'm not holding my breath." And if I did, I could hold it for a really long time.

Chad nods, and I see his tears too. “You know that if you ever need anything, you can call me. Might not be official, but we’ve been together for years. We’re always going to be partners.”

When he raises his arm, I lean in and hug him.

“Thanks, Chad. That means a lot to me.” I hug him gingerly for a moment and lean back. “Same goes in reverse, although private citizen Sam won’t have the same connections.”

He chuckles, more sad than amused. “Whatever you do, please find happiness, okay? Take care of those kids of yours, and keep that Danny on the straight and narrow.”

I nearly ask why he said that, but let it drop. I nod. “My family is all I think about these days.”

We sit in silence for a little while longer.

“So, how are you holding up after that Navy SEAL stunt you pulled?” asks Chad.

I laugh. “Handling it as best as possible I guess… for having to shoot someone.”

Honestly, it bothers me more that it doesn’t bother me. I hope this vampire situation doesn’t come hand-in-hand with a lack of empathy… or worse, grow into a love for killing. All things considered, vampires are (so it seems) designed to prey upon humans, so it stands to reason that some degree of detachment at death would be included, but there’s enough Sam left inside me that I intellectually regard it as troubling, despite the lack of emotional freak-out.

"I'm sure you'll be cleared. If I know you, even when you break the rules, you stick to policy." Chad winks.

"Heh, maybe. Thanks for the vote of confidence."

He makes a finger gun at me. "If you change your mind, call me to testify on your behalf."

I grin… and steer the conversation into happier topics as I need to keep my mind on something else.

My career has just run naked into the sun, and turned to ash.

Chapter Thirty-Two
Monster

The Damocles' Sword of termination hanging over me fills my days of sitting around at home with dread. I'm happy to be with my family all day, but I can't enjoy it. Every minute I spend *not* thinking about what I'm going to do with myself feels like I'm wasting time.

I do a little looking into other possible jobs that would let me work a night shift and offer enough money to be worth pursuing. Though, I do circle back to wondering about Danny's suggestion of private investigation. It's a crazy/scary thought, the idea of not having a 'real' job. But, I suppose in some way, it might prove liberating. But when my kids' security is on the line, I'm not quite willing to take that chance if I can find something more stable.

It's been four days since I left Nico's office, and I haven't had any contact from HUD other than my visits to Chad in the hospital. That's another bit of anxiety I'm dealing with. There's still the (albeit remote) chance of them charging me with a crime or suing me. All things considered, either of those outcomes are pretty unlikely, but I *can't* go to prison. It would literally kill me the first time they left me in a cell with a window. Of course, I am uniquely equipped to be a fugitive. But, that would mean being away from my family…

The sun bath it is.

But, those thoughts aside, I have to focus on my immediate circumstances, and do everything I can to avoid losing the house we put so much sweat into.

Danny's picked up a potential boon of a case, snagging a well-off client who's being sued by a number of women. Whenever I ask him about the case, he goes bright red in the face and won't come out and tell me who the man is. I've got no idea where it came from, but the idea that he's representing some kind of porn kingpin or a sleaze peddler gnaws at my brain.

Are we really that desperate?

I sigh at the darkened curtains in the living room from my seat on the sofa. Yeah. I guess we are.

He's typing like mad on the laptop behind me in the dining room, having continued working after arriving home from the office.

"Oh, crap," says Danny, at a sudden lull in the clickety-clack of computer keys. "I forgot to swing by Albertson's on the way home."

"I got it."

"But you're, you know..."

"I'm what?"

"Unwell."

I kill the TV and stand. "It's dark out. I'm fine now. More than fine. Besides, you're up to your eyeballs. I think I can handle picking up milk, cereal, and a pack of diapers." At the thought of diapers, my heart grows heavy. It won't be too long before Anthony's done with them, and I'll never have to make another diaper run again. Like, ever. Okay, that thought sucked.

"He takes after me, you know."

"Took you forever to potty train, too?" A grin spreads across my lips.

Danny shakes his head. "No, silly. I think our son is just sort of lazy. Why take the hard way when you can take the easy way?"

"Crapping in your diaper is the easy way?"

"Takes less effort to let it out wherever he happens to be at the moment instead of walking to the bathroom. In a way, I envy him."

Now I'm laughing. "You? Lazy? I never could've imagined."

"Then we're even. I still can't imagine you streaking around the woods as a hippie child." He leans back in the chair and stretches, yawning. "I grew out of it. When I was a kid, I think I had sloth genes."

"Oh, I usually put clothes on if I planned on going more than fifty feet from the house. It was

Clayton who streaked all the way to town. Okay, need anything?"

"Uhh, how about a win in court?"

"They don't have that at the store, I'm afraid."

Danny leans forward and resumes typing. "Nothing I can really think of."

Except, I get the strangest notion he's running a short list of groceries through his head that he wanted to ask me to get, but he feels bad sending the bloodsucker to pick up food that I can't partake in. I guess he figures it's as cruel as asking an ex-smoker to stop and grab a pack of cigs. It annoys me that he's basically lying, but because he's trying to spare making me feel like an outsider, I let it drop.

"Okay. Back soon."

After checking on the kids, kissing Danny on the cheek, and grabbing my sneakers, I head out to the Momvan. It's a little after nine, so Albertson's should still be open, and best of all, I don't have to worry about sunblock. A mile or so away from the house, oncoming cars start flashing their lights at me.

Oops.

I turn on my headlights and squint at the brightness on the road, but eventually, my eyes adjust. Technically, I'm still a paid employee of HUD, but despite going to buy food for the kids, I can't help but wince at spending money, like I'm stranded on a desert island and rationing my last canteen of water.

After parking, I stroll across the lot, enjoying not having to hurry out of the roasting glare of the sun. The inside is painfully bright, but I keep my head down and tolerate it. Overpowered fluorescent lights and mirror-polished white floors are *way* nicer than sunlight. Soon, I've got a basket on my arm and I'm running around collecting a few necessities we'd run out of. Shopping is such an automatic, normal task, my body runs on autopilot while my mind gallops off on a tornado of worry about what I'm going to do with myself once I'm officially terminated. Or resign. Or… whatever.

A tantalizing aroma filters out of the background din of uninteresting people food when I near the cooler aisle in search of milk. Like a salivating dog, I find my head turning to the left at the meat counter, my attention honing in on a middle-aged worker in the meat cutting area upending a plastic basin into the sink, dumping blood.

It's about time I have a meal… I've been so worried about work that I've gone two days without eating. Guess anxiety works on vampires too? It's tempting to leap the counter and swipe the basin away from the guy, but I have enough control over myself to resist making a scene. Plus, I've got plenty of blood back home.

I turn away from the counter, hurrying around the endcap into a cooler aisle.

A shrill high-pitched scream startles me to a halt.

Five feet in front of me, a little girl about Tammy's age is leaning half-inside one of the cooler doors, her hand on a carton of ice cream. She's frozen stock still, staring at me and shrieking every ounce of air out of her lungs.

"I'm thorry?" I lisp, and realize immediately what's wrong.

She bursts into tears and runs away, crying out for her daddy and shouting, "*¡Papi! "¡Papi! ¡Es una diablesa!"*

Crap!

My fangs are out.

Cheeks burning, I duck out of sight around the corner of the aisle and huddle against the endcap, a case of frozen pizzas, hiding my mouth with my hand. My God… what if that had been one of my kids? Overwhelmed with shame and horror, I squat to the floor and bury my face in my hands, shaking. A little girl screamed and ran away from me like I'm some kind of monster.

Aren't I?

I'm not even human anymore.

If my kids ever looked at me *like that*, I couldn't handle it. Nope. It would break my heart into a million pieces. I can never ever let them see that side of me. Hell, even I'm disgusted with myself, by these daggers in my head. The tension in my facial muscles relaxes not two seconds before an agitated man appears at the end of the aisle and starts machine-gunning me with Spanish. I follow enough that he's pissed off and wants to know what I did to his daughter.

"I'm sorry. I'm not sure." I peer up at him, probably looking like a terrified little girl myself. As soon as we make eye contact, all the venom drains from his expression. "She just saw me and screamed. I have no idea."

The man rubs his forehead while the child cries in the distance. A woman, perhaps her mother, whispers "*Todo está bien,*" and "*Cálmate, cariño.*"

A sniffly, tiny voice replies, "*¡Vi una diablesa!*"

Yes, I can hear voices whispering from halfway down the aisle.

The man before me lets his arm flop to his side with a sigh, and switches to English. "My kid thought she, uhh…"

"Saw a devil…" I flash an apologetic smile, wide enough so he can see my *normal* teeth. "*Entiendo un poco*. I've got a lot on my mind, maybe I looked angry or something. I'm sorry for scaring her."

"It's all right." He offers me a hand, to help me up off the floor.

"Thanks." I feel unworthy of his kindness after what I did to his daughter, so I stand without accepting his offer. "Sorry."

The man nods at me and hurries off to his wife and daughter at the far end of the aisle.

Head down like a scolded child, I collect two bottles of milk and make my way to the register.

I can't let that happen again. Never. This isn't 1498. It's the modern age and I can easily get blood in bottles. These fangs are a holdover from days gone by, and I will *not* let them scar my children. They're not coming out to play again, if I have anything to say about it.

I may be a vampire.

But I'm a mom first.

Chapter Thirty-Three
Cheers

It's going to take some planning to work out the logistics of being a stay-at-home vampire mama.

For now, Mary Lou has been watching the kids until about five in the afternoon, so I can rest in a dark bedroom with heavy curtains. Danny's kept the fridge stocked with at least two bottles of animal blood for my nutritional needs. That's one good thing. Now I don't have to go prey on people. Doing that still feels wrong, despite it likely being what God or maybe the 'other guy' intended for vampires to do.

Staying up all day and all night doesn't appear to be having any long-term effects on my 'health,' though I can't say for sure if it will affect my sanity down the road. Continuous wakefulness isn't what our minds were made to handle, after all. Oh, and even with Danny's big case, we're going to lose the house in a few months if I don't find work.

Geez. This stinks. Count Dracula didn't have a day job… or even a night job.

Fiction, Sam. That's a character in a book.

Real world. Real worries.

Six days after my night raid, I have a moment at home with Danny while the kids are at Mary Lou's. He gets all the truth. Me throwing Renton around, Eva shooting me, the whole nine yards. By the way, the ATF boss, Frank Baker, was happy about what I did. Saved his people a lot of work and they found a serious amount of not-civilian-legal firepower in that armory building. M60 machine guns, M249 machine guns, grenade launchers, land mines, claymore mines… holy crap.

Danny nods through my story, and laughs when I comment how much like that video game it felt when I snuck into the place.

Truth be told, he's been acting a little weird around me, especially when Tammy and Anthony are close by, so I talk at length about how I couldn't bring myself to hurt Eva, even after she shot me. She's just an innocent child poisoned by a hateful set of parents. I really hope she grows out of that mindset. If anything sugars the pain of my resignation, it's remembering the look of astonishment on Eva's face when she held Terrell's hand after realizing he saved her life. I'd like to think that's the facial expression caused when a bunch of bullshit preconceptions shatter.

My husband's smile gets more genuine as I go

on and on about not being willing to harm a child, but he can't fully conceal a note of worry. I don't blame him too much, though. It's not every day a person comes to terms with creatures like vampires being real… and living with one, not knowing for sure how much of them is still the person they knew and how much might be something else pretending to be them. I know I'm me, but he's not inside my head. No, something else is in here with me. I'm sure of it.

"I've decided to resign," I say after finishing up the story of the raid. "There's a chance I would've been fired anyway, but since I'm willing to resign and not make any kind of stink about it, they'll probably just let me slip away quietly. This new existence of mine doesn't seem compatible with being normal anymore."

"Oh, that." Danny grins. "I've got a surprise for you."

I raise an eyebrow.

He takes my hand and tugs me to my feet. "Your hands are cold."

"Your hands are hot." I attempt a smile. "Hot and cold. Yin and yang."

Danny chuckles and leads me out to our detached garage. I haven't sunblocked up, but it's a short dash and doesn't hurt *too* much. We go inside, and he approaches a large rectangular block under a sheet. "Ta da."

"The ghost of a dead appliance?" I ask.

He chuckles. "No, silly. I haven't had any luck

finding any real information about your, umm, condition, but I have been able to help a little."

"Oh?"

Danny pulls the sheet away to reveal a small refrigerator, the kind of thing bachelors put in their basements to hold beer. "Look inside."

I lean forward and tug the door open. It's full of plastic pint bottles, all containing blood. "Oh, wow… Danny, what is this?"

"Blood."

"Obviously." I poke him in the side, and decide *not* to mention I can smell it through the plastic. Lately, it seems reminding him how inhuman I've become hasn't been going over so well. "I mean, it's so much…"

"Remember that butcher I defended in a drunk driving case? Jaroslaw? I've made an arrangement with him. Up to a reasonable cap, I've agreed to represent him for future litigation should any arise, and waive my remaining fees for his old case. In exchange, we get blood. He's only going to dump it down the drain anyway."

I blink. "What on earth did you tell him we are doing with it?"

"Gardening. Not sure if he believes me, but he didn't seem to care. Saves him the trouble of dumping it, and saves him on legal fees. Win-win."

"Hmm." I select a bottle, pop the cap, and sniff. It's quite a bit weaker 'feeling' than the blood I remember taking from Dale, but it's also guilt-free. I don't have to hurt any people. "Hah. This is like the vegan version of a vampire. No humans were harmed in the production of this food."

He smiles wider than he has since the attack.

Guess I passed some kind of test. *Yes, Danny, I'm happy to exist without harming people.* A sigh slides across my brain. It's not reassuring that he doubts me, but given the supernatural element, I can't really fault him too much.

"This is great," I say. "Thank you, Danny."

"You're welcome, Sam." He stoops to pull open the drawer at the bottom inside the fridge, and pulls out a can of Heineken, which he taps against my blood bottle. "To us."

"To us." I tap his can back.

"Cheers," he says before taking a giant swig.

I glug down a few mouthfuls. The little bits of flesh and hair are irritating, but again… no one is getting hurt for this blood. It's not gourmet, but it's survival.

Danny nudges the door shut with his foot. We stand there for a moment in the annoyingly-detached garage of our dream home, staring at each other like we did so many times during the year of fixing up the place. Every time the stress just got too much, we'd wind up ignoring it all, skipping a day of work on the house and just be there for each other.

This feels like one of those moments.

Money-wise, we're still barely getting by. I can't sit around doing nothing or we're going to get foreclosed on, and I refuse to let what happened to me take anything more away from my life. First, I need some income. The paid suspension won't last forever.

Time for Samantha Moon to fight back.

"So," I say, with a hint of a smile. "Tell me more about that private investigator thing."

The End

About the Authors:

J.R. Rain is the international bestselling author of over seventy novels, including his popular Samantha Moon and Jim Knighthorse series. His books are published in five languages in twelve countries, and he has sold more than 3 million copies worldwide.

Please find him at: www.jrrain.com.

~~~~~

Originally from South Amboy NJ, **Matthew S. Cox** has been creating science fiction and fantasy worlds for most of his reasoning life. Since 1996, he has developed the "Divergent Fates" world, in which Division Zero, Virtual Immortality, The Awakened Series, The Harmony Paradox, and the Daughter of Mars series take place.

Matthew is an avid gamer, a recovered WoW addict, Gamemaster for two custom systems, and a fan of anime, British humour, and intellectual science fiction that questions the nature of reality, life, and what happens after it.

He is also fond of cats.

Please find him at www.matthewcoxbooks.com.
~~~~~

Made in the USA
San Bernardino, CA
11 August 2019